A HERO OF OUR TIME

"Ruthnum's language is graceful and hysterical—often in the same breath. His deft hand makes this sharp, propulsive skewering of corporate hypocrisy a rich read. "

—Mayukh Sen, author, *Taste Makers: Seven Immigrant Women Who Revolutionized Food in America*

"Naben Ruthnum captures a side of modern employment and work culture that is so funny, so accurate and so specific—but somehow makes it feel incredibly universal. *A Hero of Our Time* made me laugh out loud and cringe, all while holding a mirror up to my own workplace experiences."

—Sarah Hagi, writer

"A shot across the bow and a major literary achievement, *A Hero of Our Time* is the most relevant work of satire this country has produced in years. In Ruthnum's hands, the state of political discourse and the value of the education sector has never looked so etiolated or more deserving of a life preserver."

—Jean Marc Ah-Sen, author of *In the Beggarly Style of Imitation*

"Savage as *A Hero of Our Time* is, I'm not sure it can fairly be called satire. Naben Ruthnum's assessment of corporate culture—and the academy, contemporary religion, the politics of identity, and so much more—is withering but honest. The novel nails so much about 21st century life; what can you do but laugh?"

—Rumaan Alam, author of *Leave the World Behind*

A

HERO

OF

OUR

TIME

ALSO BY THE AUTHOR

Curry

Find You in the Dark (as Nathan Ripley)

Your Life Is Mine (as Nathan Ripley)

A HERO

OF OUR

TIME

a novel

NABEN RUTHNUM

McClelland & Stewart

Copyright © 2022 by Naben Ruthnum

First edition published 2022

McClelland & Stewart and colophon are registered trademarks of Penguin Random House
Canada Limited.

Library and Archives Canada Cataloguing in Publication data is available upon request.

ISBN: 978-0-7710-9650-1
ebook ISBN: 978-0-7710-9651-8

Book design by Kate Sinclair
Cover art: (man) stocknroll / E+ / Getty Images, Dean Mitchell / E+ / Getty Images
(building) Marco Di Stefano / EyeEm / Getty Images
Typeset in Sabon MT Pro by M&S, Toronto
Printed in Canada

McClelland & Stewart,
a division of Penguin Random House Canada Limited,
a Penguin Random House Company
www.penguinrandomhouse.ca

1   2   3   4   5   26   25   24   23   22

For

Kris Bertin

Part One

1

Certain stories are for wielding, not telling. I used to have one before it was taken away.

It was more of a joke, a few lines of generic airport experience and television borrowings honed into a minor weapon for use in business situations. But I counted on it. The final time I used it was at the AAP Conference in October 2018. Seven listeners and I were on a sickle-shaped couch in the lobby of a generic hotel implanted into the superstructure of a retired castle in Montreal. The couch was upholstered in washable light gold fabric that rasped against pants and skirts and felt like Kevlar against my palm as I pushed myself deeper into the cushion, hoping to discover a secret angle or groove free of the rigid springs that were pressing into my tailbone.

"I don't blame them, I'd pat me down too. I am always, no exception, late to the airport, sweated up when I get there. The air conditioning freezes it on my face and gives me that hospital or strapped-with-plastique sheen. Then there's the whole 'this' thing."

I added, as I did every time, to the invitation of my smile with an up-down displaying wave of hand over face. The downstroke acknowledged the skin that caused the airport situation and the unease of my listeners. The upstroke, a toss like I was flinging salt or a spell, dismissed any tragic significance, sent race into the ether, let my listeners join in a laugh if they were brave enough to start it.

Anyone who takes pleasure in rendering even brief power from goodwill and fear is shit. When I used this story, I was no exception. I want to make it clear that I understand this, and that it doesn't prevent me from discerning that Olivia Robinson was and is much worse than I am. She's also, in the sense that matters to her and to our world, much greater.

The six listeners who weren't Olivia reacted exactly as I wanted them to. Mouths balanced between self-evaluating smile and moue of concern, quickly hidden by a mug or glass held up like a quivering masquerade visor, eyes shy to meet mine and saturated with a compassion begging for transmutation into accepting, accepted laughter. The features of these people have vanished now, from AAP's offices and from my memory. Eye colour, ruddiness, dental details—all gone. Enough of them were white for me to have deployed the story, remarkable considering the company's diverse employee pool, which Nena Zadeh-Brot called a "rainbow whirlpool of mediocrity blending into a calming diarrhea tone when stirred with the correct human resources stick." I only remember that they were watching me correctly, that they were doing what I wanted them to do.

But Olivia Robinson just looked like me. Her expression. She looked like the person telling, not the person listening. Her appearance, classed by Nena as "tolerable Aryan prettiness," has nothing in common with my aging Indian softness, other than the strip of upper gum we now both reveal when we speak. I say "now" because this first meeting took place during Olivia's closed-mouth speaking period, when her lips only allowed the occasionally flickering sight of tongue against darkness, never a gap or archwire or elastic or point of enamel. And now that she's speaking with her new mouth, with its perfect teeth, I'm in recession. If I still spoke to people and cared about how I presented, I'd have to reprogram myself to talk through the same flat pucker she mastered. As my gums retreat and blacken, the teeth look like they're growing into my head, as though they mean to bite my brain, also shrinking and darkening in its nervy membrane pouch.

"What about the power of it, though?"

"Of what?" I scratched my thumbnail against the cushion just in front of my crotch, then turned the motion into a brush at the immovable pills on the knees of my suit pants, in case anyone thought I'd been subtly gesturing toward my dick. Olivia saw the gesture, and beyond it. I am myself when I'm inside a doubt.

"In the airport. Instead of feeling abject, targeted—which, totally, I understand you are—what about feeling how scared of you people are? Isn't it powerful that there are spaces in this world where you're not you, but a menace? No one's ever scared of me."

None of the others saw how much smarter she was than me, and I hadn't yet understood, either. But I did feel it. Olivia played it perfectly to look like she had no sense of humour, which people are always ready to believe about a person like her. Perhaps it is true in her case, but she at least has a sense of senses of humour, or she wouldn't know when people hope she will laugh, and that would be too great a tactical weakness.

I couldn't see how this exchange benefitted Olivia until the next day, when she allowed me to know. But I did understand that it had been fair to rob me of my pathetic charge of control. The drinks in our group's hands were appropriate to an early afternoon with two conference sessions left before dinner—coffees, club sodas. Olivia had a lemonade. She was younger than me, perhaps twenty-seven to my thirty-eight. I chewed ice. My story died, not because Olivia had exposed it, but because she had begun to consume it, at the outset of a long game that began when she indicated a pretend path to power on that acrylic couch.

I'm going to try to avoid making these pronouncements with the false sense of distance and ironic knowingness I want to slip into. The truth is that my airport story's morsel of leverage was meaningful to me, and I was sad to lose it. I'm still sad about it. Sad that I am a person who wants a tool like this, sad that I no longer have it.

As I mentioned, no one else in my audience for this impromptu conference-adjacent seminar on race and terror still works for AAP. In pursuit of the ideal of efficiency that our leadership requires, and with any of the many who have attempted to form a union paid off or terminated long before their organizing can come to term, there is a lot of churn. It's painful, because AAPers are hired for their devotion, their programmability, their willingness to pronounce their liberal arts degrees both useless and crucial, their servitude to the ideal of technology making knowledge masterable and advancing education beyond the cave. When AAP leaves these employees behind, they are so completely indoctrinated that they are cut off from their pasts. They can only move on to one of AAP's lesser competitors, begin doomed start-ups, or fling themselves into the pensioned, shutting maw of university administration.

After Olivia routed me, I left the lobby and skipped the afternoon session. This was still possible before the enforced scans that were instituted at the January 2019 AAP Edu-Jam. A point of AAP structure that we present to clients as proof-of-efficiency is that there are only ever 100 upper-level employees. Thus, there should be exactly 100 people in the room at every central AAPC presentation. When we talk up this streamlined aspect of our business to schools, we're very careful not to let them think we're critical of their own inflating administrative position numbers. The more people clustered at the broadening top over there, the better chance that one of them will subscribe to AAP. The suggestion is that we stay lean so they don't have to.

I went to four used bookstores and one bar. There, I laid out the books I'd bought on the artificially distressed but genuinely beer-stained table in front of me and took a photo to post in the near future, when none of HR's freelance social media hawks could make the connection between my browsing time and absence from Dr. Bobby Merchant's "Your New Paperless Memorybank: A Digital Communications Action Intensive" seminar. My co-workers would be repeating to Dr. Bobby, who had been an early champion of AAP at our crucial first two Ivy League scores, that his product wasn't a shockingly obsolete rehash of the Palm Pilot and that the stylus was indeed an essential and neglected connectivity tool. Dr. Bobby had retained enough money and influence for his irrelevance to be denied in every zone of his life except the market. He constantly mistook me for an AAP programmer named Amandeep who'd been deported months earlier, two days after the FBI came to our offices for his hard drive. Amandeep wasn't deported, really: he flew home with a cousin's passport to avoid prison or ICE detention. The cousin was then deported. My superiors didn't tell me to accept Dr. Bobby's ongoing error, but it was made clear that I should prevent him from feeling embarrassed, or worse, asking what had become of Amandeep. Dr. Bobby presented with that tech mogul eyebrowless squint and isosceles lip-purse that suggested an unattackably itchy anal contusion caused by excessive scratching. I wanted to spend my afternoon looking for modern firsts, for J.G. Farrell and V.S. Naipaul, and so I did. I would post the photo and the prices I'd paid two weeks after the conference and a fellow collector in Devon would call me a lucky cunt in genuine rage, and I would feel happy. I drank three beers, ate two dinners, and waited until midnight to come back to the hotel with my books and bottles. Nena was only a couple of floors away, but hadn't messaged me all day, which wasn't unusual when we were about to see each other.

The next morning, Olivia apologized for being insensitive.

She was ponytailed and her clear eyes spoke of at least a decade of sobriety, disciplined sleep and exercise. I was sure she'd spent the morning in the hotel's gym or pool, while I roiled the sheets and coughed into consciousness. Perhaps forty other AAPC attendees could hear me forgiving her repeatedly, in a voice I had to drag from hungover glottals into the precise, gracious speech that Olivia knew I was capable of if only I tried. Nena Zadeh-Brot was across the lobby, speaking to two AAP board members and pointing at an iPad, but also watching me. We wouldn't speak until after the sessions were over, but her glance pulled me out of the final lingerings of sleep, forcing me entirely into conversation with Olivia Robinson, to witness the creation of repentance as product, to contain the apology that was being forced into me.

"It's totally okay. I feel embarrassed you've even been thinking about this, truly." The lobby smelled of fresh tile adhesive, except when a guest disobeyed the signs to use the revolving doors and let in a gust of October wind cool enough to have an immediate freshening effect, even if it was polluted. But I stayed lodged in the smell of my own head, its plaque and necrotic mucous and trapped air. From Olivia came an insistent scent of pennies and mint.

"No. Osman, I know nothing of your past, of you, except what I can see and imagine. And that I—that I just *interrogated* you like that, told you how to process your own experience like I had any conception of what it is to live even a moment in your skin—it would be like, oh, Jesus, it would be like you telling me how I should fucking deal with PMS."

"It would not—I didn't see it that way at all. We were two grown-ups talking about ideas, which is always okay." It is not okay, especially at AAPC, but I was too disoriented to figure out how to claw this remark back. Olivia didn't lean in, but her right forefinger, a questing E.T. digit with a bumblebee-yellow manicure, landed at the apex of my shoulder, the place where the hollow between muscles would be if I had a proper body.

"I'm sorry. Please feel that," Olivia said. Her expression hadn't changed, but the eyes were clearer, wider, the pupils refracting with dark sincerity. The crowd of forty was quiet. Even the people who were speaking left pauses long enough to take in what Olivia was saying. And while I understood exactly what she was doing, finally, while I knew that she was speaking past me to an audience, that she always would be, she still made me want to try to live up to her earnestness in that moment.

How the fuck does that work?

That exchange is only remembered by Olivia and me, except in the subconscious of every man and woman who'd seen me dominated with such ease. It is generally forgotten because Olivia made herself unforgettable moments later by hijacking AAPC's keynote presentation, dominating a stage she wasn't even standing on, and reducing the speaker and anointed next leader of our organization, Elodie Chan, to just another audience member.

Planted questions are part of the house style of an AAPC presentation. Every session has to come in at under twenty-five minutes, including Q & A. This time-efficiency is also part of AAP's public face. Part of what we offer to colleges and universities is a guarantee to increase potential enrolment by packaging their existing lecture and seminar offerings as compressed online-delivered courses with an optional in-class supplement, an offering that we assured the schools was "just as beneficial to end-users," leaving out the statistic that somewhere under 17 per cent of enrolled students actually viewed and completed the entire online package. But the profit stats and test cases were undeniable. Tuition income rose by the millions at each of our four pilot schools, and AAP's earnings swelled on our 5 per cent ask in return for upfront-costless implementation and administration of the program. The inescapable five-year contract for sign up had been conceived of and written by Nena Zadeh-Brot in conjunction with two long-vanished members of the legal department; Nena had taken an enormous bonus instead of a promotion after its successful implementation. That's when the board knew she planned to leave AAP, someday, and she was never offered a promotion again. 2019 was Nena's planned final year, in fact, but only our end-to-end encrypted chat knew that. I wasn't ready to escape so soon, but was naturally unremarkable enough to avoid offers of promotion.

That same quality kept me safe from being asked to be a question-plant at AAPC. Olivia Robinson was assigned to raise her hand in minute seven of Elodie Chan's keynote, which would end up being her last as VP, two months before her total release from the company. A particular trick of Elodie's was to avoid cramming in prepared questions at the end. She had them peppered throughout, so she could hit minute twenty-five with a judicious wrap-up that included everything that the audience had brought to the idea. It was a reusable innovation: simulated dialectic fit the AAP tradition. It was an organized display that we could replicate and use in sales pitches out in the field.

During Elodie's wireless-mic-and-chin-thrusting speech, her arms ran through a sequence of four postures—summoning, inquiring, pensive, embracing—that she had memorized because her instinct was to leave them hanging apelike at her sides. Her set-up to the fatal question was: "What can we tell these institu-tions of *higher* learning that they're all, from Sunnydale Polytechnic to *fucking* Cambridge,"—Elodie paused for the laugh here, as the top reaches of AAP were expected to display frankness and practi-cality by swearing in their presentations—"what can we tell them that they're, without exception, doing wrong?"

She pointed at the person who was about to depose her. Olivia rose from her middle seat in the second row and stumbled over the first set of knees she encountered, laughing at herself for the rest of her trip to the mic in the aisle.

"I can't believe I'm about to make a serious statement to y'all when I can barely walk." The "y'all" sounded so wrong in her mouth I wondered if it was a bit of Swedish until I figured it out.

"Please, go ahead," Elodie said. Olivia had eaten perhaps forty unplanned seconds, and Elodie's arms assumed their natu-ral slaughterhouse dangle as she mentally cut sentences from her remaining time.

"Elodie's asking us what the schools are doing wrong, and I totally see the value in that. Absolutely. But—and I'm sorry—I just don't think it's the question we need to be asking right now. In this company, in this world. We need to be asking what *we're* doing wrong."

The tremor of a hijack in progress passed through the room, as tangibly as if the aisle Olivia was standing in was airborne and she'd stepped into it with a clever wood-and-rubber gun. Elodie could edit, but she couldn't improvise. Her jaw hung open a half-inch, matching her slack arms perfectly. We all saw it. She fixed the mouth but the arms stayed.

"And I think that how we choose the questions we ask is *exactly* the issue," Olivia continued. "Who we think of as our customers, as our clients—that's the issue. How limited our idea of inclusion is. That's the issue." The mic was cordless, and

Olivia had silently unholstered it from its stand and turned, started to back up with perfect smoothness. She moved slowly. If you were sitting, and not exactly in line with her at the back of the room, as I was, the glide to being flush with the stage would have looked like a wedding or funeral procession: dramatic, inevitable, ending in the right place. The movement made the stage, and certainly Elodie, invisible. Even the camera tracked down to record Olivia, leaving Elodie as a pair of calves ending in grey heels, the gradual zoom briefly revealing a scuff that looked like a wad of white gum on the tip of the left toe.

"End-user is such an impersonal term, but that's what we have to think about. It's what our clients, the schools, think about. The students. That's ultimately who we work for, am I right? And what we're leaving out is their *humanity*. That's what *we* are doing wrong. I am so guilty of this myself, and I know it resonates for a lot of people in this room.

"Connection is what we sell. Accelerated connection, yes, but in order to be accelerated it has to be deep, profound, immediate, true connection. Do we really understand how valuable what we're doing is? We are the only company in the world that is both mining and enriching the *same* resource: students. Young humanity."

I cannot express to you how well this went over, and how well it still does—a combination of disingenuous self-criticism and laudatory descriptions of our mission. Now that Olivia was up there, everyone in the room collectively realized that this was one thing, one essential thing, that Elodie Chan sucked at. She didn't know how to take the right shallow dips into shame and corporate self-interrogation to illuminate the glory of AAP's path forward. This was a crucial sales and motivation tool that no president could be without. Elodie's career ended right then, but Olivia continued with another few strophes on students, and then a transition that included my name.

"Osman—is it Shah? Could you please stand? God, I didn't even have the—I really hope I got your last name right." She blinked self-consciously, the eyes closed for an extra moment of penance. There was a gathering of flesh around the mouth in her otherwise sharply cut face, a poised cluster of skin that suggested the protrusions her braces were correcting. Olivia summoned me to stand, looked for me in the crowd instead of behind it. I walked a few steps forward and waved, then receded back to the wall. Elodie watched me as though I were advancing with a rifle and her blindfold had slipped slightly.

"Osman was telling me—telling us—a story yesterday, about his mistreatment at the airport. He couched it in humour to make us all comfortable, but it was just so clear—this was, this *is,* a person who deals with daily humiliations on a scale that I can't even contemplate, and comes to his colleagues with the expectation that for us to be open to his emotional state, he has to entertain us with his despair.

"This is a man who carries the certainty that even AAP, with our perfect diversity statistics, can't be a home for his pain, unless he smuggles it in under his labour and good-hearted humour. We need to ask what we are doing wrong. We need to ask: are we really valuing diversity? Are we channelling the fullness of the experience of our Osmans—I see your faces now in this crowd as I admit I never have before—if all we're asking is for you to help us with specific sales strategies, and not to come to us with all of your experiences, freely and with openness and the expectation of understanding? Are we working with you or just using your work?"

I watched her subsume my story, annex it to her ongoing enlightenment narrative, a grander tale that she was offering AAP the chance to be part of. I've since read my first name twice in interviews with her, an altered telling of my tangle with security now embedded in her pruned and arranged answers about diversity, power, grace. This is the real reason I don't tell that story anymore: it's not that I saw the truth of what a manipulative turd I was when I told it, but because Olivia liked what I said and decided to take it away and make it useful. Now I can't take it back without being correctly accused of theft, because she did more with that airport scenario than I ever did.

While AAPC applauded, and Elodie waved redundantly behind her, Olivia Robinson unfurled a hand toward me, as though she had manifested the brown lump of tragic heroism who was leaning against the wall to take pressure off his shitty spine with its slight curve and two herniated discs. The audience turned to applaud the person who had been conjured for them. Randall Dunn, the biometrics chief analyst who worked in the chair next to mine, mouthed an apology to me as he shook his head. Our *obviously curry* lunchtime bit died forever that day.

Olivia's move to topple Elodie would have been laughably obvious if she hadn't made laughter impossible by hiding the coup in an apology. The audience accepted her bid at concealment. They saw the attempt but also the quality of its packaging, and they allowed that exterior to become the reality. It's the reaction they would hope for if they ever strategized assassination plans of their own. They would want their goodness to be believed, their ambition ignored.

No matter what came to pass in the year after that summit, Olivia will always be fond of me, because her gambit worked. And Elodie, long absent from AAP, is rumoured to have died of the big flu or to be running a non-profit. It's generally agreed that she moved to Denmark.

I asked Nena Zadeh-Brot about Olivia Robinson when the afternoon session concluded. Nena had seen the performance, of course, from the end of the first row. I'd taken another shower after the putsch-presentation, and was sitting naked on the hotel duvet, looking with dislocated recognition at the rolling mounds of brown flesh and black hair in the mirror above the dresser as I phoned Nena, who I would be able to face once I was under at least three layers of thick fabric.

"You must have known about her," I said. "This never came up? You never thought to tell me there was a demon at HQ? Did you guys manufacture her?"

"We were friends when she started out with AAP. For a few months. And we didn't make her, but I did hire her," Nena said. We were speaking over the hotel phones, and the pure hard-wired connection reproduced her voice with a dimensionality that I wasn't used to from our cell calls and conversations in rooms crowded with noise.

"You knew a creature like this existed and didn't tell me about it. What are we even talking about in all those chat hours? You can't have been actual friends with her. There's no way I can accept that." The sharpness of the connection enhanced a truth: my attempts to banter with Nena were frantic outside of text. I tried to emulate the amused gaps we used as occasional punctuation. I kept my speech relaxed, slowing down just before "actual friends," causing it to emerge in a NyQuil-sluggish drawl. Nena was aware that I loved her and wasn't as disgusted as she should have been, simply as confused about what to do with that information as I was. Next to AAP, a collection of hatreds, and our focus on securing an iron-weighted blanket of financial security, the dilemma was something we shared.

"I don't know what we were, I guess. In retrospect. At the time, we were absolutely friends. I never brought her up because I don't like thinking about her, and now that I'm mostly remote or at the Boston office, I don't have to." Nena said. "I'm over Olivia, and after I tell you this horrible saga I suggest you get over her too. And I'm not saying her name again in a room where I'm going to sleep later, so tell me where we're going to meet and otherwise shut up, okay?"

As I remember it, the only recurring name in the story Nena was soon to tell me was Olivia's. This can't be right, obviously, as I'll find out when I prune the memory of what she said into what I will write down. But the important thing is that when you begin to understand Olivia, you wish to retain her and to know more, even if you profess detachment, even if the face behind the acts you describe never quite attains definition, even if the jaw is light and bevelled or has a projecting underbite, even if the cheeks shift through the correct seasonal level of inflation or gauntness, even if the eyes are almond-shaped and reptilian or manga-flared and curious. Even if you hate her, even if you can't say exactly what she looks like, eventually all you remember is her. I didn't believe that Nena was over her, then or in the months that followed, even when she feigned detachment from what I was planning, what I was doing. Nena just needed me to be the vehicle of her interest in Olivia, needed me to increase the gap between them.

2

I found a proper place to drink near the hotel, through diligent googling of dive bars and investigation of photos. In the review site JPEGs, this bar had black walls striped with torn white remnants of paste-fused posters, tables that looked well-chewed but clear of debris, and no top-rail liquor. There were reviews from students complaining about prices, which confirmed its suitability. I took the stairs down to avoid running into any AAP people. With the president's excruciatingly named and unskippable closing session on "The Self-Administrating (We Wish!) Online Classroom," at eight the next morning, only Nena and I were likely to be drinking at this hour, which illustrates exactly how far from the academy our company had floated. I took the elevator down and crossed the lobby in only my T-shirt and pants, very slowly, to make sure I would sweat as little as possible. Once outside, I let the cold dry and neutralize what had come out of me. I stared at the ground as the doorman evaluated my stiffening nipples, then put on my sweaters and coat. My hips, assaulted by the tight cinch of my belt, hurt so sharply that I took a taxi the three blocks to the bar.

A couple of kids, the ages and races of the students that AAP showcased in our literature, entered before me. They were upset that the band was just wrapping up their patch cords and stepping off the tiny stage, while I was exultant. Nena had once punched me in the arm hard enough that I worried about hairline fractures when I brought her to a bluegrass night at a bar near my apartment in L.A. A purple patch spread over the skin for the next couple of hours, the flesh tender and delicate with the memory of her fist. I kept a photo of the bruise on my phone as proof that Nena had touched me.

I ordered at the bar, a gin and soda that I could drink quickly and pay for before Nena came. The bartender, bearded with a thick chest and clean fingernails, didn't look at me when he gave me the drink, didn't tell me the price before he broke my ten-dollar bill. I said, "with ice," twice before he said, "Rocks," and I nodded. He would always hate me.

Finding a table with two stools, one of which was in a shadow that would hide the worst of me, I sat and found a spot on the empty stage to stare at. It was late on the evening of the punch that Nena and I were explicitly kind to each other for the first time. While my non-bicep throbbed under the subtle hematoma that Nena had made, this brief colourful organ that marked new intimacy, we talked. We stopped arguing and joked only intermittently, eating peach pie in an all-night diner that was patronized by teenagers, sober stand-up comics, and old men filling their wallets with sugar packets and drinking coffees that were half milk. Nena told me about the particular collisions in her racial makeup, then about her mother's unspeakable childhood, then about her own remote and luxurious one at a Swiss boarding school where she had read *Don Quixote* in Spanish at fourteen and had two male teachers fired for their sexual misconduct with her classmates at fifteen, at which point the entire student body and most of the teaching staff stopped speaking to her unless it was impossible not to or she was being interviewed after another tennis win. She kept reading and campaigned for a false grade in mathematics if she agreed not to drop all of her athletics, a bargain the headmaster agreed to.

At AAP, she used an alternate childhood history, mostly New Jersey–based, where her single father worked as a handyman for the Persian expat community. This one was partially true as well, but Nena allowed most of her listeners to believe that was the whole story, leaving out her and her mother's nighttime departure to live with an uncle who worked for the UN and took nauseating risks on the stock market with repeated success. After she and her mother left for Switzerland, her father immediately returned to Iran, abandoning the apartment and power bills as his family had abandoned him, forcing Nena's mother to do paperwork across international lines until Uncle Azar made exactly two phone calls—one to a lawyer, one to a bank. Nena's mother received an eighty-three-dollar cheque from PSE&G that she framed and hung above her desk, and an apology from the IRS.

Nena didn't ask me any questions about myself in the diner, and soon it became too late to offer any information without seeming like I was wanting to make it my turn. The next morning, I wrote down everything she told me about herself so I could bring up details later. The bruise turned yellow, then green, then vanished.

Nena came to the bar with an emerald scarf around her neck, walking fast and looking down, finding the table without seeming to look directly at me once. Her blue eyes looked digital against her skin, which was a brown close to driftwood. If I told her that driftwood thing, she would take a cab to the beach to find a long piece to shatter over my head. And the eye part sounded fetishistic, with a suspicious racial undertone, suggesting that she had attained a precious measure of whiteness through a genetic, cellular campaign to be Aryan not just in the regular Persian way, but in one that counted here in the world.

Nena took in the drink specials before turning to me, apparently as disappointed by my face as by the catalogue of shooters she'd just dismissed.

"You were really good being show-and-tell'd today. You should've bowed."

In photos, Nena looks like a hastily anthropomorphized eagle, either because she has never learned her angles, or assiduously memorized the wrong ones and assumes them anytime a lens is levelled at her. She does not look that way in life. A man at the nearest table, white and wearing wooden-framed glasses, was watching her sit and gauging whether I was somehow an obstacle. Nena touched the scarf around her neck and quickly tied it over her head, apologizing to me in an accent not her own. The man turned away, then left his stool and went to sit at the bar.

Nena pulled the scarf back down. "A piece of silk or rayon and you vanish. Or at least become some sort of oriental cypher. They get scared or they want to find a quiet bathroom where they can have an aggressive jerk off at me."

"Fuck," I said. Nena took the curse as I'd intended it, a compaction of laughter and applause. Inwardly I was wondering if it was possible to masturbate "at" instead of "to" someone when you were alone, and decided that yes, it was. A server arrived—twenty-eight from a distance, forty-two up close, a man with his mouth permanently ajar from the juiciness of a lip pout that would someday become a droop. Lean, in a pale blue Samhain T-shirt ventilated by nickel-sized laundry-chewed openings, he was white but white-sand Mediterranean white, that drip of olive-oil exoticism that opens many doors and shuts none. I wished for the courage to be rude to him. We both ordered gin and sodas, Nena widening her eyes and emphasizing "gin" in a way that suggested former-service-industry-worker solidarity. Samhain laughed and left.

"How are you?" I asked.

"You'd only be pretending you cared. You want to hear about Olivia, and that's okay. I knew she would do *something* this year to make sure everyone understood that she wasn't just back at AAP, she was ascending. You're so mercifully isolated from the actual company culture in L.A., you wouldn't understand. It was generous of her to use you. I know she probably thinks so."

"I do care how you are," I said, "I also care to know about the woman who pulled my spine out and dangled it from the stage like Predator."

"I thought more about what you asked. And yes, we were friends. Just because a friendship ends doesn't mean it never existed. Olivia was my first real friend at AAP. Under me, over me, whatever. This was back when I socialized, but when I went out it was with profs, musicians, people I could be vague about my career with. Olivia was the first person I could talk to about everything, including AAP."

"So she was someone you could talk to. Okay."

"We were much closer than you and I are," Nena said. She smiled, but it was a generous smile that made her eye contact waver, and the pain I'd invited shut me up. When Nena's meanness was deliberate, it was always funny, somehow kind and validating of my opinions and my toughness. I had to work in order to feel hurt around her. Our drinks arrived and I filled my mouth with ice on the first gulp, filtering the rest of my sips through it, keeping my tongue frozen and dead.

"Olivia interviewed when we were thinking of setting up an AAP shop in Toronto. AAP thought we should have a team there for daily contact with the universities we were stoking. With an all-American staff, of course. To sort of enter meetings with admin and appear to be leaving before we'd arrived in the room, before we'd even crossed the border. We ended up deploying the same plan, but from HQ. It really worked. Canadians feel compelled to audition when you walk in with the correct American-progress angle. They hate it, but they do."

"You don't have to explain Canada to me. I've only been in L.A. a couple years." I would have been on the Toronto team if it had manifested, perhaps—I'd been doing secret interviews with AAP and its competitors for years before I finally got a position and was able to stop pretending I was going to be a professor. I'd been a part of AAP for two point five years, during which I'd lost a father and a hopeful vision of myself and gained an annual salary that eclipsed the total of everything I'd earned throughout my twenties.

"Being from a place doesn't mean you look around and know anything about it. For example, you know nothing about Los Angeles. And please don't expect me to remember every obscurity of your past."

The last remnants of the band were gone, and lights just above our heads beamed through green and purple gels to illuminate a DJ opening her laptop on the stage, the screen's glare delineating a small face in the depths of a tremendous white hoodie. About a dozen people had entered, chatting and spreading out enough to make the room feel emptier while providing a comforting damper of noise, like crickets or whippoorwills.

"I keep necessary details," Nena continued. "But the kind of remembering that people like you value, retention of those details you think make the human, the recognition and recall of which you think make the relationship, is exactly what I hired Olivia for. She was too good to concentrate on the Canadian gambit, which was taking care of itself. She took everything I said in. Just like she did with you.

"If you ever suspect Olivia's only pretending when she seems to have forgotten something, is searching for the right word, can't quite place you—she is. She always remembers. I travelled constantly in those early days and I wanted someone presentable and young, younger than me, white, who could take meetings, not offer up too much, present a blank to any client colleges or universities, but also be sharp enough to record anything I'd need to know, spout it back verbatim. I ran tests on suitable candidates, memory games with words, colours, clothing. Nothing computerized. The data I wanted them to pick up was all real-world stuff. Reactions, words spoken."

"This sounds like one of the panels. Please stop." I wish I could say that I was the only one at AAP who spoke to Nena this way, because we are friends and I am quite sure that she finds it amusing coming from me, but it's not the case. I had seen people who make half her salary, whose fast-fashion mail-order pantsuits or synthetic collared shirts were body odour manufacturers as much as garments, cut Nena off and explain what they actually wanted to hear from her. A man out of the L.A. office, Kevin Cuttner, told her in the lobby of the last AAPC that he wanted her to "focus on actionable facts whenever you speak to me, if you're not going to say anything fun." Kevin isn't at the L.A. office anymore. He went to a content mill on Sunset, writing fake blog posts about canvas bag printing shops and pet dander brushes. Nena doesn't have people fired out of spite or personal dislike, but Kevin was overheard by leadership and given his release.

"I'm telling you about Olivia the way that I want to. You want an origin story, Osman. You literally asked me for one. Like superhero movies. That's where the brain rot started with you people, even if you seemed to be too old to have your entire worldview and understanding of human character redefined. Either you want the flash-forward, skip-to-the-aftermath backwards-telling, or you want the spider bite in high school. No sense of pace." A second gin arrived for Nena without her having asked for it. It was a generous pour with fat jagged ice cubes. I'd gotten those small round ice ovals that vanish on contact with liquid in mine.

"I'm almost forty and haven't seen a superhero movie in full since the Bush administration."

"You have boxes of them in that sad apartment." Nena had come and gone from my apartment soon after our peach pie chat, thinking better of ruining a pleasant evening with me by risking the exposure of my flesh and emotions. We did a bookshelf tour and she left. I used clear tape to pull one of her fingerprints from the glass case where I kept my Andrew Holleran firsts, then wiped the case down. I kept the piece of tape in a Mylar sleeve in my wallet for less than a week before I decided that I was going to have to stop behaving like a serial killer if I ever wanted to be proper friends with Nena, or any other woman, or make any friends at all.

"Those are comics, not movies. And EC horror is not superhero stuff. It's *Tales from the Crypt*. Not the same."

"Stop defending yourself when we're trying to talk," Nena said. She'd finished all the ice and started on the drink, sipping through her front teeth, like I had. Farhad, an Iranian boy I'd grown up with in Toronto, used to drink tea that way, a sugar cube between his front teeth, the tea streaming through it. I considered bringing this up, but Nena hated attempts at cultural intimacy.

"I'm not being defensive. I just don't think I count as the *you people* you mean, even if I'm a lot of other kinds of *you people*. But forget it. Before more Olivia, tell me my origin story so I have a handle on the particular kind of shit you're talking." I didn't know why I was challenging Nena until I thought about it for a moment. It was because I was scared of Olivia Robinson, but I wasn't scared of Nena, just in love with her. I wanted to be mean to her and have her be mean but patient back, and finally as kind as she was in the diner while my arm ached.

"You just told me. You just can't believe that you're as boring as you are. It's the same thing I had to accept about myself, that we all do. But for you, it's hard. You're a mediocre, pleasant Indo-Canadian, the perfect hyphenate-union of cultures to elicit zero interest, and you moved to Los Angeles two years ago. That's the start of you. Your background—the degree, your father's transferred academic prestige—those are stats, not story. You made a move that allows you to exist in this world, to make a salary while you think small thoughts to yourself, and that's your beginning and end. At least to anyone you meet now. That and—" Nena replicated the up-down face-and-skin indicating gesture from my airport story, sweeping it larger to encompass my torso, which concealed its sad details in cotton under cashmere under wool. The bar was hot now, deliberately hot, to encourage divestment of slenderness-and-muscle-and-tit-covering cloth. Encased, I was growing moister, heavier, runnier.

"Someone who isn't anything at all can't have an origin," I said.

"A packaged thought. One of *Osman's Realizations*. You should have a pamphlet instead of a business card, one that opens accordion-style." She tapped the wet bottom of her glass against my knuckles.

"But I'm not just talking about you being boring. I'm boring. Everyone is boring," Nena said. "Maybe not Olivia, but there's a trade-off there. She gets a real origin story but that's because she became something remarkable, which is never—and I insist on this—never good."

"If Olivia's been here since you were still travelling everywhere, that's what, four years. Why haven't I met her yet? It's impossible."

"I told you. She left and came back. She was gone for almost a year, came back just six months ago. That's why you've never seen her."

"No one leaves AAP and comes back. Did something happen to her?"

"People who didn't know thought what you're thinking now. Those sexual mutterings. It wasn't that, or the gossip wouldn't have been so formless, and it would have spread."

"And there would be a name."

Nena started to count with her left thumb, getting to the extended ring finger before retracting it. "Yes. I've personally fired two gropers and one inappropriate serial emailer from the Boston office and HQ. I'm always happy to get rid of more. That's not what got Olivia her leave."

"What did?"

"You're flipping to the ending."

"It wasn't the ending or she wouldn't be back here among us, would she?"

"It was the end of our friendship, Osman. Because she didn't tell me anything about it, before, during, or afterwards. She went through HR and then talked to everyone else in the branch about it but me."

"What?" I said. I tried not to look eager, because I knew Nena wasn't being withholding, that she wasn't drawing this out to create suspense or to tease me. She stared at the DJ, who was spinning Green Day at a low volume for a soundcheck, mixing it into a country song that I didn't recognize, keeping her face far back in the hood so she wouldn't have to return the knowing eye contact that was being projected at her from the growing crowd.

"Cancer. It all got back to the office in fragments at first, no detail. Until she started visiting. But she was very sick."

"Did any of this happen while I knew you? While we were talking, every day?"

"Yeah, Osman, I don't tell you every detail of my life, especially my working life. We kept what we knew of the real story confined to the NY branch, out of decency and by HR decree. And as sort of a growing personal challenge to see who would leak the sad story first. I was never going to tell anyone, I just wanted her to return a text. I even left fucking voice mails. It never got out. She would drop by the office for the next many months, her skin going yellow and her hair going grey, then just going, then a scalp under a slick scarf bonneted under her chin or in a Rosie the Riveter knot at the forehead. We eventually just stopped seeing her. Olivia would email. Group emails, nothing personally to me. Hopeful messages that would break your heart even if she had given you the creeps, but the office was pretty sure she was done.

"She stopped emailing. We all assumed. But then she came back. About twenty pounds lighter than she looked today, if you can believe it, a heroin skeleton who told us she was drinking green juice all day and eating steaks for lunch and dinner. She needed more time away, but she was fine, she announced, speaking as loudly as she could, which wasn't very. But she still didn't want to talk to me, even when we were in the elevator together, even when I put my hand on her elbow and told her I didn't know what I had to apologize for but that I wanted to, and that I was fully in support of whatever she needed from me. She waited until the doors opened in the lobby to tell me she 'Appreciated the Kind Words.' There was a nurse, support worker, someone like that waiting with a wheelchair for her by the security desk, and Olivia sank into it so fast I was afraid parts of her had snapped inside, that she had started bleeding invisibly as the chair rolled out. But she was fine. She just wanted to get away from me.

"Now, if you'll shut up and let me do this properly, you wanted the beginnings of Olivia. The beginning was me, and I was confident in who we needed, and I had all the slack I needed from the CEO."

"Brautigan," I said, knowing I had this wrong, knowing that Nena needed a quick couple of blows on me to pull her out of her memory of the wheelchair rejection.

"No, O'Keefe. A little before your time. The turd who wanted you to know his hat wasn't just some fedora, it was a Borsalino. That was his idea of being brand-conscious. He actually started a speech to the board like that once. Establishing that he was a Borsalino-wearing-idiot, not a fedora-wearing-idiot. Anyway. This was during his eight months before permanent obscurity. He was drowning up there and knew it, but at least trusted that I didn't want his job. I laughed at him once when he asked if I did, pretending he was kidding and that it had just occurred to him. There was a fishing game open on his iPad. I could see the reflection of it in the window behind him. He wasn't remotely qualified to be in his seat and knew that I was already doing most of his duties, and so badly wanted me to be a cunt to him in private so he could discredit me in public while pretending it was equally weighted give-and-take playfulness. He wanted to cram that iPad right into my laugh, even if he lost his high score, but he smiled because my not-showing-willingness to take power was as comforting as if I'd actually been weak. O'Keefe told me I had full control over hiring for the role as long as there was a probation period when he could fire anyone without explanation to them or me."

"The memorization test you gave them. What was it?"

"There were a few. Here's one. I gave each candidate a white paper on administrative restructuring in distance ed. Immensely dry, crackling, dead as dead. I'd written it, of course, but hadn't published it yet. It made me too sad. The test was for them to take it home, commit the ideas to memory, write a single-spaced page of coverage and memorize that, their own words, unerringly.

"The last applicant against Olivia was this public policy grad with a mole under his eye that fluttered when he was nervous, which was often. He was tall but not confident about it. Stretched-out arms and a stoop that was almost a hunchback, so he sort of scarecrowed over you when he shook your hand. A goony body that was apologizing for itself. Not what I had in mind, but the people no one wants to look at can be the exact ones you want as observers in rooms where you're not, right?

"Anyway, he started stuttering by his own second paragraph but got through it, then cried when I asked my first follow-up question. Just cried and left and sent his girlfriend back for his briefcase later that afternoon.

"Olivia was in with her homework just after the failure's girl-friend left. She was carrying her written summary, warm from a printer, uncrumpled in her hand. She'd asked someone on the floor to print it from a memory stick she had in her skirt pocket, and she made a joke about skirt pockets that I'd heard on late night six months before. I laughed because I didn't know her yet and some-thing made me want to avoid being stern with her. I told myself after she left that she elicited kindness in a person through something unguarded and frank, something Christian and hickish, the way she didn't have a briefcase, or a folder, and hadn't stopped at a Kinko's or a Staples and paid twenty-nine cents for everything she would have needed in order to come into the office as the collected applicant her predecessor had been before he started weeping. I told myself that it was the yoga shorts she said she was wear-ing under that skirt-with-pockets, for the workout she intended to hit unless things went really badly in the interview and she needed to hit The Cheesecake Factory instead, haha, ha ha ha, haha. But that wasn't my effectively suppressed instinct talking. It wasn't my reasonable deduction that she would, indeed, be a perfect observer, an innocent recorder. Why I'd been kind to her, why I'd joined in her stolen jokes and clichés, was that I was afraid of getting On Her Bad Side.

"I could only admit this after the friendship was over, that it had started in this fear. I wasn't sweet because I wanted to get along with my new hire, but because I found her so undeniably capable that I knew hiring her was an error that I couldn't avoid making, that I would lose my job if I became the kind of person who passed on talent like this, and just as inevitably I would lose my job if I brought her in."

"You haven't lost your job." I heard the "yet" dangling from my phrase before I even knew it was in my mind. Nena tugged on the knot of her green scarf, not to tighten it, but to pull her neck slightly forward for an instant, suggesting a leash, then to the side for another moment, almost rotating it into a noose.

"Olivia started, handing me the sheet and reciting it as soon as I had eyes on the first line. Perfect, no errors. It was a 320-word précis that I couldn't have improved on, and when I asked her questions, she didn't cry, she quoted me back paragraphs. Not of her summary, but of my white paper. She had the whole thing, sixteen pages, pat."

"The efficiency scared you?"

"No. I'm efficient. This was freakish. I asked her what the fuck and she started with, 'I was home-schooled.'"

"Ah. Shit."

"Her father had her memorize *Paradise Lost* by the time she was twelve. And then he—or she herself—started on the rest of printed English. Novels, popular science non-fic, anything Dad could use to lure an audience to her foundational memorized mass of Bible et al. Olivia was on talk shows with him when she was a teenager who could still pass for a seventh-grader—regional shows where her father would have her parrot *The Hobbit* or something else they'd shown her scanning before the commercial break, then Dad'd start in on the Lord as the source of all talents, and if it was a Christian show the host would play chapter-verse bingo with Olivia until the next break."

"You've seen these shows?"

"Only one. A Portland counterfeit of *100 Huntley Street*, from right before her parents briefly split up because Mother refused to let Father take Olivia on the megachurch touring circuit, a high-earning sideshow of talents bestowed and disabilities defeated by the power of Christ's compulsion. Mom's refusal cost Olivia an East Coast opening spot for a retired Korean heart transplant surgeon with a ninety-seven per cent success rate."

"How do you know all of this? Any of it?"

"Olivia's your generation—"

"You're three years older than me."

"I'm not like you. Olivia was telling me her life story before, during, and after that interview. She had to finish it, even after she'd gotten the job.

"On the Portland talk show clip, there is no father. Olivia's seated across from the usual hosting alignment of desexualized Vanna and suntanned bog mummy in white cotton-candy hairpiece. She's fourteen, wearing a prairie dress and matching patterned ribbon in hair done in chaste American plaits. Pastor Wig breathes questions near her and you can sense her recoil at whatever's on his breath, brimstone or salami, but you can't *see* it. She has as much control over her face as she does over her hippocampus, this vast text dump that she starts to plunder in response to his questions, John elevening and Kings fourteening into the coffin air of the set. And you see that she's not in the room at all. She's in the camera."

"So you actually saw the tape?" I asked. Nena ignored me and turned her face down to the table, as though I had pastor breath, a term that has been part of our lexicon ever since that night.

"Olivia told me all of this in bits. Because we talked, you see, for years. Conversed. She left spaces for me to answer, she gave me something back every time I offered her a piece of myself. She found out about my father, my mother, Tehran, Jersey, Geneva. Olivia liked every piece of what I said to her, and to this day, she hasn't told anyone else at AAP any of it. But Olivia didn't show me the tape, just gave me enough clues so I'd know it existed online, part of a legal archive footage dump from when the show itself got sued for misallocating funds, spending Philippines hurricane money on Macau plane tickets. There she is, total proof, the kind that makes you stop looking for any lie. She's even wearing the outfit she describes every time she tells the story.

"But there were lies in what she told me. Huge lies, none of which you can see in the tape. I found these out after she stopped speaking to me, after she vanished from the offices, after I could only have conversations about her, not with her. Olivia's parents were addicts when she was a toddler, in and out of jail on petty drug and occasional theft charges. They're out and Christian now, but they were never around when Olivia was supposedly being trained for the holy sideshow circuit. She was adopted by an Oregon aunt out of a Depression fantasy musical, with 120 acres to live on and three textile factories that she'd shut down, outsourced, and converted into condos in time to catch a real estate boom just before she took on Olivia. She had as much safety as I did in Switzerland, she just wanted nothing to do with it. This aunt, Cecilia Govington, was secular, born Anglican. Nothing to do with evangelism.

"The church and memorization weren't forced on Olivia, they were her first steps into independence, driving hard against Aunt

Cici's wishes that she have a normal childhood that included no tour circuit, no miracle men, no collection plate profit potential. There was a father figure in there for a few moments, a youth pastor that I can only assume was a pervert. A guy named Ogilvie that Cici spits and whispers about. Pastor Ogilvie was crude, grasping, stupid, a man whose greed Olivia could harness. She basically used him as stilts and an overcoat, a moving adult costume she could use to mask her negotiating position and gain entry into arenas of evangelical power she couldn't enter as a lone teenaged girl. He was sloughed off somewhere in flat western Canada and stayed there, leaning against a pulpit and staring at front row legs. Olivia raked in personal savings of $35K from exhibitions before she realized, by the end of junior high, that if she stuck to the religious circuit, there was a ceiling, or at least a set of determined outcomes she didn't want. Pastress of a megachurch, political office in a state she didn't want to live in, or an alliance with a private-plane public-bathroom closet case that she'd rightfully sap millions from in a post-scandal divorce. By fifteen she'd renounced Jesus and embraced public sector education. As a senior, she was advocating for Ph.D. grads who were starving out of the academic market to be shortcutted into high school teaching positions. She was an AAP dream hire in gestation, postering Portland City Hall with students-first measures that funnelled government money into employing institutional leftovers."

"You found this out how?"

"Research. Work. I sent film crews down to the families of ten core AAP team members for a branch doc that I commissioned for last year's holiday party, in that period when Olivia was out of office, before we assumed she was dead, and before she came back."

"That thing turned out really well."

"The director was expensive and I supervised the edits. Anyway, I did it all to find out about Olivia. I have three hours of tape with Aunt Cecilia, none of which were ever intended to make the cut of the video that we projected behind the punch bowl, but which was the whole reason I had the video made. I wanted to know everything I could about Olivia Robinson, so I could find out why she stopped wanting or needing to have anything to do with me."

While Nena could speak like this in a chat window, in narrative torrents usually embroidered with personal insults and jokes, I had the sense that this was the longest speech she'd made in some time. I have noted it all down as I remember it, with adjustments, and you must believe that I remember it very well. I was fascinated and knew that any knowledge of Olivia would be crucial to my future, and was also exulting that I had found an arena where Nena could relate to me and only me, that I had created a new place for intimacy. But it's the interruptions that are crucial in these situations, when a relationship is about to become a different sort of relationship, or not. That's when the transformation from audience to confidant happens, when the information is processed successfully and emerges as a comment that invites and achieves closeness, the kind of empathetic proximity I could strive for in the absence of the physical attraction I would never be able to create in Nena with my oily face, impregnated with its sebum custard, and the souring mollusk pheromone stench that drifted through the helpless cloth over my armpits.

I couldn't interrupt Nena with a question about herself. And I didn't know how to leave the right kind of fecund space, the kind Nena meant when she said Olivia could leave spaces when they spoke. With me any pause is a gap. I knew it was time to contribute. I could see the expectation in Nena's handling of her glass, the loosening of tension in the jaw, the sense that she was no longer onstage, that it was my turn to speak. I had to interpose something about myself. Not an invention. Something related. Olivia's father,

Olivia's invented father, Olivia's pastor-prop father, it was natural to introduce some talk of my dad, of Ajit. A confession that could complement Nena's—because that was what I had just heard, a confession of culpability, an admission that she allowed the creature to pass the threshold and that if Olivia had an origin, part of that origin was Nena Zadeh-Brot's invitation.

"You know my father stopped speaking to me when I came to work for AAP," I said.

"Did he? That's sad," Nena replied. "My mother won't ever stop emailing me about climate change or cellphone towers. Parents are hard."

I didn't say anything. She waited.

"Osman, it's too late to do anything about Olivia. She's just going to happen."

Nena got up to go to the bathroom, leaning slightly toward me as she got off her stool. I tilted back on mine and turned to the side because I was afraid of her smelling my breath, but didn't turn back in time to prevent her from seeing my Hitchcock wattle in profile.

"Thank you for telling me all that," I said. She nodded and started to walk toward the washroom arrow, then turned back.

"You didn't even care to ask why I'd be friends with this person that you loathe and are becoming obsessed with. You start to talk to me about your family, like this nucleus of boredom and disappointment you grew up in has anything to do with where I came from. We talk for hours a day online and you still have no idea how to speak to me."

"I'm sorry," I said. That was all I had. I wanted to defend myself by telling her I'd been close to offering what she wanted from me—that I was going to say that Nena and Olivia and I were haunted by our families in triplicate, that this was a shared if not terribly uncommon situation, that I could draw closer to Nena if she would detail her own distanced relations with her mother and father and if I told her about the death of my father and the upcoming total dementia of my mother. That if the story of Olivia's broken childhood and reclaimed adolescence and her lies about both were of any use value to Nena, it was as a spur to connecting with me, now. I continue to believe all of this, but I know it was correct to shut the fuck up, as I did. Nena was back from the bathroom in a few minutes. I spent this time in my glass.

"I don't need you to ask me things or to understand how a conversation is supposed to work. Just pointing it out," Nena said. She was staring at the DJ again, who had taken off her hoodie to reveal black Bettie Page hair and vivid tattooed arms extending from a sleeveless pearl-buttoned blouse. I know this because I was staring at the DJ too, to avoid looking at Nena, who did at least sound fine. Believing that she was hurt by the failings she had observed in me took more arrogance than I could access.

The bar had revealed itself to be awful, a protectorate of the rockabilly people who were filing in, every man a once-skinny tattooed musician turned fat tattooed barber, every woman a bartender or librarian with progressive politics melded with nostalgia for an era when Black people weren't allowed to make eye contact with them. Nena and I watched the crowd and traded observations like the above, which I may have stolen from her.

We shut up completely when we saw Olivia enter. She was wearing a vintage dress of lime silk under a black leather jacket that fit her autobiographically, the way blown-out jogging pants fit me.

Nena and I didn't even have time to make meaningful eye contact before Olivia saw us, eyerolling an *of course* to go with her smile of delighted surprise. She scraped a stool into place between us, somehow sitting at the head of our round table.

"I shouldn't be surprised that the only other edgy AAPers are in the only cool bar for eight square blocks. I need"—she pointed at Nena's empty glass—"one of those, and so do both of you."

"It's gin," Nena said. "You hate gin."

"People grow, girl," Olivia said, and went off to the bar. Nena looked at me and tried to laugh.

"You're scared," she said.

"You are too. Girl." We weren't accusing each other, just commiserating. At the bar Olivia turned with the three drinks, clustering the highball glasses together in a two-handed grip, like she was holding a thick bouquet. She walked back as though on a tightrope, watching the glasses while I watched her.

"I feel like she heard everything we said. Like she's got a chat-log of any verbal exchange about her that may be of value."

"She did advocate for keystroke monitors on all company-issued laptops for new hires, just after she cleared her three-month probation period," Nena said.

Olivia set the drinks down and leaned against her stool instead of sitting on it. Nena and I were her slightly shorter audients. I was grateful to Olivia for being drawn into alliance with Nena in a physical context.

"Wasn't that fucking wild in there today, Nena?" Olivia said, bringing her glass up and poking the straw aside with the tip of her tongue before taking what appeared to be a brash pirate swig that left the glass exactly as full as it had been when she picked it up.

"It was."

"I was up there and it just came to me. I was like channelling it. Osman, I don't think I've ever been so sincerely in touch with myself and my role as when I'm explaining myself to you. Does that sound insane? I mean, I know this is not bar talk, but I just wanted to air this so we can actually hang."

I wanted to tell her that it sounded calculated, that her appearance here seemed calculated, that I hoped the DJ would start an assault of something unlistenably lame and incredibly loud so I didn't have to exist in the naked reality of this conversation.

"I really appreciated what you said," I answered. A trombone triplet burst out of the dented Yamahas hanging from the ceiling behind us and hoop skirts started to spin on the tiny dance floor. Olivia looked back at Nena and widened her eyes, inviting the same reaction. Nena's face, in emotive motion except at work or when she was being surveilled by men, was now just skin and lips. This dose of late twentieth-century uncool—the brief resurrection of poorly executed swing music a moment so culturally embarrassing that even an unstoppable appetite for retro hadn't hearkened back to it anywhere outside this Montreal bar—confirmed the futurity of what Nena and I did and discussed every day. These horns made AAP feel modern, of the future, almost cool. I met Olivia's eye roll with an attempt at a wry lip twist that made my nose hairs twitch and a rear molar cavity announce itself with a nervy bolt of pain.

Nena reached under the table to hold my hand. She started talking to Olivia. I touched Nena's knee. I did not want to owe Olivia for this but I needed it too badly to let it go. A small line of other AAP employees appeared at the door, dressed in T-shirts and jeans and dresses that looked to have been purchased that day at the mall across the street from our hotel. They came to our table once they had beers. One of them was biometrics Randall, who looked like he wanted to add to his mouthed apology from the afternoon's presentation. I arrested the words by patting the hand he put on my shoulder and nodding solemnly.

"Why's everyone out?" I asked him.

"Halloran's deferring his speech to the evening. Said he wanted to rework it in acknowledgment of what was said this afternoon." Randall nodded, including his torso in the movement: a slight bow in the direction of Olivia. Nena caught what he said and the gesture, too. The president was rewriting his presentation to compete with Olivia. This was defeat, an admission that he was a follower, and that he was too stupid to prevent this intelligence from spreading through AAP via the incontrovertible fact of the rescheduled talk. He would be out within a month, a tenure shorter than anyone's since O'Keefe.

I left too long a gap and Randall decided to apologize after all.

"Osman, I'm sorry. If you want to have a talk with HR about the way I've been with you, I want you to know I completely understand. I'll fucking go in with you to confirm. I mean, if that wouldn't just make you feel intimidated. Out of support, I mean, I would love to go into HR with you to sort this out. The jokes, they're allowed to be just jokes to me, and it was arrogant to assume that they would be that way for you."

"I don't want to talk to HR. Please."

"It's—I know that jokes can be a way of speaking truth to power, and I'm hoping that that's what was—"

Perhaps, no, obviously, because I was drunk and also because I didn't have the courage to say anything contradictory to Olivia, because I was never able to assume any sort of authority in conversation with Nena, I decided to try the truth out on Randall.

"Speaking truth to power is allowed because it affirms that you can sit and listen and be more powerful than me. It's soothing, Randall. Were our jokes about lunch an exercise in you humbling yourself? Were you just allowing me to talk to you as an equal, and now you're not?"

Randall shivered, the meniscus of his beer rimming over and dribbling his knuckles. Something happened in the area of his knees. His penis, and this I could only sense, not see, was fleeing into his body, shrinking so quickly that it seemed to be inverting.

"Dude," I said. "Kidding. Ignore me, man. Come on." I spilled a few drops of my drink into his beer, which struck me as a way to re-establish friendly male intimacy until I was actually doing it and it just seemed very strange. I sank back into my own voice again, the one he was used to. When I'm honest and confrontational I'm doing an imitation of someone honest and confrontational; I'd been doing Nena, with an involuntary leach of Olivia that I didn't notice until writing this down. Randall and I toasted and talked about the shitty pillows in our suites until it was safe to turn away.

I ignored everyone except Nena for the rest of the night, which was an active effort that involved much back-turning, stool rotation, and helpless cupped-hand-to-ear looks. Nena asked me to come back to her room with her when we were outside. She kissed me, and I recognized in the flutter between my balls and esophagus the ghost of the apology that would be born from our sex.

I didn't know if I could ever reconcile owing this to Olivia, and Nena probably couldn't either, but I did know that I wouldn't ever have had the courage to touch Nena naked and to let her see my accruing bulk, even in the darkness, if we hadn't already both been bound deeply by our shared fear and knowledge of Olivia Robinson.

In the morning I told Nena I was taking the Toronto train to visit my mother. Nena, still in bed, was turned toward the blackout curtains. Her hand emerged from the sheets to grope for clothing.

"You might as well while you're up here," she said.

"It's not a fun trip. She's in the earliest stages of dementia. Sort of pre-dementia."

Nena stopped reaching for the clothes, and her hand receded under the sheets. She pulled them over her head, as well. Her phone illuminated, casting a shadow of her head and hair against the wall of the small white tent she'd made.

"I've got to get back immediately," Nena said. "They just gave me—do you know who Brody Beagle is? This is a lot."

I sat on the bed and felt the spectral shoulder under the sheet. Nena didn't move, but I felt the recoil in her voice. There was something in my grip that evoked Olivia's eye-widening at the bar, its prescription of reaction.

"Osman, you can't change what we talk about because you suddenly feel like it. You can't just tell me about your mom losing her mind in a stupid fake-joking voice and expect me to become a sympathy machine. Don't do this to me."

I dressed, left, and cried. Okay, I cried, dressed, and left.

3

I couldn't follow Nena to her essential meeting, but I can simulate it for you. I thought about Brody Beagle during the slow train ride to my past, a five-hour trundle that I spent with my first of *The Siege of Krishnapur*. And with my detailed reconstruction of what Nena and I had tried to do when she had her clothes off and I'd exposed as much of myself as I could endure. I know Nena must have been forced to recollect our acts as well, to take herself through what she had done and how, even though she was never cruel enough to discuss it with me. There has to be a toll when a Nena fucks an Osman, beyond pain from the hulking pressure that had been above her, or an ache in her abdominals from trying to make something, anything work below her. An emotional bite, a sense that the natural order has been violated, that even if this particular Nena at this particular moment wanted to fuck this Osman, it wasn't right.

We talked about everything else later, including Brody Beagle. We're always talking, at least four hours a day of secret chat in an app possibly funded by the CIA, writing small and often extremely witty and worthwhile bits of prose that are swallowed and scrambled into indecipherable data every forty-five minutes. Mostly it's our shared earth of rotting low-culture garbage sprinkled with dandruff flakes of literature and Bach, the AAP employee index of cruel nicknames, detailed jokes and inventions about our differently broken homes and futures. The layers of reference and irony would make a leak inscrutable to all but the most dedicated codebreaker in HR, but I have seen people fired for a screencapped sentence about the hairline of an AAP VP who was himself on the verge of being fired.

When Nena's out of the office, away from our shared virtual space, I find myself watching her, as from a drone, a perfect Steadicam without an operator, hovering six invisible feet in front of her, staring until I feel calm enough to risk entering my own body again. After the impossible occurred and our bodies became involved that night in Montreal, our digital contact and my imagination of her, my constant consideration of where she was when she was away from our conversations or my sight, deepened into a form of narrative contact. I was telling myself the story of her day when she wasn't telling me herself. I would have explained this to her if it wasn't so impossibly creepy and high-pressure, if it didn't sound like something scrawled in a spiral notebook recovered from beneath a blood-soaked mattress. While I read my J.G. Farrell and when I later spoke to my mother, I reserved room for what Nena was living through at the same time, for the hours I would be able to resurrect when she let me in at the end of this difficult day.

The assignment email that Nena received in the hotel was from her direct superior, Lottie Roth-Yu, who did her best to be ominous about consequences if the meeting didn't go perfectly. Lottie wasn't in a position to make any threats, but she was able to pass them along. Behind Lottie's text wasn't just the soon-to-be annihilated Elodie Chan, or Halloran's flaking authority, but the board, the true seats of AAP power before Olivia's ascent.

Lottie had ordered a black car and was waiting for Nena, who had concealed part of her hangover with Italian sunglasses. Lottie smelled like the discontinued bubble gum vape pods she stockpiled. She talked Nena through the day ahead as the Lincoln's tires occasionally half-vanished into immense Quebec potholes on the way to the airport. Nena's earlobes reddened, charting the rising heat of her alcohol-burning digestive system. The recall of Olivia saying, "People grow," or perhaps a traumatic flashback to my greasy, breakfast-sausage fingers in her hair and on her neck made her shiver.

Lottie told her to take a breath.

Instead of unbuckling Lottie's seat belt and opening the car door, Nena nodded.

"Sometimes I can't even handle it. I mean, I can, but I'm watching everyone and wondering how we're all doing it. It's just go, like, beast mode go, every second, right?" Lottie said. "AAP, You-Own-Me. But I think this one could be kind of fun, and most importantly, it's an assignment that is totally you, Nena." Lottie had formed an early liking for Nena because they both had hyphenated last names. Nena's name was her own creation, which didn't occur to Lottie, despite the extremes of artifice that defined her own reputation, appearance, and curriculum vitae. Nena had chosen "Nena Zadeh-Brot" with the indifferent approval of her mother, as it sounded old world and pan-cultural and unplaceable. Her mother had been fine with it because Nena sounded enough like "Nina," the only bit of her original name that Nena has let me know.

Nena had been doing both of their jobs for about three years, and Lottie was fearful that Nena would soon stop inscribing reports with a shared byline, or would speak up when Lottie presented Nena's research at the monthly general meetings. Nena was not worried about this, because she'd been personally assured by the two board members she'd spoken to in the lobby while Olivia was apologizing to me that Lottie would be given her exit package before December. Lottie was twenty-one and had been offered her position and a four-year contract at eighteen in a symbolic hire by AAP's then-president Colleen Farmington, signifying their support for tech-and-entrepreneurship-focused students who chose to swap out an undergrad experience for invaluable real-world experience. The press release had infuriated AAP's clients, losing us two West Coast schools that had been on the *Forbes* Top Ten. Lottie kept her job, but Colleen, who co-owned a spa chain with Lottie's mother, was no longer with AAP.

"This is all in an email that we'll get to you before you fly out, but I thought you'd appreciate being onboarded face-to-face." Lottie's nose had recently become too small for her glasses to properly rest on them, so she kept her head tilted slightly upward.

"Oh, thank you," Nena said, meaning that she was thankful she could stop listening to Lottie entirely and just read her assignment on the plane. When Nena arrived at the airport, she would be sick in a private bathroom in the first-class lounge, and would take off the tight white GapKids T-shirt she had worn as a sop for the booze sweat when she knew she would be riding with Lottie, who had been sober her whole life and was fascinated by other people's vices.

There was a fund to access. A huge one. And Nena was ideally placed to access it. It belonged to professional start-up founder and abandoner Brody Beagle, who had one unicorn exit in his past. BeagleScreen, his first company, had two patents that Samsung wanted, and had paid for.

Since then, Beagle had been on eleven boards of directors and been CEO of six start-ups. All were service-related, none with a physical product. He and colleagues that had vanished onto eternal beaches or into family life or suicide had made abstract sums of money. He was twenty-eight, had dropped out of high school after watching entrepreneur YouTube for a summer, collected bourbon and VCRs, owned two apartment buildings in Greenpoint, and his wife was a wellness influencer who had recently died of breast cancer.

"I'm sorry about all this, but we need to strike right away, and since you've already met him, you're it," Lottie said, in the last few minutes of the ride, when Nena started to tune back in. Nena remembered to be generous and nodded in solemn assent, thanking Lottie for trusting her. Elodie Chan had recently been bypassing Lottie altogether, and would have given Nena this job directly if she wasn't combatting the early processes of her exile. This had been part of Nena's case for firing Lottie when she spoke to the board members in the hotel lobby—even Lottie's function as a pair of texting thumbs or an oral compressor of emails was almost moot. Nena's analytical focus became too tight as she absorbed Lottie's blather and prepared to scroll through the emailed brief. It didn't occur to her to ask whether Elodie had been behind this assignment at all, or if it was the board, or Halloran. Lottie may not have told her anything, but there would have been an enlightening silence. Elodie Chan's emails would be bouncing back with a boilerplate out-of-office by Monday, as her digital working life at AAP was requisitioned by IT for the careful harvest of lawsuit-deflecting details, which could be used in court or spread as rumour.

"Beagle may not know who AAP is, but we all saw you corner him at that event we did at the St. Regis," Lottie said. "It was almost scandalous, you two were talking like there was no one else there."

"He owns my apartment building, we talked about that. He didn't realize he still had those holdings," Nena said.

"Oh, we know," Lottie said, going for omniscience but landing on petulance. She recognized the tonal error and tried to adjust. "We were just so impressed that he turned up at all, and that you could keep him interested for an hour, and—"

"Okay."

"This is exciting," Lottie said, grasping Nena's hand, which was baking hot in the palm and coolly damp elsewhere. Showing resolve, Lottie kept the amphibian claw in her grasp. "I wish I could tag along and watch how you execute."

Lottie would vanish from AAP by mid-November. She reappeared during the 2020 lockdown to promote Ferrommune, a line of iron supplements that, when combined with a magnetic weighted blanket, were promised to reprogram the human immune system. Her family bought the company out from under her immediately, but were not able to delete the screencaps or the compressed infomercial she'd paid nano-influencers to link out to, in which an AAP-less Lottie Roth-Yu halts before each off-screen prompt in her earpiece, every silence a void of purposeless longing. She was bad at her AAP job, very bad, but Nena would eventually agree that it had been cruel to take away Lottie's only source of direction or purpose.

"Don't front-load this, but maybe Beagle'd be excited that we're switching to a model that reflects his past whatever-many start-ups, where we don't want to be dependent on sales for income," Lottie told Nena. "I think you were part of generating this take, yeah?" Lottie was referring to a report with her own name on the byline alongside Nena's, which she had written none of but possibly read up to the halfway point, where the statistics began.

"Yes. Abandoning the twentieth-century methods of bringing money in. We need—"

"Funding," Lottie said. She had kept her sunglasses on in deference to Nena's hangover mask, but now removed them to signal that her consideration allotment had been filled. Lottie had large-pupilled but extremely sad eyes, as though she were on a permanent misfiring ecstasy trip. They swallow light in the Ferrommune infomercial, making her look like she's just been pulled over and is remembering in the Maglite glow that her license is suspended.

"We missed out on being a start-up, but now we want to emulate that energy and ability to attract growth funds."

"You're quoting me," Nena said.

"No. I mean, sorry."

"I won't be saying anything about our financial aims, Lottie. He's not interested in our workings, he's interested in what we can do for the schools, right?"

Lottie hadn't thought about this, and wasn't going to start trying. She let go of Nena's hand and took out her phone, finding whichever text or email she was using as cue cards.

"Beagle doesn't do traditional meetings, nothing in a conference room, nothing by Skype, very few calls. He's all about actual one-on-one. Anyone who's gotten anywhere with his wallet can confirm. That's why we're excited to have someone in-house, you, who's actually gotten significant face time with him. This is precious, we're in a precious place, Nena. Brody's been a donor before, but never an investor at this level. His wife died six months ago but he's just started to really free the money. It's moving."

Lottie, or rather her commander's perception, was correct. Nena was the only choice for a lead on the Beagle attack. Brody Beagle had been in the news the week prior, for a donation to the hospital where his wife underwent early treatment that amounted to the budget of a second-tier Marvel film. He was currently, according to his final tweet before a self-imposed mourning exit from social media, angling to donate the same sum as an endowment to the right university, one willing to aggressively unroll gender balanced enrolment across every department within ten years.

"The university donation is sort of a last offering to his wife. To Gwen Geffen. He didn't even make it tech and business development exclusive, the money. He said outright that Gwen had done a History and Lit double major and that it had made her into the person he loved and would love forever. They ran this in TechCrunch. It's strange, Nena. So old-fashioned—like donating to a symphony, something like that, weirded everyone out. AAP can really use him. We need him," Lottie said.

The Lincoln they were riding in had a tank-like stability that delivered the physical data of dips into the scarred highway and off-ramps to its passengers as slight quivers, moving Lottie's bangs, clicking Nena's teeth together. "The hidden news, what everyone's acting on today, or like yesterday, is that Beagle's going to tie the recipient announcement to news of his own education venture, a college-disruptor that will deliver constantly updating curricula and personal interface with subject experts to a base of subscribers paying subscription fees that will make tuition seem—blah, blah, right? Okay?"

"I can work with that. Absolutely." Nena was unsure if Lottie knew that at least half of what she had attributed to Beagle was part of the AAP mandate document that Nena had prepared and leaked days before the conference, causing a gentle rise in stock prices and furious internal gossip about who the author was, after Elodie Chan had unwisely said it wasn't her. If Beagle was already ripping off Nena's ideas, it would be extremely easy to convince him that AAP's goals were his own.

To Nena, Beagle's name had long been familiar in more than the cloying way it is to all of us, a juvenile alliterative ring emerging from feeds and newscasts in a wash of other data. Nena still lived in the Greenpoint building he owned, while renting out the Manhattan condo that she acquired after her first serious year of AAP earnings to her senior assistant. That night in the St. Regis bar, two years prior, Beagle had asked her to describe not her unit or the exterior of the building, but the lobby, so he could remember which piece of his real estate portfolio it was. "I'm a lobby guy," he'd said, as though this reflected something about himself, perhaps that he was sensible and grounded.

"Let me know how it goes," Lottie said when she let Nena out of the black car and waved the driver back into his seat, taking out Nena's suitcase herself. Her tiny hands quavered beneath her wrists, which were exposed under the sleeves of an inadequate wool coat. Neither of Lottie's races were marginalized enough to help her survive her contract renewal period, and she still hadn't understood that ingratiating herself to the people who seemed to work beneath her protected her from nothing. Nena would never see her again.

"I will," said Nena, who wouldn't. "Bye."

In the bathroom, Nena put the Gap undershirt in the garbage can, then rinsed herself at the sink. Two white women who had heard her vomiting watched her, looking for an opening to commiserate.

"It's from drinking," Nena said. They didn't believe her.

While I was on the train to Mother, Nena flew to JFK, napping her hangover off. When she arrived at the apartment she paid Beagle to live in, she took a second shower and drank four litres of Evian with a jar of living algae distributed between them.

Nena took the risk of emailing Brody Beagle directly, drawing his contact from the immense AAP black book of tech and educational contacts that was given to all 100 upper-level employees.

Condolences aren't enough, Brody. I know it's been
months since we had that drink, but it would have felt
wrong to contact you sooner. I used to see Gwen in
the bookstore on Franklin, often . . . it was so close to
my building lobby, or your building lobby, that is, that
I would drop by there almost every rainy day when
I didn't feel like walking further. And Gwen would be
there, too. I know I'm babbling. I'm just sad I won't
ever see her there again. I can't imagine what you must
be . . . I mean, everything that she was, down to your
name, even. Up for a coffee if you want / need / are
intrigued to talk to a near-stranger with no stake in
your life right now other than concern.

The message was a risk and would not have survived company
vetting, which is why Nena sent it from a personal account that
ghosted an AAP address.

There was enough truth to the message she sent to Brody:
there had been drinks in hand in the St. Regis, and she had seen
Gwen Geffen at the bookstore, twice, and had nodded at her in
the way you nod at someone who seems known to you but is only
familiar because they are beautiful in an archetypal way, like a
Rodin or an image from a dermal-filler-specialist's Instagram.

"Beagle" was a name that Gwen had chosen for Brody, for his
first company and for himself. Nena knew this from an interview
Beagle had done for an online magazine that she ran on evenings
and weekends a decade back, when her pre-AAP salary at a media
analytics company wasn't close to what she needed to escape her
New Jersey basement suite. As far as she could tell, this interview
was the only place where Beagle mentioned the invented name.
The hook of Nena's fake magazine, *FutureLens,* was that AIs did
all the reporting, and it was a hook that had gotten responses

from 80 per cent of the top tech CEOs of that moment. *FutureLens* consisted of zero AIS, one email address, Nena and an employee. Nena had hired Bobby, the boy who played their fake AI in the online interviews, because his natural syntax mimicked the mistakes humans thought computers would make in language. He was quite smart if totally uninformed on anything other than classical drama, Fugazi, and the cultural history of rock climbing. Nena had given Bobby *FutureLens* when she started working at AAP. He lost it within a few months, which Nena only found out when she discovered that the URL directed to a camping mattress company. Bobby lived in his station wagon and various national parks now, and would keep climbing stone walls until he fell and could stop.

Nena assumed Brody Beagle's candour in this extremely low-profile profile must have come from pills or a weak mental state. Beagle talked about his anxiety and near-sobriety in almost every presentation he did, but never his meditation. This made pills more likely. Fluvoxamine, citalopram, paroxetine. Lulling ovals or circles, paired with the dull inquiries of an unemployable writer pretending to be a sophisticated social robot, had led Beagle to reveal that his wife had invented his name, and then refrained from taking it.

Brody Beagle answered Nena's email within five minutes.

> I'll recognize you. Meet me in that Franklin bookstore
> at two if you want.

Nena looked at hundreds of Gwen Geffen photos before the meeting. She wasn't sure if she wanted to avoid dressing anything like Gwen or make an effort to come close. She pocketed her phone, deciding that this wasn't where the calculations needed to take place. She put on black jeans and an ancient New Order

T-shirt that billowed and clung and felt more like a constellation of spores than cotton on the skin. She wore an unbuttoned wool coat overtop, and was absolutely not warm enough when she went outside. But she would fit Brody's vision of accessible cool, and the band imagery would negate any sort of threat from her ethnicity, would only make her light westernized brownness pop.

In the store, Brody Beagle had the lost look of a person who has left books behind along with chalkboards or Etch A Sketches as a viable media format. He was the only man over thirty who wasn't also wearing a toque and attending a stroller. Nena watched him being watched by another woman: young, with an elaborate mullet and thousand-dollar Valentino combat boots that were either brand new or had been polished that morning. She was taking photos of Brody Beagle with her enormous phone while pretending to scratch her face mid-text, with the smoothness of a drunk taking subway upskirts. Beagle was erect, radiating powerful bereavement. His trembling humanity had loosened the firm flesh from his skeleton, putting him in a permanent subsonic shiver where he seemed to be floating apart until an inspirational slogan or the recollection of some tremendous sum of money brought his electrons clustering back around their protons. Nena made the photographer vanish with four seconds of eye contact.

Brody handled Hillary Clinton's campaign memoir, tilting and weighing it as if it were the unidentified egg of a rare species, then circled the shelves and did the same with a Larry Kramer book, staring at the title in puzzled malaise. He opened neither. Nena did her best to glide into his field of vision, striding long and pausing, looking around like a pony that got loose a season ago and was now tentatively nosing its way toward the ranch fence, missing its stable. She wanted to look as lost as Brody imagined himself to be.

"It was books that actually got her the name," Brody Beagle said. Cinematically, he skipped any greeting.

"What do you mean?"

"For my company. For me. I figured anyone who even knows it's not my born name thinks it comes from the dog. That's what I thought, that Gwen had beagles when she was a kid, but her parents were allergic, you know. Of course you don't know that, but that's why. She was a total animal lover, which is how—" Beagle gestured at his own black jeans, which were striped and dotted with furs of various hues, from retriever gold to tabby silver.

"But it was a book. Her favourite book. *The Last Unicorn*, by Peter S. Beagle. That's where she took my manifesting-name."

Nena's commitment not to AAP, not to herself, not to decency, but to the institution of work itself allowed her to swallow her spit and paralyze her diaphragm and chest muscles, imagining the deep sting of a jungle insect plunged into the hollow of her throat, never allowing her to laugh again. She made it.

"That's beautiful. I can't believe it, but I totally can. I read that book twice when I was a girl in Tehran." Nena saw a flicker in Brody's eyelids that denoted he didn't know whether she grew up in a war zone and he was supposed to offer condolences of his own, or if she'd been torn from a place of ancient truths and forced to live her adult life in an alienating urban sewer. She was quick to get him off this track.

"We only spent summers over there, I grew up in Jersey. And *Unicorn* was one of the few books they let us get over the border. Because it was about wizards and witches, they didn't think there could possibly be anything dissident inside, but they never understand what something beautiful and deeply felt like that story can do to a child's heart." Nena hadn't read the book, had only been to back Tehran for an awful adult visit to her father, and was quite sure that she'd exaggerated Iranian censorship codes, but wasn't afraid that Brody would know this or that the republic would hold it against her. This had to be her next-to-final lie, she reminded herself. Three, or at most four more, and the entire structure of the deal would crumble before it could get to paper. This one could be partially truthed by reading *The Last Unicorn* before she saw Brody again.

"I never did read it." Brody looked at the Kramer book in his hands as though someone else had placed in there. He put it down. "I wanted to keep the story hers, right? And the title, you know, unicorns, billion-dollar exits, I immediately understood how that worked for my company and also as a philosophy that could carry me through my life. Gwen told me the plot so many times that the book was more hers than this Beagle guy's. And when I took the name, making it not just the company's but mine, it became mine, too."

"I know," Nena said. "I mean, I understand."

"You live in one of my buildings. I remember, from our talk. I half-remembered, at least. I'm sorry. My mind's been, it's just vanished, for some things, I had to send some texts, but I remember you."

"Don't apologize," Nena said, touching her temple, shaking her head.

"It was Gwen's idea to buy the buildings, you know."

"Smart lady." Nena had glitched here. This Nena wouldn't have said "lady," because Gwen or Brody wouldn't have. She pushed through. "You feel like you're drifting. Right? I don't want to assume, but that's what grief has been in my life. But it can be so different for everyone, even though no one really, really talks about it." She waved Brody toward the kids' area of the bookstore, pushing past the Grief shelves in the Self-Care section, and they each took a seat on a crenellation of the castle wall that sealed the toddlers off.

"Drifting," Brody said. He said it dreamily, whether he intended to or not, and Nena knew she had him. Brody stared at his hands, willing them to stop shaking, then clutched the thick, lawsuit-proof plastic on either side of him. He wiped his hands on his dark grey athletic sweater, a completely unselfconscious act following a completely self-conscious one. A trail of mucous so pure it seemed to radiate light snaked out of his nose. He let it.

Brody looked down at the dual traceries of dirt he'd left on his sweater and back up at Nena. Bringing up grief had made Brody look more like someone who was grieving, and he was grateful.

"You agreed to a meeting with someone you've only met once, not long after one of the most impactfully upsetting, life realigning moments of your life. You're Brody Beagle. You're impossible to meet with. That is one of the things about you that people talk about—you're the most inaccessible of the accessible guys in tech. Seeing you at that St. Regis event was so unexpected, everyone just knew that you must have been there as a favour to one of your juniors, or a friend."

Brody smiled at this, at the floor, at his past generosity.

"You know what I mean, Brody. You're incredibly honest and no one ever gets close enough to find out, except when you're on a stage or with a camera in front of you. No one can believe that someone so open, so giving of himself up there, can be so guarded in his private life. But I know because I'm like that too, in my small way. I know what it means to keep a pure part of yourself safe, because practising the kind of active openness you do would burn you out in ten years if you had to do it with everyone, all day. People would take everything that you were, everything that you are."

"That's what happened to Gwen," Brody said, just as he was supposed to. He lowered his head, and Nena extended a consoling hand above his leg. She made sure he saw her hesitate, close her hand softly, and set it back into her own lap.

"People think the stuff that makes a person a person happens in childhood, Brody. Sometimes. Sure. But I think for people like us, like Gwen, it's that first step out at as an adult that colours everything."

If you think it bothered Nena on any level to use an origin story as part of an overture the very day after she scolded me and our generation for being childishly addicted to them, I haven't done a good enough job of rendering the difference between her self and her working persona. But that is the purpose of this part of the story, to add to your knowing of her. And even though I do know her, I still tried to give her a hard time about it in chat. The false Gwen connection stuff was so obviously ghastly but necessary that we passed straight over it and into the origin thing. She explained to me that she didn't have enough time to explain why I was a failure, and that the chat was for jokes, interesting stories, and brutal insults only. I didn't answer, because I was doing a rare few minutes of work. She added a placating line: *I was navigating it like I would any business situation that involves vast sums of money and the emotional maturity of a man who has never been subjected to philosophy beyond Instagram poems, memes, and the first fifty pages of* The Alchemist. *There was genuine sympathy there, yes, but the best way I can indicate that I wasn't sharing anything true and originating about myself is to tell you that I was telling him about my past like it mattered to me.*

What was crucial in her speech to Brody Beagle was that she didn't damage the digestible exoticism that her skin tone and outfit had established. Nena's teeth are small and American, her nose and chin, something else: something Beagle could respect and fear, something that suggested wisdom and judgment, hieroglyphics and a scimitar.

"That's why I can't get over this name thing. Giving a choice like that to Gwen, letting her take a role in your everyday existence. An active symbolizing of your trust for her, and this new birth into adulthood. This seizure of your future, together. It's beautiful."

"I've been meditating ever since it happened, you know?" Beagle said. "I haven't actually replied to many emails. I've sent plenty, absolutely. I still spend the first two hours of each day making decisions, asserting, owning, being. That's how I built every single one of my companies. That's how I weathered all of what Twitter nobodies call 'economic shifts.' There are no shifts, only systems. A funding round has a weather pattern to it, that's what I've learned to see, what others have also learned to see, but not enough to act on. I spend those two hours acting. Decision, move, conclusion. I do that for two hours straight. Two hours. I understand when we're looking at a wintry investment climate, and I plunge expectations, only to come out on top when we clear the estimates. I've gotten reams of condolences and meeting requests, just sitting here next to you. My phone's blowing a raspberry in my jacket pocket, I have to lean away from it or I'll start vibrating. I don't give any assistant access to this inbox, the one that matters. I answered you because I decided to. It was after my two-hour window. I've been giving the one hour afterwards entirely to thoughts of Gwen and anything that arises from them. I slept in today, so your email came in that slot. That's Gwen communing with me. Same as three days ago when I heard from the one nurse on the cancer ward we took Gwen out of before doing home hospice. The one nurse we both really loved. I wrote the cheque to the cancer unit that day. Because in those moments, every message that opens me up is from Gwen. It's Gwen telling me not to just walk the dogs and come home, sit silent. It's Gwen telling me to live."

This flow of babble emerging from a combination of meditation apps and organic Adderall simulators was familiar to Nena. Instead of nodding, and certainly without ever opening her own mouth to interrupt his freestyle, she stared questingly into Brody's eyes and occasionally closed her own in an extended blink, as though staring inward, checking in on herself. Nena had experienced the apps and the uppers, but never at the same time. It was an extremely common tech and education sector weekend cocktail, especially among the growing numbers of non-drinkers in leadership.

There was an empty circular bench near the tills, and Nena considered bringing the conversation over there, but was worried the silver thread of it would snap on the ten-step walk over. Brody was still receptive, not quite dreamy any longer, but engaged. He had a few visible nostril hairs, like strands of copper wire, that blended with his stubble and sometimes moved with his small rapt breaths as he stared at Nena.

"You know what you're doing? In those long moments, that hour of silence? Of course you do. You're creating, Brody. That's what—I mean, this is conversation, I don't have a goal, but if I'm getting at anything, it's that invention has too narrow a definition. That's what I think of when I think of Gwen and you. Whenever I saw her in this bookstore, hovering at that display with her leather tote, her curiosity would take in the whole place, not just the book she was opening. Invention. This age, this era, is changing that concept for us. You and Gwen knew that, from the moment you invented a new mode of being yourselves by uniting over that name. Beagle. Beagle meant you weren't attaching yourself to the idea of a union that our parents would approve of. No. She kept her name, and gave you yours. You were aggressively detaching yourself from your pasts to make a truly shared personal future: *Beagle* was an act of mutual creation, not the reinforcement of tired hereditary and financial bonds you get from keeping your old name, from giving it to her, from doing any sort of shit with a hyphen. *That's* invention. And that's your career, too, isn't it?"

Nena was glad that Brody Beagle was wearing a sweater, and that he'd watched her not-touch him moments earlier. It allowed her to cup his elbow in an utterly unsexual way, to create an electric juncture of contact at his ulna as she made a fist with her other hand and opened it gently, like a slow firework. She let go of his elbow and he looked down at the joint. Nena risked a pause. Brody said what people on uppers rarely say.

"Go on."

"Invention used to be synonymous with product. There had to be a *thing*. So we made that the artificial point of origin for companies, for decades. The Edison or Tesla or Ford making *things*, things that had been conceived of with tubes and soldering irons and plans over sloping tables. The things that would redefine how life happened, and that therefore everyone needed to buy.

"But that isn't how culture and life move now. That was the millennia-long infancy of invention. And you and Gwen understood that. That's why none of your companies—and it's hilarious that you actually get criticized for this—ever made anything concrete other than money.

"Because you got it. Got it without needing to be taught. Companies, companies now, invent a space for creativity and connection. That's what Brody Beagle does. That's what Beagle means. It's what you and Gwen did in your relationship. And that's why you thrive a decade after your first billion-dollar exit, instead of being retired. These fake icons of hardware and software are flailing around trying to start relevant charities, and the app makers exit and suntan twelve hours a day pretending that was always their dream. They never invented anything. They modified existing products and made a mirage of temporary newness. You've been making up entire worlds from the moment you got into business with yourself, from the moment Gwen found you that name."

The mulleted young woman who had been taking creepshots of Beagle had only been warded off by Nena, not dispelled. She would later tweet her shots with the hashtag #TechBroMourning. They were not well received, neither funny nor interesting enough. Even the most brutally sarcastic of leftist post-irony anti-capitalist posters and podcasters passed over them in silence. Nena was holding Beagle's elbow in one of the four photos, her features scrawled over in violent digital red, as though she had been airbrushed with a knife.

Gwen Geffen was beloved by a narrow but important demographic. She had a wellness subscription box company that continued to grow posthumously, despite fears that Gwen's cancer would damage sales. But black salt and white charcoal continued to land in dormitories and two-bedroom, four-tenant apartments across the continent. The expansion into Europe and Asia was delayed but not cancelled by the coming outbreak and subsequent recession. The packages were carefully peeled open by consumers who would never be able to pass beyond the realm of sample size. Gwen still has fans who will always hate Brody and blame him for her death, calling attention to their early withdrawal from the cancer ward and the couple's decision that Gwen should die at home, where she was attended by two purchased doctors and one twenty-four-hour nurse.

Olivia Robinson surfaced during the second part of the pitch, when Beagle's driver was taking Nena and Brody to a shuttered Queens sweatshop that had been Gwen's last purchase. The sewing machines had been donated to various makers of activist couture, Gwen cleared the space to make an enormous greenhouse, then died.

"I want to bring this up before it gets weird," said Brody. "I'm quite close with someone you might know at AAP. She was on the ward with Gwen, left at the same time as we did. She even gave us some weeks at the house. She was with us for the hardest days." As soon as Olivia was named, Nena felt her conjured, as though she'd oozed in through the vents. Nena wished that Lottie Roth-Yu could appear as well, so she could take off her Cartier sunglasses and thumb both eyes deep into her skull. Of course Elodie Chan hadn't commissioned Nena to take this project on. Of course Brody hadn't just agreed to meet her because they had chatted once, two years ago. Of course.

"Olivia Robinson," Nena said, refusing to remember until quite a bit later, when this was all over, when I was interrogating her over a dish of Szechuan green beans that I would mostly eat and entirely throw up, that she had been the one to say the name.

"That's her. You know her?" Brody asked.

"Yes, AAP is very streamlined, so I know everyone, if not actually that well. Olivia recovered. She's back with us."

Brody looked out the window. "That seems quick," he said. "I should call her." They were driving through a brief cloudless rain, and Nena watched Brody seeing God or Gwen in the shimmering drops. His low constant tremble geared up, shaking his forearms and then his shoulders. Nena unclasped his clenched fists and joined them as namaste emoji prayer hands. He let a tear fall on them. Nena stared beyond his head at the spectre of Olivia, who couldn't have taken this meeting herself; she was too healthy, too recovered for Brody to see her without being hurt.

Nena didn't go through that portion of the analysis at the time, but when we argued about it later on over chat, she conceded I may have a point. What she did understand is that Olivia had formed an extremely temporary allyship with Lottie Roth-Yu to secure this fund for AAP and to reconnect with Brody, at which point Olivia would immediately and forever cut Nena out. And if Nena tried to exert any control again—how the fuck was she expected to compete with cancer ward veteran bonding? She couldn't. She would perform this portion of the task, meaning that Olivia would never be remembered as the one who'd asked Brody Beagle for money. Nena would receive a bonus for securing the fund, perhaps, if Olivia allowed it. But none of the credit, once Olivia was managing the money, managing Brody. In that car, as Brody's chest and shoulder blades expanded and hollowed from the pressure of unspent sobs forced back into a body, Nena recognized that she didn't have a year to get her retirement money gathered up. She had as much time as Olivia allowed her.

Nena released Brody's hands. He looked up, his face red and boyish, a Little League swinger who's just waffled in front of his family.

"Olivia's just finding her feet at the company again, but I'm sure she'll want to speak to you soon. She doesn't know about me reaching out, of course. This isn't business," Nena said.

To pull Brody out of a potentially deal-queering misery spiral, she talked about Tehran and her difficulties with the version of her father she had decided to tell Brody about, a man who still drove a bus in New Jersey, and had never happily migrated back to Iran to found a prosperous property management company. A reverse voyage with a good outcome was antithetical to the kind of arc that men like Brody wanted to hear from immigrants: they enjoyed tales of oppression left behind, of the humble glory of work, told in a light, comfortably American tone with an occasional accented proper name glowing with desert warmth. She'd used bus-driver-dad professionally for much longer than I'd used my plane joke.

"I'm sorry, I feel like I can talk about this stuff around you," she said, after concluding with the incident of her father nearly missing her MIT graduation for a union meeting.

"That means something. Don't apologize. Thank you for telling me."

Inside the warehouse, a group of twenty workers were finishing a complex irrigation system. Two white men in Dickies commanded a Central American crew. The scent of huge barrels of fresh earth overlaid the old rust and burnt fabric scent of the cement-floored factory. Brody tilted one of the barrels over, prying off the lid with an Opinel knife that he had in his jeans pocket and likely used fewer than six times a year.

"This is Amazon earth. From after the fires. Incredibly nutrient rich, an entirely new resource for South America. I have six partners in Brazil." The dirt, replete with invisible insect carcasses and cremated sloths and carbonized bark, did indeed look blacker than most black dirt. As Brody walked on and Nena followed, a small brown man righted the barrel and restored its spilled contents with a tiny shovel and paintbrush-sized broom.

"Tell me something unique about AAP," Brody asked, in a voice Nena hadn't heard before, perhaps the skewering one he used on anyone who came shuffling to him for money. For a moment, she thought she'd failed, that Beagle had interpreted this whole meeting as a disguised appeal for money. *But that wasn't it*, she typed to me. *It was his embrace, what he did to bring the conversation to full maturity. It wasn't something he was trying to catch me on, and it wasn't something he just had to get out of the way. It was part of his objective, too, his half of getting close.*

"AAP works on a philosophy of the individual-as-team. If workflow interests you."

"It does. And I've never heard that term."

"We hire in batches of four. And you spend every moment that isn't sleep—so work, meals, exercise, social—with your pod for a full two weeks after hiring. We take care of childcare, arrange occasional spousal meals, and of course everyone goes home at the end of each night, but the point of the intensive is for you to absorb the working methods, philosophy, skills, and strengths of the other three people in your pod. And at the end of that two weeks—it's a probationary period, too—you're tested on the skills that you *didn't* come in with, and your knowledge of your podmates. The goal, and we build to it by re-forming an expanded version of the pods every six months—"

"Each new hire absorbs and becomes that miniature team, and you apply that philosophy to a company as a whole, so eventually the ideal employee contains—"

"AAP. We want each cell to be a whole. Yes. It reflects our interactive educational packaging, too, one of the products we bring to schools."

"It's incredible," Beagle said, shaking his head. He was right, it was incredible, and we had forced the practice on all new hires for the past year and a half. Nena had modified the proposal I'd written for it myself, my first big organization-wide coup. Leadership and management didn't have to come close to practising any of it, which made it immediate-implementation-friendly, and Nena's polish on the theorem I'd come up with made it sound less like the cautionary science-fiction story it had started as on my laptop.

Nena inhaled deeply, commented on how sweet the dirt smelled, and talked about her mother's hanging garden of planters in the kitchen of their tiny apartment in Summit, where there hadn't been enough square footage on the ground for them all to sleep, eat, and work.

"She took a trellis off a trash heap—not at a dumpster, just a sort of pile of garbage at a median, lawn chairs and coat hangers—she cleaned it, sanded it, gave me five dollars to paint it, and mounted it to the ceiling with a stud finder she borrowed from the building super, telling him she was hanging family pictures. Then you'd look up into this absolute glade, these flowers and especially these herbs—she'd reach up and pull down parsley, dill, sabzeh—we'd eat from heaven."

"That's beautiful."

"I've tried to keep that element of the natural in my life since childhood. Effortlessness starts with concerted effort, you know? Getting those herbs up there in the kitchen took real work, but after that, my mom would look like she was casting casual spells or flicking her hair while she was putting together these amazing, complex dishes."

"You cook?"

"No. I meant that I want that kind of naturalness in my life, all of it. That's why I could never have a conventional job. Just like you. AAP isn't the office I go to, it's the way that I think, it's what I believe. Reshaping education to be as pure and accessible as checking your phone, as walking into a new day outside your apartment and deciding to run, knowing you can because you instinctively put the right shoes on. Being natural is hard, and it's how you do business too, Brody. And it's what you and Gwen did with your marriage, bending this institution to your will. How you live, how you create—it's always going to be a testament to her. You queered marriage by doing it your way, and we're queering institutions like universities by just pointing out that it doesn't have to be the way it always has been. And it shouldn't." Nena didn't have much left at this point, and hoped that she was connecting themes, not just repeating them. The "queering" bit had been a risky improvisation, and something that Nena found deeply unethical to say about two white heterosexual rich people getting married and staying that way, but she knew Brody well enough by then to believe it would stick, that it would take, that he would adore being called queer by someone who thought he was straight and progressive enough to take it as a compliment. Brody was watching the workmen. The two white ones had become far more animated when they saw that it was their ultimate leader who had entered the workshop. As Nena spoke he was also eyeing the curved roof, and she knew there would be a garden hanging there within a month whether Brody pushed money in AAP's direction or not.

When Nena got to this part of her conversation with Beagle, I interrupted the unbroken column of telling on her side of the chat to ask if this detail about her childhood apartment was true. There was a digitally transmitted hesitation before the bobbing ellipsis of her response began.

You're asking me that? That's what you're interested in? Okay. The herbs were there, but it was pure utility. And part of that utility was to help mask the smell of dad's pot plants, which took up what would have been my bedroom if the weed wasn't his main income outside of disability. We sucked power in from an outlet on the side of the building that the ancient Portuguese landlord didn't know existed. My dad ran a black extension down the side of the brickwork then put up a fake drainage pipe over and around the outlet.

All that dill and every garlic-heavy meal we made was as much to mask the pot as it was to feed us. When he dried it, the smell got so intense I vomited. Mom made him do that part of things somewhere else after that, probably the attic of his friend Kourosh's store. This was a year before we took off for Switzerland.

Do you like this, Osman? More interesting than what I was talking about? I'm not hiding anything. I just don't want to be actively bored when we talk. Usually you allow me that.

"What do you think of Olivia, Nena?" Brody Beagle asked. He gestured for her to sit down with him on the cool, upward slanting cement floor at the north end of the warehouse, where the scents of sawdust and old, unmoving air were still perceptible under the overwhelming smell of wet earth.

"I think she's great," Nena said. "Anyone who meets her can tell they're in the presence of someone pretty remarkable, quickly." Looking into Beagle's eyes, seeing this unconfident face that somehow inspired and birthed confidence in others, this man who had a dense philosophy of slogans that he would need to add to selectively until he found three or four that contained and dispelled grief, she didn't want to inform on Olivia Robinson.

The lies that Nena had discovered about Olivia—the alternate childhood, the abandoned pastor—they wouldn't even be interesting to Brody Beagle. Pointing to a lie is only exciting if it directly indicates a concealed truth that has value. It can be intriguing if it merely opens the question of what the truth could be, but unveiling Olivia's hidden past would only lead to Brody asking Nena about hers, and perhaps asking Olivia about Nena. And Olivia knew important truths about Nena, ones that Nena had never given me.

Brody, leaning back on that cement slope, was probably thinking he could make an excellent half-pipe in the space. In one of his keynotes, he had talked about skateboarding as an urban design hack that kept him constantly rethinking who the end-user of any product really is.

Nena admitted to me that she was thinking of battle. This was in odorous fleshy life again, over that plate of Szechuan beans in the aftermath of my long battle with Olivia, the one I hadn't started yet, the one that Nena left before it began. I argued that her decision to effect no resistance against Olivia's takeover of AAP, of her use and marginalization of us and of the Nenas and Osmans to come, was an internal surrender. I ate two beans without chewing, the slick sauce matching the viscosity of my saliva exactly. Both slid down my throat in a chokeless coast. The enemy you imagine is as important as the one that you actually have, I told Olivia. The unwitting foes we obsess over online and in dreams, the ones we picture scheming against us, wanting to absorb us and our place in the world: some of them forget our names and faces after the first meeting, if we meet them at all. But that doesn't mean it isn't essential to hate Olivias, to have hated them. How else would we decide what's important, what our values are, who we can safely share with, how to live?

"I still don't hate her," Nena told me. "I won't." Perhaps she didn't tell me this over the beans, but she said it, or typed it, somewhere.

"Olivia's always been great. Super sharp," Nena said to Brody Beagle. "It was heartbreaking to see her momentum at AAP interrupted, and I can't wait to see what she's going to do now that she's here again."

"I don't like to use 'brave' for survivors, because that implies that someone like Gwen didn't have the guts to get through being sick—"

"No one would think that," Nena said.

"But Olivia really did have bravery. I saw her with a shaved head, she got that stick-thin, that, you know—" Nena watched him wonder if "Auschwitz" was offensive in this context—"that sort of prison-camp thin. Even Gwen didn't get that far. We stopped chemo before that when, we, when we knew."

Brody slumped to his left slightly, as though he were having a neurological event. His right side descended to the same level a moment afterwards, and he drew his knees up to rest his face against them. Nena moved her body away from his slightly, so that when she put her hand on his shoulder, which was moving in those gentle shudders again, it would be comforting, not intimate. When Brody established the Beagle Generation Knowing Fund the following Monday, AAP was a contractual partner, and Nena Zadeh-Brot's administrative oversight was part of the contract.

But Brody added a clause that Olivia Robinson would take on this oversight role should Nena ever leave the company. When everything was already signed, Nena texted Brody a thank you.

Nena ctrl'c'd his reply and v'd it to me: *Committed to it. So happy. Olivia you and me, drinks soon.*

Olivia got to him sometime on the weekend, sometime after Nena rested her hand on Brody's quivering deltoid, before the lawyers processed paperwork. Olivia found a crack and turned it into a fissure. That contract became a guarantee that Nena would vanish when Olivia decided she wanted her gone.

4

I rang the doorbell and waited for Sameen, knowing she could take as long as six minutes to appear. This wasn't because Mom was slow, but because she wouldn't open up for an unexpected caller who didn't demonstrate unusual persistence. I was rested but nervous, my nose clogged and my teeth buttery and reeking in my mouth. After I'd stopped pretending to read on the train, the trip passed in a near-constant brood interrupted by apnea naps, from which I would awake gasping with visions of Olivia y'alling and saying "channelling" repeatedly until the word began to sound like a fused verbing of "anal" and "anneal."

I rang again and backed away, kicking dirt and leaves clear from the walkway. Our front garden, which had been a battleground between natural growth and mother's long jags of lethargy on one side and rigorous planting and bursts of energetic pruning on the other, looked its best in autumn, in this particular kind of October. The chalk maple crimson, its small trunk tender and white, the purple mouths of morning glory in their early-afternoon slouch as the leaves and vines around them browned.

I paced the cement path, invisible under crackling autumn skin. Mom never raked, not out of laziness, but because the dead leaves fed the roots once everything was beneath snow. That's what she said, and I never questioned it in case my father were to buy and thrust a rake in my direction.

There were three grinning-arrow packages and a seed catalogue leaning against the front door. I picked them up and leaned against the doorbell. Two packages were books. Not novels, but psychology or psychoanalysis. Mom hadn't worked since university summers, but she continued to read everything in her field, and could have made her fortune as a straight analyst or combination guru-shrink, depending on what outfit she wanted to wear. We used to joke about it when I was in college, feeling Ajit's low simmer if he was in the room, as he imagined the humiliation of his wife either directly embarrassing him or, worse, outstripping his notability and success. So Mom stayed at home and read for decades.

Dad had banned Amazon from the household, but Sameen broke the embargo when he went into hospice, at first to bring in ras el hanout and urfa pepper from a spice warehouse. She spent hours with NYT Cooking on her phone as she watched him being cared for and waited for it to end. Sameen told me these things during our late-night calls when she got home from his dying room. They were the longest, kindest, most dissociative conversations we'd had since my childhood—two-hour, whispered, headphones-in exercises in lulling small talk, grains of chat that could safely drift around or blow over the great subject of Ajit's final departure, while Sameen fell asleep with a cooling mug of chamomile on her bedside table.

Those spice tins were still untapped. Mom continued to Amazon every lamp or book or blanket she felt she needed, and had also discovered delivery apps in the post-Ajit era. She attacked her stomach lining with West Indian roti and Scotch bonnet hot sauce three times a week, then recuperated with a two-day cycle of water and penitential avocado rolls. She ate tiny portions at each sitting, which was why she was still so small, and getting smaller. She went through the psych books she ordered with unbelievable rapidity, consuming as much as she could with the brain time she had left, but each time I asked her about one she treated me as though I were quizzing her on comprehension and recall.

Mom opened the door and gazed at the jut of my stomach, which I tried to heft up and forward with Jolly Aplomb. My actual feelings about my appearance came quite close to the puzzled distaste I saw on her face, which was like a beakless sparrow's with tiny jowls shaded in by an English children's book illustrator. Sameen was wearing neon-purple framed glasses that a salesperson must have convinced her were daring, not just unsellable stock to be foisted on the elderly. She stared at the gap between my third and fourth shirt buttons. I usually wore a white undershirt to avoid the eyeless flesh-and-hair wink effect created by a torso like mine crammed into a garment built for the tall, broad-shouldered human male who had earned my garment size and not merely eaten his way into it. But this shirt didn't hang right with anything on beneath it. Mom banked the sight and decided to open the conversation with mercy.

"Hi, sweetie."

Surprise had vanished since Ajit died. This wasn't a dementia symptom, nor was it the wife-on-the-pyre hollow-existence routine. Their marriage, not arranged but certainly not an accident—two Northern Indians of a certain class background in a certain university town in the U.K. with certain family encouragements that would leave them unable to entirely trust the purity of their love—had started distant and become cordial, mocking. Hierarchical with irruptions of instability, but occasionally warm. They slept in separate beds but burped and yawned in the same rooms. They pretended each day was different from the last, or at least that they woke into an alterable reality, when eventually neither of them could possibly have felt that way. With Ajit dead and me gone Sameen hadn't suddenly stopped being surprised by things, she had stopped pretending she viewed any event as a disruption of the natural order. We had talked about it on the phone in the hospice era, once, just before Sameen fell asleep and left me to silence the line. She had always accepted her life and the occurrences within it as fated manifestations, successive happenings in a string reaching back to the beginning of her reality and toward an ending that was drawing close, the final expectation. The widened eyes and shocked smiles of past decades had been Sameen's chosen, conscious acts, always for our benefit, mine and Ajit's.

I kissed the top of Sameen's head, the line of skin that ran down its centre, noticing as I pulled away that it was thinning toward the front, almost gone, as though the parting had finally managed to start an uprooting coup. Mom's hug was fond, substantial, a more forceful and accepting hold than her body should have been capable of offering. Sameen is more human than I am. Perhaps this thinking is a generational mega-trait, a sense that the purity of the species is diluted with each mating and reproductive cycle, that the former batch of humans in every family has more of the real right thing in them. But it was certainly present in her half of our embrace. I stared at her budding baldness with sympathy and satisfaction, and with a dumb speechless love that made me want to back away, push a thumb far under my rib cage and pull up and outward. We walked into the living room, which mom had stripped of my father's profusion of rugs and wooden furniture. This left two couches, a television, a plush tray for her tablet, and bare floors.

"You should wear sandals," she said, pointing to my feet as she sat. I set down on the edge of the TV stand, felt it about to tip, and rocketed up, hitting the screen with my ass but catching it with my right hand. Sameen let me settle the television and myself.

"If you still had the carpets I wouldn't need sandals."

"Sandals keep the cold out better than carpet. They surround the foot, trap air." She cupped her hands as though she was holding something in them that moved.

"No one wears them anymore. And especially no one travels with them. Clean sneakers inside, maybe. Don't people who come over complain about how freezing it is? Ranjeet, Mrs. Eckhardt?"

"They don't come unless I ask them."

"And you don't ask them," I said. Mom smiled, and her eye roll was magnified under the silly glasses. "I understand why you don't want Mrs. Eckhardt over here. I've seen her Facebook. The Russians own her brain."

"I don't look at that," Mom said, lying, her Facebook open on the tablet below the tray, which she'd placed halfway over it while I dealt with the television. "But she has become very boring in real life."

"And she hasn't aged like you have. Hard to look at. Those awful yellow-brown patches on her hands make it look like her all of her skin would blow off in a bad storm."

This, a joke I'd come up with on the way over, worked well. We'd been making fun of Mrs. Eckhardt as a family for years. She and her husband had once lent Ajit twenty thousand dollars after he'd made a tax error and gone deep into the wrong investment in the same quarter, and none of us had ever forgotten or forgiven the gesture. Mom rubbed her smooth, uniformly coloured and patchless hands together as she laughed.

"You're terrible. I like the place cleared out the way it is now, Osman. Not just the carpets, all of it. If you have guests over, they expect to have things around to sit on, to inspect, to rest their cups on. I was tired of walking around here when it was crammed like a bazaar. I like some space."

"It's depressing. Like you're moving out." We moved into this house when I was eleven and incredibly lonely. I had used the occasion as a temporal and physical marker for the era where I would no longer be Close With My Parents, because I wanted to be comfortable with solitude and also ruggedly cool and detached for when the high school flood of friends and a girlfriend or two arrived. None of these characters appeared. But through successive evenings of turning my father down for viewings of DVDs he'd special ordered for us and telling my mother that I was tired of our weekend trips to eat and shop in Scarborough, I did manage to alienate my parents enough that I became a genuinely alienated teenager myself, so unused to conversation that I would need to take slurping salival pauses into my retainer when talking to a teacher or the mailman, eloquent only on MSN Messenger and LiveJournal. I later watched the other adults around me recover this distance with their parents, saw the dual-sided acknowledgment that it was a phase. In my family, we had silently determined that it was an evolution of the relationship. My dad and I focused on discovering ways to disappoint each other, he unconsciously and I consciously, developing the mutuality of opinion that allowed us to finally part. Mom and I continued to drift in a natural pattern, tugged back occasionally by circumstances that wound us together like a linking tendon that only existed in periods of stress, such as death or the onset of terminal dementia.

"We're half–moved out. Your father's moved out. This is what a house with half the rubbish in it looks like, and I think it looks lovely, Osman. And don't convince yourself I thinned it out because I was afraid of colliding with things and breaking a hip."

In her seat, Sameen did a small dancing shake, a joyful movement between shrugging and shimmying that was alarmingly quaint and filled me with a sense of how old we both were, and how much of that time had been spent together, even if we'd usually been in separate rooms.

I'd known that with no Ajit here to force the invitations, large gatherings would be over, but I didn't think individual friends would go as well. Sameen was damn good at it—hosting—as I'd observed from the upper floor, staring down from the darkened hallway as she served platters of appetizers that had been baked to emulate the mini-quiches and sausage rolls of the era's popular catering, occasionally invigorated with a round of samosas or an oyster bar if the company was of the type to appreciate it. At those parties, Sameen spoke with her own cheerfully uplifting version of Dad's faux Britishness, an Indian valley girl Katharine Hepburn in which the rasp was the only identifiably false part, but also the most charming. Between their two forged voices and a few imitable television actors, I shaped the way I speak.

That day, Sameen didn't even offer snacks or tea. She relaxed into the silence of my expectation, a flat harmonious smile on her face, and I went to the kitchen for glasses of water. The cabinets had brass handles that tinted toward green between the treatments that my mother used to order every two years. It had been long enough since the last one that the turquoise verdigris looked to be patterned into the handles in the kettle's steam path. The handles were one of the few interior details that hadn't been erased by renovations. The cabinets were the same light bevelled elm, but the secret slumbering tiger pattern on the long one by the fridge that had been worn by age and patina and the work of my own thumbnail was gone. Its body had been the scratches, its stripes the unharmed wood. Vanished now under sandpaper and an insipid but glossy chocolate milk shade of paint. The corner of the countertop just under the fruit bowl, where the peeling rim once allowed me to insert four fingers, was gone along with the rest of that counter, replaced by a contiguous slab of silver-black marble that looked like the fretboard of a tasteless metal guitarist. But the glasses that I carried back were recognizable pints, thick and Guinness-logoed, stolen by my father from the graduate student pub, where he used to carry his drink out while he smoked a cigarillo, walking straight out to his car when he was finished.

Mom asked me about travel first. The train from Montreal to Toronto cost me an expensable ticket and five hours. I had intended to make it an AAP-related trip by looking up a client, any client, to have lunch with, probably at a steakhouse three blocks away from the faculty club where Dad freed me from his life, and only four blocks from the office that the English department kept for him until his death. (It is now shared by six sessional professors on a rotating schedule. Dad's immense Scandinavian desk, purchased by the school in 1972, has been sold to a hotel.) But I decided to pay for the train ticket myself, making a personal division that allowed the mental space to take care of this mother business, to consider a possible Olivia Robinson plan, and to dissect my ongoing panic about Nena Zadeh-Brot, who had just seen me crying, and worse, naked.

"Are you here about my brain?" Mom asked, watching the dewlap under my chin judder as I tried to find a way to get into the subject. I swallowed dry, dustless air that turned my throat papery.

"Discussing what needs to be done, Ma."

"I wanted to have the conversation, sweetie. You didn't have to get on a train, or a plane, or a bus to make me talk about what we need to take care of. Come on."

When you're altering daily reality for an elderly person, you can't make a phone call, even a video call. You have to deal with them in the same reality that is being taken away from them. Sameen wasn't erratic yet. Since my first and only meeting with her doctor, months after Dad died of his sudden illness (which was actually a long-diagnosed and untreated tumour that he had told no one about, nourishing both the cellular growth and secret until he was in the hospital), I had visited Sameen four times. And she seemed nearly fine. There had been no planting of wrapped cabbages in the garden, no four in the morning phone calls to friends. But it would happen, and I needed to speak to her about having someone come in. Not a caretaker, not even a nurse, just a support worker who could check on her welfare and also recommend a cleaner.

We'd been told Alzheimer's, but she preferred dementia. The doctor, an East African gentleman named Otieno with long but extremely clean fingernails who met me in a restaurant near St. Joseph's the same Christmas I went home to witness her SkipTheDishes addiction, said it may possibly be mixed dementia. Perhaps he never said Alzheimer's, I can't remember. Mom reported a scene in which the previous neurologist, Akhtar, had been dismissed after a long argument with my father about her care, when Dad brought a sheaf of highlighted WebMD printouts to her appointment, pointing out conditions that Akhtar had neglected to test for. I had missed Dad's email forwards more frequently than I'd missed him, his strange all-caps subject line slurry of *Guardian* reviews of books he'd never read, junk medical science, borderline climate change denial, and occasional anti-Muslim screencaps from WhatsApp that he presented without any context or commentary. His politics were inscrutable, except in the classroom, where they were exactly what his students needed them to be from decade to decade. He would never allow a belief to interfere with his ability to bloviate about his favourite novels.

My father stopped screaming at neurologists when he began his own hospital to hospice to grave journey. But Akhtar, who Mom described as having the affect of a gulag guard when he wasn't administering memory tests in a singsongy market vendor's voice, refused to take her on again, even when Sameen told him that her husband was dead. Perhaps I could have changed this if I had still been involved, either by yelling at Ajit or placating Akhtar. But I'd removed myself.

Dismantling a family bond by inattention isn't just a matter of turning away. It takes consistent work. Ajit and I both got tired of our unacknowledged combat, and ended it through AAP. Ajit put the separation into words. The moment he did was the first time I'd felt properly like a character, not just a reader, a true dislocated Indian protagonist who had been cast out, even if the details didn't quite fit. Dad, Dr. Ajit Shah, was a University of Toronto professor who called Harold Bloom by his first name and had been invited to his house twice. He manipulated all the necessary committees to get me into the Ph.D. program and shepherded my dissertation on Anthony Powell from his emeritus coffin. My failure to get a job he blamed on the market, on the techno-capitalist savagery that turned society away from the liberal arts, on the sprawling might and size of the administrative divisions, on the influx of money from other shores and the dominance of financial ideals that had turned his Socratic grove into an educational-industrial complex. But my decision to quit a bookshop job and take a position at AAP, a chief devourer of humanities departments, he blamed on me. This was beyond the scion of a military family deciding to vote Democrat. It was like the son of a Purple Heart recipient taking a summer job with ISIS. I was cast out, not from a tangle of clutching hennaed auntie arms by a stony moustached face that turned to reveal the flat plane of a kurta's back, but by my dad on the steps of the faculty club, both of us wasted on Scotch while my mother waited in the car. He had gravy on his tie and I was holding a bag of Yorkshire puddings, items I skipped from the buffet but planned to eat the next day when my carb fast ended.

"You don't care about what I do. How I make money, how fucking abject or shameful or unlettered it is," I told him. "Not really. You want me to complete *your* project. You want me to stand by, failing and less than you, while you complete it. You just want me in the room."

"You're—I can't properly come to terms with how someone so inarticulate could have leaked out of me. My 'project'—and to hell with you for saying that in disdain, in dismissal—is beyond you. I just don't want you to humiliate me, your mother, and myself."

Two Indians, one who would never have children and the other regretting the one he did have, both stinking of roast beef, screaming that the other didn't understand the world, hitting the diasporic end of our line. I didn't ruin the perfection of that terminus by seeing him again, and I know he appreciated it.

"Have you talked to Dr. Otieno since last winter?" Mom asked. "I have, Ose. I talk to him every other week. I know what's happening. We're very realistic about it all. The pace. The process."

I inhaled, put the tip of my tongue into the roof of my mouth where the smooth inorganic comfort of my retainer had once been, and said what I had come here to say. Since the intimacy, borrowed from death, of our hospice-period phone calls, we'd returned to our old way of speaking, of not speaking. Sameen took her glasses off and pinched the deep, darkened indents they'd made at each side of her nose, the same mark each pair of glasses she'd worn for decades had grooved darker and deeper with the gradualness of living. In her presence I was gripped by a helpless fondness, which kept my mouth slightly open and my brain performing both sides of a conversation we had in an alternate relationship that had grown after the mid-night whispered calls during Ajit's death. The unspeaking love I had for her and the dumb fog that emanated from my mouth while I listened or just stared at her smudged living face with an overmastering sense of Sameen's oncoming death, a reassuring, dreadful, definite moment that would allow us to stop trying to know each other.

"We need to have someone come in to check on you, Mom. Just once a week, at first."

"I know. Otieno and I discussed it last month, he gave me a list of ten carers that I've narrowed. You can help me decide on one. You're here for two days?"

"Yes." The minimum, as she expected. As I didn't expect, my task was nearly over, the reason for my visit expended. Sameen wasn't just unsurprised, she had already done it, and was offering me this chance to rifle through the CVs of doubtless interchangeable care workers and nurses in order to let me feel involved.

The refurbished diner booth where I sat and waited for Dr. Otieno last December had a table that cut into my torso and a bench seat that wasn't just uncomfortable but seemed to be actively attacking my thighs and buttocks. Otieno hung his white coat on the rack by the door, ate a kale Caesar and congratulated himself for making time for me on his lunch break. He told me the symptoms were still slight, but that experience and the MRI Mom had been given after a minor stroke told him to expect steady decline. I drank tea and made it clear that I would be paying the bill, but didn't thank him. A small stroke had already been explained to me in text accompanying the cross-section image of Sameen's brain that arrived in my inbox, forwarded by Mom. To me it looked like a gap, an uneven pathology that would soon widen to take in the rest of the brain, grey meat and synapse sparks sucked over the gravity of its expanding rim.

Mom drank her water faster than I did because I did all of the talking for the next half-hour. This was our dynamic on these post-Ajit visits, though this time I had expected that my demand for home care would derail the process. The usual had been me blathering for minutes or hours while she sat, draped in various shades and fabrics of blue, blouses from Fairweather or delivered salwar kameez, looking as calm as a retired actress or culinary-adventure author or Merchant Ivory screenwriter being photographed for a 1980s magazine profile that would teem with words like matrician and doyenne. Today, instead of bickering with her about managing the inevitability of her aging collapse, I started telling her about Olivia Robinson. I inserted myself into the story that Nena had told me not by pretending that I had been there, but by pretending that I was Nena. I had told my mother many stories this way when we had our midnight calls. Not to make myself seem important, but to avoid having to describe other people in my life and their importance to me. I would have told this story without Olivia Robinson in it, if it could still remain a story, but she was impossible to eliminate. And without her, I couldn't think of anything else to talk about.

"So I hired her, because I had to. I set the tests, she passed the tests. I either had to take her on or disregard this entire system that I'd told my superiors was the only way to discern the correct candidates for the position, their profile tests and online pre-interviews being useless for a role that needed this sort of flex. And now she's gone and, I don't know, surpassed me but in this very insidious manner, as though she doesn't think I've noticed. As though I don't know that she'll run out of uses for me soon, as well." Speaking to my mother about myself and Nena as one collapsed entity waiting to be crushed under Olivia's reclaiming-femme-power-heel or quirky-casual-Keds was another way of drawing close to Nena. It was the best version I could deliver of introducing her to my mother, for now, now being a time when Nena would never want to meet her and my mother had no inkling that she existed.

"Osman, can you be quiet? Please, just for a minute. Two minutes." Mom, still possessed of her impeccably poised, lensed-by-Annie Leibovitz collectedness, delivered annoyance through a rasp of her sharp knuckles against the muslin skin of her forehead and extra air around her "two." I checked the angle of the light cutting through the room's particle-free air, then my watch, wondering with a bit of pique if she was sundowning.

When I'd taken away those weekend Scarborough trips from her as a kid, I'd taken the last meaningful companionship Sameen could expect from within the family, and it wasn't long before I noticed that she was utterly relieved when I vanished on Friday nights. She compensated by cultivating deep friendships with a series of women that she contrived to keep away from me and my father. The last, Linda Hill, had been a personal shopper for the rich and housebound elderly, someone who would have been handy to my mother in this present phase of her life if she hadn't disappeared from Sameen's life about five years before Dad died. Linda, then, was about forty—much younger than my mother, a very unexotic and Canadian white, a figure whose eyes looked past me with a purer indifference than what I met daily in my high school hallways. She would wait for my mother in a boxy Mercedes made just before I was born. My father, drunk enough that his phone voice raised in volume until I could hear it through the door, insisted to the wife of Professor Volpetti, a woman that he tried and failed to have an affair with twice, that Sameen was "up to nothing dykey, only the usual female games of attention and repulsion." Dad said this both because he was a terrible dick and because his wife's friendships, for as long as I had been aware of them, had the lifespan of intense flings. Sameen did not let me know their nature, making it clear through laughs and vagaries that she wouldn't share what happened, but that she had made her own way into talking to people when her family proved inadequate. There had been something fascinating in this, a woman in middle age stepping out not into adultery but the intellectual life she'd deprived herself of at the tacit request of an intellectual husband and a son of consuming needs he himself didn't understand. I would have to read about it elsewhere, because Mom would never tell me, and I certainly would never figure out how to ask, or to talk to her with enough focus and time to get a satisfying answer. All this to say, I know that she had something to compare me to when she said I was being dull.

"I don't wish to live through another long story about your work," she said. "I want you to be okay with me saying that. Are you? And I don't feel the way your father did about that place, either, that's not it. It really is just—it's foreign, even when you think you're making it interesting for me. The villains, the occasional hero that I never hear of again. I know it's important to you."

"It's not important-important, it's just a way of—"

"Yes. But I just don't care about your days, right now, sweetie. I want you to be doing well, to feel whole and centred and everything else that's desirable to a man your age. You're going to be out of that job, and soon. Moving on to something that matters to you. I feel it. I feel that it's temporary. I love you, I care about you, but not these characters you are inventing out of nothing, out of speeches and tests and whatever else you've been telling me and yourself."

"If I matter to you, then what I do every day has to be important to you. Or your caring is abstract, Mom. I'm sorry, that's how it works." I tried to be emphatic but the hypocrisy deflated me. My face heated up and sweated, except in a razor burned declivity between jowl and jaw, where the warmth just made the rash glow with itch. I scratched, hoping for blood. I pushed my tongue into one of the spaces that had opened in my top front teeth in the years since I'd lost my retainer. The tongue and gum tissues nestled into each with a comfort my briefly aligned teeth had never felt in their gapless rows. It was an aging decomposition that I could accept, my body drawing closer to true.

"I studied this, Osman. Long ago, but at a quite good school. The self. The person you are before and after what you're doing. Having no notion of that, existing entirely as these bland, these pointless actions you tell me about from your office, that's not a good way to be." Sameen wasn't afraid of pushing toward the metaphysical in an argument, even though that's where Ajit would most frequently trap and ridicule her, as though he gained power when they left the earthly arena of conversation and battled in the ether of ideas. She was out of practice and he did it in the classroom and in his office every day; thought and speech were closer together for Dad, but if I had kept a careful record of the fights they did return to—Kashmir, child pornography, my student line of credit, Mom's potential enrolment in a Ph.D. program, Afrobeat, the moral difference between burying a stillbirth and an aborted fetus—Sameen won, but was careful to never let Ajit notice, which was quite easy.

"It's the only way I can actually live and thrive, if you haven't noticed, Mom. Being someone that can do a fucking job that pays me at a level that I can have something resembling security, so I'm not in permanent freefall and at the mercy of banks and landlords. There's nothing easy for someone like me. The life you had, the ease of it, would be impossible today."

"You could have a home life that isn't just an apartment with no one inside it. That doesn't seem impossible today, I see it all the time. On TV. Across the street. It happens, sweetie." Mom sat back in the couch, the softness of it eating into the smallness of her. She hadn't been able to get back to her middle-aged fighting weight after a mis-prescription led to a ramp-up in her thyroid gland that began a burn process no amount of roti or buttered toast could quite compensate for. During my Christmas visit, there'd been hollows in those sparrow cheeks, at the base of her throat, and under an ancient midnight-blue Irish wool sweater that once gripped at rib and waist and wrist but now bagged out over her like a fashionable vintage tee. Supplements and powders had filled the gaps somewhat, but the gnaw of those pills and time still had her floating in clothes and furniture.

"Sure. Thank you for that. And yes, I could. If I get to a point where I feel I can afford kids, I'll let you know." This last bit would have worked better in an argument with the kind of brown mothers I read about, but never had. Sameen meant a wife, and that's all. She never raised the prospect of grandchildren.

I could feel us both quitting at the same moment, on the edge of passion, on the edge of communication. I didn't want to yell at her ever again. The memory of my teenage screams made me tired and ashamed. I don't think either of us sighed, but we both smiled, and the conversation ebbed into a chat about food and real estate that was almost silence. After a certain age, and from a certain distance, arguments in a family have no vital function. Even in the face of accusations, false analyses, and the ultimate hurt of being thought boring, I couldn't care for more than a few minutes. My face was cool again, burning only in the scratch. The battle had been won by the admixture of indifference and love that I felt for Sameen, the indifference only forgotten when I was in front of her and she was pissing me off, and even then, only briefly.

A pigeon descended outside the bay window to land on the garden fence, chewing dumbly at the seeds that a man from the care home at the base of the street threaded along every fence rail on the block. My father had once thrown steak knives like darts into a cluster of pigeons who were nesting at the gutters. Elaine Herring, a four-foot-eleven classmate of mine who had been vegan in junior high and by senior year was listening to political hardcore and panhandling near her grandfather's walk-in clinic, saw him from the streetcar stop on the corner and called the SPCA. Nothing came of it.

Mom made me write down a brand of frozen naan she had discovered. It gave me a chance to take out my phone and see zero new messages from anyone, a zero that included Nena. I'd forgotten the brand name but wrote "naan" in the notebook app out of respect for what had been said.

I went to the fridge and extracted tinfoil containers with cardboard lids, warming the contents in pans, bringing them to our seats in the living room where we ate in front of a muted Fareed Zakaria. Resuming the actual conversation, I chose a tone of self-blame, a slightly Edwardian clipped speech pattern.

"Maybe that's the problem, my distance. Not actually turning up enough to show you that I care. Dad got tired of me, and I suppose it only makes sense that you'd get tired of my blather about work, but I'm just clearly carrying that Dad baggage into this—"

Mom laughed. Just a small laugh of warning.

"Don't—please. Let me talk. I think it's good that we try to be honest with each other in the time that I still have." She held up her thumb and forefinger an inch apart, then squeezed the gap into nothing. She had taken more food than she wanted to. I could see by how much was left after ten minutes of eating. I had taken less, but would put her leftovers back myself, placing them where I could come downstairs after midnight and eat them straight from the fridge without risking a clatter.

"That neurologist was so good at letting your father scream at him that I wanted to catch him in the hallway and give him a tip. But that is something only your father would have done, not me."

"Unneeded, insulting generosity. Yes," I said. Sameen was quiet, in what I took to be assent. But that wasn't it.

"You. Osman. You needed every moment, and every dollar, of generosity that he gave you. What you didn't need or want was our company, our personal presence, and you should think about how Ajit perhaps understood that. I do, sweetie. I see it. You could have come here when your father was alive. You know you could have spoken to him, but you didn't want to. You could have come to the hospice. You could have had one of those phone calls with him, at least. His mind worked until the last day. But I know you think that not speaking was his choice first. Fine. There were times—probably a dozen stretches of many months, over the years—when he and I didn't speak, either, not in private. And he didn't ask for you in hospice, and he should have. That was all his fault.

"But you think you're coming here now because you love me? Because you need to tell me about medical essentials that I could take care of myself? Four times in one year, not including the funeral? Love, yes, but it's more than that. It's territory."

"I've been coming because I want to see you. I thought you were just bored about hearing about my job, Mom, not with everything to do with me."

"That's not it. We just have the opportunity to really say something to each other, Osman, okay? Just please, listen."

I groaned and leaned back into the sofa, which groaned as well. That is not a fat joke at my own expense, it is a joke about the cheapness of the furniture that my mother chose to retain when she cleared my father's decorative ghost from the house.

"I'm not trying to embarrass you, Ose, it's just true. Territory. You think you're surprising me coming here, but really you're *walking in here like you own the place*. Because you do! I'll be gone soon, your father never would have wiped you out of his will, and if he had I would have put you back. This is your den.

You're reclaiming it. That's the only interesting thing in your work story, sweetie. You made up fear of this woman, the fear has become real, and you've run back to your den to regroup. I just happen to be here. And I love seeing you, but I don't need to see you to love you. And soon I won't even know it's you, right?

"And you know what else is a part of this territory business? Let me tell you about your Olivia," Mom continued.

"She's not mine. I was just telling you because you used to like knowing about different kinds of people. I haven't adjusted to you being devoid of interest in anything or anyone, so I've been trying to bring a bit of the world in."

"All you're bringing here is a manifestation of yourself, little boy." She called me little boy in a fond way, not a condescending or ironic one, but I still balled up a portion of my intestine. When your parent is a psychologist, and worse, one who never practised, it is almost a gift when they lose their mind after decades of trying to unravel yours. Mother was collected, enthroned in the v-dip of a middle cushion, her face and mind steady as she read me. It was what made her feel best, and when I saw her, the purity of her young big-brained self, intact as she had been before my father and life eroded her, any consternation I had vanished.

"I inflate this stuff. For entertainment."

"If you're going to make something up, write it down. Why don't you make a film on the cheap, something, Osman. You love movies, you have money now. You live in Los Angeles!"

"That's not how it works, and I have no time. And I don't really watch movies anymore." I put a hand on the couch arm and noticed that it wasn't the upholstery I was touching, but a green piece of velvet. I looked at the arms of Mother's couch and saw two pieces there as well, mismatched swatches of red and black.

"We're not finished speaking, Osman," Sameen said when I stood up.

I went to the bathroom and did a brief lap of the downstairs rooms in the process. I saw the velvet reproduced on the arms of every chair, hanging, cut not raggedly but not evenly, either. From the chair at the head of the dining table two scraps in blue hung like alien lichen, the one on the right stained with a patch of tomato sauce, a seed in its centre. I pissed and contemplated. Walking back into the living room, I saw Mom, looking vacant in profile, the presence she had during her minor and partially perceptive hectoring session gone, petting the patch of black under her right hand like it was a flattened cat. This dementia slippage after her analysis tirade. She wouldn't want me to believe what she said in her lucid moments when she was already capable of acting like this, I was quite sure. So I repeated that I'd stay a couple of days to pick the support worker and to drive Sameen to Costco. And to the dentist, which I was sorry to inform her she was in need of, with that black crack in her right front tooth turning into a fissure. Her hand went up to it, she laughed. Then she stopped, keeping her hand over her mouth for a moment.

"I want to give you more time. What do you think of that?" Mom's habit of leading had been exciting when I was a child, excruciatingly annoying as a teenager, and distantly charming as an adult.

"I think I want to know more about what you're talking about. Is this about your 'territory' crap?"

"No. I was giving you that explanation because I think it can help you, but also to put you at ease." I watched Sameen ponder, pause, as though she was rejecting a friend who thought there was something more between them. Her patience looked different than it used to, more effortful, less natural. But perhaps that was because I was older now and realized how horrible it might be to deal with me.

"This place is yours, Osman. The papers won't change. Now just work with me on this little project. I don't want just a support worker from a service catalogue, which is why I've done the work to get to the suitable ones. What I want is for us to find a nice caretaker, together, someone you can trust personally—and we use them as a go-between. A middle. So you don't have to come here anymore." Mom came closer and put her hand on my stomach. It wasn't intimate: it was as though she was thoughtfully resting her hand on a globe before spinning it to pick a random destination.

"You were away from your father for his bad time. I know it was just because you were shot of each other, but I also know—he talked more, toward the end, finally it was like he found me interesting enough to speak to again—that he was happy to leave you with, what did he say, 'vigorous memories.' Maybe that's what we should want for ourselves, too, Osman."

I've read about grown children who are offered this bargain insincerely in a pantomime that is meant to force a redoubled commitment of love and constant presence. No one has told me about having the exact experience Sameen enacted in her careful speech, but I'm sure if I'd kept or deepened any of my friendships from my twenties, it would have happened. A poignant severance, a pre-plug-pull plug-pull. Sameen was offering the kind of challenge that a Carol or Ginny or Robert or Chan would respond to with a promise to take a leave of absence from work, to move back home, to enjoy every last second of the mentally decaying, dissociated, diaper-changing cycle of life. But Sameen, with her flat hazel eyes and a mouth positioned to be annoyed but hoping to smile in mutual understanding—she meant it. There was no game here, only an order. So I nodded.

"No one should ever have to live this long. No one was ever meant to," Sameen said. "I like that idea of sannyas, just walking into the forest after you retire. It was one of the good innovations, but of course, it's for the men. And your dad did it, even if he wasn't conscious of it. Letting you go was part of that, even if he was too much of a boy to resolve things with you first, do it clean. He stopped using his office that year, too. He was like a wounded cat, hiding from you and his colleagues under the deck. Me he kept around for service and because he barely loved me. But he taught me extraction, in those last few months. If we can't die on time we can at least remove ourselves from all the parts of life that used to matter to us, that will continue on with us irrelevant. We can choose when we end our relationship with the world.

"Let's keep Ajit with us when we shop for someone we both can trust. His spirit of wanting to stay independent, himself to the end, only we do it right, honey. With this talk we're having right now." Sameen's feet shuffled together, emerging from their slippers to rub sole-to-sole against each other, a habit that I had never been able to pinpoint as nervous or triumphant, as it always emerged at the end of debates I had either happily conceded or forgotten in a miasma of flooded-frontal-lobe upset.

"I think I get it," I said. She wasn't offering me the chance to imagine her lost in a romance of dementia, where forgetting was kind, where her brain would unravel in candy-floss layers that would uncover the childish wonderment at the core of every human mind. She knew I'd imagine the forgetting, the humiliation. She just didn't want me to feel I had to be there as she began to fail, to scream in the night the names of the people she had actually loved, to wake into suspicion and anger, to gain the ability to be surprised but find no pleasure in it. To rot.

"You do get it, sweetie. We say our goodbyes before I start thinking you're my uncle or the mailman. We love each other the right way."

By the end of this she had her hostess voice, the one she used to make the visiting professors laugh. This was the first time I'd been the solitary audience, and in that moment, it was meaningful insincerity, a sort of trench-war joking, something that let us intimately skip tears and pain. It was the way she would talk to another adult.

Every childhood home becomes a treehouse, a clubhouse guarded from elements including the future and the present, as long as your parents keep it. And this is where I would be sure to return when I was finished with Olivia. I knew then, looking at my mother in her last viable weeks or months of condescension. I would come back because here is mine, because it is safe, insulated by its place in my past, even if that past was uncomfortable and humiliating. Keeping the house as a destination was important to the rest of my developing plan for the future. I kept fixed points, among which I could now consider my mother's absence, now that she had generously cancelled herself out as anything other than a financial spreadsheet cell. Olivia the villain was also a touchstone. Nena, who I was sure was already recasting our sexual experience as a mistake as major as her pleasure had been slight, was a crucial element of my receding present that allowed me to see ahead, her virtual and physical presence a resource that I could use to make sense of my own life until she inevitably tired of me, the way this house never could. I don't come back home because it is my territory, but because I belonged to it once and I will once again.

"Don't make me promise not to kill myself again," Sameen called after me as I started up to my room. I stopped and turned back.

"I talked about that just once! And I didn't ask for any promises, I was talking about if it was me going through what you have to go through. But if you don't have to cope with me, why would you want to kill yourself, at all?"

"Not funny, Ose. But you just have to believe me, that's all. I want to see it through, every day of this. I'm going to be writing notes throughout, and that's where I want you to come back in. Make a little book called *Signposts* that you see about having published when I'm gone. Would you do that? We can talk about it later, not us personally but maybe I'll get Barry's firm to email you about it when I work out the last bit of my will. Later. I want to keep living, for as long as I can. I'll walk into the early-morning mist in my long T-shirt, I'll let myself be led back in by the girl we hire. I'll take being cold when I sit in front of the turned-off TV for hours. I'll accept never making sense again. I'll bake a cat. I'll forget why I came into a room, I'll forget what the room is for, I'll forget who I am. As long as no one I ever knew can see me."

"It sounds lonely."

"It would be lonely for you, but it's the life I want, sweetie. Take your nap."

I went to bed in the small downstairs room that Dad used for his last nineteen years. The two small bookshelves draped with lace cloths were gone, and so were the side tables and carpets. They had been there for so long they were still the first things I saw. The closet was empty and so was most of the dresser, but the bottom drawer was still full of his pyjamas. I eased it open with my toe, hooking it into the old-fashioned handle that swung and rattled like a doorknocker. At first I thought a rat had been at them, but then I realized that Sameen must have been scissoring off strips to use as cleaning rags. The perfume coming from the drawer didn't smell like Dad. I learned from a summer working at a retirement community, a job I took both to defy Dad's embargo against work that didn't contribute to my education and to impress a girl named Holly Illium who quit on the second day to take a job selling ice cream at Sunnyside pool, that an old man's pyjamas, no matter how hygienic he is, will invariably smell like three of the following: mothballs, cum, dust, urine. Here, dust predominated, and I didn't inhale testingly enough to class the other odours. The pillow did smell like Dad. Discontinued pomade, dry teeth, and cinnamon. I slept for ten hours.

I dreamed of the pho restaurant down the block from my apartment. It's in a strip mall, the one where I drop off my laundry and pick up my packages. I would pick up the pho as well, a bowl of lemongrass and bone broth and spring onions steaming up, pink beef turning grey and brown as I opened the package on the teak table that I had stained and flecked and dented into worthlessness with fluids and utensils and the blunt edges of tumblers during years of involved, passionate eating and drinking. Inhaling the steam and staring at my books, on shelves angled away from direct sunlight and protected by swinging doors of UV glass. Eating the soup so fast the beef cooked in my stomach under gouts of still-boiling broth, searing the papillae on the sides of my tongue. Later that night I could park near my favourite taco truck and bring my takings back to the car, eating off the plastic tray I kept under my passenger seat. I'd stolen it from a Wendy's when I first moved. I wanted to wake up in the smell of that fat and cilantro in my hatchback, the steam in my mouth, the windows fogging to hide me.

5

I did eat the pho when I got back to Los Angeles, the first bowl
so quickly that I couldn't properly taste the second until I added
enough garlic chili paste to access viable tongue tissue. I could
feel the soup, even if I had to reconstruct most of the flavours
from memory as it coasted, slid and seared down my throat. I
would have an unspeakable hour in the bathroom later, whether
I made it to my taco truck fantasy or not. Despite my consistent
heartburn, I somehow didn't produce enough stomach acid to
compensate for my lack of chewing, but I couldn't think of a
solution that would allow me to get the food down fast enough
while breaking it down sufficiently. I had pasted my long chat
with Nena about the Beagle meeting into a document, and the
printout was on my kitchen table, spattered and sauced but still
readable. Nena wasn't angry at Olivia at any point in the chat,
treating her as an inevitability, treating her own inevitable oust-
ing from AAP as a certainty in the way that melting ice caps and
declining literacy are certainties. "Two more bonuses and I'm at
my x million," she kept saying. "I can do that. I can earn that."

I walked to my other apartment after my phos. It was also in West Hollywood, but was a tiny bachelor box that I scored during a market dip after my first absurd bonus at AAP, the one they gave all senior-level employees who made the one-year mark. Nena advised me to collect apartments, and I listened. I lied to her and said that I had a tenant, a young ESL student named Shin who was secretly taking acting classes instead of language lessons, which Shin defended as not-exactly-a-lie because they were a better way of sharpening English skills than rote chats with bored, ugly instructors. This was a fiction I pulled from a distant summer job when I was a bored, ugly ESL instructor. Nena told me I was a moron for taking on a leasing tenant when I could be making five times the rate on Airbnb.

The apartment collecting was our temporary right, Nena argued, as it was a compressed version of immigrant striving: one that complemented our careers, which would necessarily be briefer and less secure than those of our parents, and the economic moment, which was a plateau between endless caverns. "Each of us gets five years of peak earning to suck in all the money we possibly can and make that money explode into wealth that will sustain the rest of our lives. Or we're fucked." It didn't reflect her immigrant experience, at all, but it was still sound advice. I kept my second place empty because I was against short-term leasing but also afraid of taking on a long-term tenant, and I thought that if I started doing some serious writing or another form of plotting, I could use it as an office. The only furniture inside was a futon. I kept it in permanent bed form after once hurting my knee trying to convert it back to a couch.

I went there with my laptop in a canvas grocery bag, and my walk began to smell of cilantro as the still-hot computer warmed the leaves on the bottom. I had chosen the street the condo was on because men slept outside on queen-size mattresses that they propped up in the alley every morning, considerately clearing the sidewalk in exchange for remaining unmolested by residents or cops. I thought I could use photos of this to lower the asking price, and I was right. One man, new to the block, slept with an enormous genericized Snoopy with a green nose and ears.

Olivia Robinson added me to LinkedIn and a new Slack channel at AAP as I stared at a diagram in the true crime book I was reading on my phone. The notifications from Olivia intruded on the auk detail of the tattoo on a murder victim's wrist, which would later prove to be a link to the boardwalk caricaturist who had killed her.

I feared writing about Olivia so early in this story because if you are like me, you will be waiting for every conversation or scene or thought to come to bear on her. You will impatiently skim entire characters or revelations or weeks waiting to get to Olivia. After AAPC, even with what happened between Nena and me, what we started to make between ourselves, I began to feel that everything in my life and work was a distraction from the game of Olivia. She was haunting me, like she, as my grad school classmate Isaac found a way to say every fucking seminar, is haunting this text.

Before I left Toronto, I couldn't stop thinking of Olivia as I flicked through the CVs of carers with Sameen, especially after being enjoined not to speak of my job in the house. Olivia was going to become my job, if she hadn't already. Mom and I settled on a carer named Angela something, who was about fifty and took on only one client at a time. She was white, which Mom had insisted on. I called Angela, then Ajit's benefits provider, then two or three banks. I left forty thousand emergency dollars in an account and told Mom's lawyer how to access it. I had that steakhouse client lunch and charged the flight I took two hours later to my AAP Amex.

The passages of my bachelor's Ikea-rejuvenated low-rise were always empty save for perhaps two actual residents and a cycling assortment of vacation renters whose screamed conversations about Disneyland and Trader Joe's were as distinct in the hallway as they would be behind the plywood doors. Inside I tethered the laptop to my phone and typed a message to Nena: *has olivia been promoted yet.*

The message went unseen for a half-hour. I gave up and masturbated to an old picture of myself in college with my longest-term girlfriend, Liz Butcher, on my lap at the DJ night my friends used to host at a gay club. My father had attended, once, with three of his students. He was wearing an open-collared shirt and the grey pants from the suit he'd left the house in that morning, meaning this visit was genuinely impromptu, or he would have costumed himself for it. He waved to me in a practised, casual way, as though we saw each other clubbing all the time, and I realized that he was embarrassed of me, that he dreaded my coming over to talk to his proteges.

I ejaculated. Not in the memory, but after coming back to a vision of Liz and I fucking from a side angle, as though video-taped from the closet of her apartment three blocks from that club, a place that was about as small as this one. I fell asleep on the futon and woke an hour later to no message from Nena. I hadn't exactly dreamed about Olivia Robinson, but my thought pattern about her was unbroken by the nap. She was still with me. Olivia had been so freshly delivered from her leave before AAPC that she hadn't attached to herself to a branch, yet, and her promotion-claiming execution of Elodie Chan could mean that she would be a free-roaming executive or would ascend at HQ. Just now, she could be anywhere.

Waiting until I could hear no one in the hallway, I left the bachelor and started to walk home. I saw the mattress man

sleeping pantsless, embracing his false Snoopy. There was no
sense that anything sexual had occurred. I just think this was
how he felt most comfortable. I envied his comfort in exposure
and immediately felt like a ghoulish tourist, bringing a pang of
shame that almost had me walking over, offering him a shower,
sitting him down for a conversation about what we could possibly work out about him living in my unit. Caretaking in exchange
for toiletries, food, detox, inroads into programs that could help
him, lessons on computer literacy, a disposable cellphone that I
would reload with minutes on a reasonable biweekly basis. I
stared into the enviably hairless cleft of his ass and envisioned a
life that I could build for him, something I could look back on
and say that I'd done. I couldn't remember what his face looked
like. For the purposes of this benevolent, depersonalized fantasy,
his ass would do just as well.

He turned onto his side and Snoopy's ear flopped backwards,
allowing me to see the man's face. It was Kevin Cuttner, who'd
been fired from AAP for being rude to Nena and had landed in the
content mill. This was the next step down. We looked at each
other for a long moment. Dried sweat and weight loss made his
cheekbones emerge beautifully, while he had me at my worst
angle. Here, with his ass, cheekbones, and stuffed toy, Cuttner was
still the team-as-individual, now a concentrated representation of
what being deprived of AAP could do to a market entity. I walked
past Kevin and let a fifty drift from my wallet onto the mattress,
and never approached my second apartment from that side of
the street again.

By December, only Snoopy and the mattress remained.
Snoopy was gone before the new year.

6

To avoid participating in office culture I put in a reservation for one of the lobby booths. There were four glass cubes between the security desk and the elevator bank, which visitors to AAP-LA were told were the only non-communal workspaces in the entire building. I watched Javier the desk man's broad back over my monitor and pretended to be on constant speakerphone calls, joking with and screaming at myself. Javier had that superhero triangle back, the broad shoulders tapering to a ballerina waist. A chest instead of tits when he turned around to point when giving directions to guests.

At the slab tables and in the conference rooms upstairs, the fizz of unspoken suggestion and daring discussion would be about the upcoming transfer of power. Elodie Chan had vanished after AAPC. Halloran, our president, had been spotted in Portland over the weekend. He was almost certainly visiting the HQ of ZoneIN, the study-focus app he'd founded and sold before debarking for the top seat at AAP. ZoneIN was now foundering in North America, which they could not explain, and was totally ruined in the rest of the world, because a Russian company had lifted most of their code and sold an off-brand app for half the price and no subscription fee. Halloran was racing against his own termination by the AAP board to negotiate a salary for his Oregon comeback. He ended up making it, his retirement announcement coming at the end of November, the board leaving an interim hiring gap for a fake search before the inevitable announcement of President Olivia and her key role in the Beagle Generation Knowing Fund in January 2019.

New hires boarded the elevators in their pods, the men still not understanding the correct balance of casual and respectful in their garb, the jeans too worn and the T-shirts not sufficiently limited-run. The women understood sooner, always erring formal early on, then correcting. The new kids did most of the speculative talking in these moments of power shift, understanding that catching up to the specific fears of their seniors on the floor was crucial to successful integration. Fear and certainty define AAP culture. Certainty that AAP's mission is benevolent and necessary, that our reinvention of a shattered system that is victimizing the most remarkable generation the world has seen isn't merely progress, it's salvation. The certainty can be attained through faith, but getting the fear right requires knowledge. The new hires are at least young; they have that advantage over us, and it's our pleasure to teach them fear. Youth is worshipped at AAP not for beauty and certainly not out of sexual interest, but for its purity and inborn, ultraconnected knowing that the broken schools AAP was determined to repair were eroding with the wrong kind of learning.

In my smudgeless cube of ventilated plexiglass, as I moved from fictional work and conversations into my afternoon load of actual labour, as I typed emails and confirmed contractual terms freighted with millions, with neighbourhood-purchasing sums that would appear as an unidentifiable $13.23 line item on thousands of undergraduate tuition and fees notices, I turned away from

Javier's back and watched a flow of workers dedicated to the maintenance of purity. Workers who accepted that the enshrinement of tutorial dialogue and the cleansing nuclear wind AAP turned on faculties and class-size restrictions was also part of our company's perfect immunity, that this abrading blast also tore through our own body, evacuating and replacing incompatible elements. The fear was the ultimate part of the belief: arriving at fear meant you understood that AAP was right.

I tried clasping Javier's left shoulder in companionable punching-out solidarity as the lobby darkened and the last of us headed for the door, but he didn't feel the thick lily pad of a hand that I rested on his deltoid. The muscle felt too intimidating to actually grip, and I worried that he would react instantly with a coiled blow that came through the trunk of his rotating torso and emerged as a life-changing fist. I kept walking and told myself that I would tell him I'd brushed a bee off him if he sir'd my back.

At home I arranged darkness behind myself and the laptop and dialled Nena, immediately accepting the failure of the video call plan when she picked up but continued typing, attending to something else on her computer every few moments. She rarely looked straight at me. She was wearing a red bathrobe and chewing a straw or takeout chopstick. I hadn't counted on the extra light from the white wall behind her illuminating my pits and pustules and pouches and bags. I straightened and leaned back, like a cornered jungle spider trying to make itself look larger by rearing up. The conversation eventually began, but the possibility of future calls was over. This did not work.

Nena started. She always did when things were difficult. Telling me about her takeout first, then back into a topic she knew would warm me.

"I thought I didn't tell Beagle more about Olivia because I didn't know enough to tell him something that would matter, that would be meaningful, that wouldn't just be a drag on this memory he had of a woman who had been close to his wife and to himself at a real time. And because I didn't want him asking her about me, and because I couldn't fuck up this deal. But I realize that it was the closeness to Olivia in particular that I didn't want to damage, because it was the only thing that Beagle and I truly shared—this deep link to an absent person, this closeness to someone who isn't who she appears to be."

"But it wasn't a real connection. You don't even get to speak to Olivia anymore. You wouldn't want to."

Nena took a quick off-screen bite of food, and dabbed at the keyboard with the corner of a napkin. She was frustrated. I could not stop forming my questions as accusations. I apologized and she said nothing, then looked back into the black eye of the webcam and threw me an explanation, a kipper to a manatee.

"I'm not close to her as she is *now*. As she was, though—that relationship is unchanged. That person, that iteration of Olivia, I'm still with. The bond is there. When I came back from seeing my father in Tehran, that Olivia was a complete system of support. She came to my apartment and ordered fleece blankets and food from couriers and cleaned up the mess I'd made and held me like she was trying to pull me into her body. I know that it's a time and a memory that meant as much to her as it did to me, and that she'll never tell anyone."

"How can you think that you weren't being manipulated if she's been gaming everyone since—"

"You wouldn't know that that's a stupid question because you've never experienced or given that level of support. Okay? I know. Olivia knows. It might have been fleeting but it's reality."

Nena went on to tell me that there is a difference between determination and bravery, and that you could be determined and a coward at the same time. She was talking about herself, about how she hadn't answered Brody Beagle's question about Olivia with any portion of the truth she knew about the friend she had or the enemy she had made.

"I focused on securing him, then left and thought about what had been taken from me. I've done everything I could to leave AAP on my schedule," she said. "It's fucked to lose control of that. All I can do is grab my end-of-year bonus and try for one more. I still won't hit my x million. My pyramid money."

The x hurt. Total financial transparency wasn't possible from Nena, as much as I'd offered her full insight into my own holdings, down to screenshots of my accounts. She knew everything I had and how much I wanted. I knew some of what she had and had no idea how much she wanted.

"Pyramid, like scheme?"

"Like tomb. Enough money to be buried with, to hide with forever, to let sit in the ground and be nourished by for the rest of my entire life," Nena said. She took the chopstick out of her mouth—I knew it was a chopstick now that she'd told me about her takeout, Buddakan dumplings—and used it to type something quickly on her laptop. A short word, or a number.

"What happened when you went to see your dad in Tehran?" I asked.

"I've never called him 'Dad.' Don't ask me things five minutes late. Don't ask me at all. Telling you about talking to someone else about my actual life isn't an invitation for you to plunge in at your leisure."

"I'm sorry. And I understand the pyramid thing. Liquidity and assets. Property and piles of gold coins in vaults. Scrooge McDuck swimming pools. Divesting stocks into farmland and energy windmills. We'll get there."

Nena didn't answer. She typed with the butt of her chopstick. I regretted my "we." Is it possible to integrate two visions of total retreat into one ideal of union? Not if either member of the couple properly understands what retreat means and what society is. I should have said that out loud, provoked a laugh or an argument, perhaps, but I didn't. I let the silence, then Nena, end our conversation.

"I have to go. Sorry if I was harsh, okay? It's the money, it's the comedown from pitching Beagle."

"You did it."

"It doesn't matter."

The sense that we had begun the ending of our relationship by fucking, by committing the act that I couldn't possibly live up to but would need to repeat, fogged the call like a crisp, thin, endlessly intensifying fart.

When I hung up I started writing this, the first scraps of it, some of which survived the next few months to become part of what no one will ever read except myself and this machine. It was when Nena disconnected that I understood that our lives would not be essentially different if I had spoken all my words to a screen without her face on it. I engaged with the monitor, listened to the replicated lagging bits of her from the speakers, not her. This machine that I did all my AAP work on, that I masturbated to, that I moved investments around on—sometimes in tabs on the same open browser, monitoring Nasdaq then flicking to a banal sexual act that allowed me to imagine myself as a different body in a different body before the moment when I didn't have to imagine anything at all—I was speaking to it, listening to it. Nena and I never interacted through our moving images again, except in AAP mass meetings, where we were silent tiles in a wall of passive leadership as Olivia Robinson spoke to and for all of us. When I chatted to Nena in the cozy box program with its built-in erasure, the temporary words had a purity that was closer to communion than anything I could do with my tongue or body.

But I did start to write when the call had ended and I thought of screen-Nena's pyramid money, of my lack of a plan for what to do other than build a similar edifice of tangible assets. And of her inability to talk to Brody Beagle about what Olivia actually was. I don't think I'm being arrogant in saying that Nena doesn't understand what cowardice is—her experience is too actual, too lived, to understand the depths of inaction that define cowardice. She simply does, has done, too much.

What reading thousands of novels has taught me is that I am a coward. You may think that my consistent failure to call Sameen after midnight or at any other time in the day, to defy her wishes in a way that she may have really wanted me to, also taught me that I am a coward, but I'm telling you, I needed the books. Knowing you are a coward is actionable knowledge that cannot be gained quite as thoroughly on the street as it can from the page and in deep classroom discussion or tutorial one-on-ones with a professor versed in the history of literature and the concomitant history of cowardice. I would place the use value of this internalized knowledge on par with most trade diploma skills, outside of plumbing and electric.

If you say there is more than that to learn from literature, I say: fuck you. Of course I know that. That is my coal-compressed-into-diamond deliverable take, the moral of 2734 books (I made a spreadsheet) teeming with subtleties, details, characters boringly relatable, fascinatingly unrelatable, or such a mirror of the worst in you the pages start riffling against your fingers like the legs of a house centipede. And those are just the human lessons, detached from the aesthetics and purpose and art that are the true point of the fucking things.

But that is not what people want to read. They can't read. They don't quite regard reading as a debility, but I can assure you that they hate people like you and me with a cryogenic coldness that it is AAP's job to thaw. That is what most people think of us, and when I say people I mean the sales demographic that comprises the entire useful segment of humanity. Useful as opposed to the Wildean "all art is quite useless," if you follow. I'm not being a casual eugenicist here, and am in fact a great devotee of the useless and absolutely belong in their ranks again. People don't want to read. People want a warm, vivid capsule of any idea, situation. They think your inability to deliver in telegram form any human situation or condition, from depression to abortion to Israel–Palestine, is either stubbornness or a limitation.

Compression and summary are real skills with real value. They are what allow me to live, along with that primary self-knowledge I took from novels. You think it's integrity that prevents you from working for AAP, but it's not. It's the limits of your ability and understanding of yourself that prevent you from filling my chair. You're limited. You're limited, not me.

Before I switched from reading to collecting, I also learned that I could find and conceal myself in novels, inserting myself as a shade slimmer than a bookmark and vanishing from the world. This, I imagined, would also be true if I were to write one. But the shadow could only acquire dimension if I lied to make myself seem worse as much as I lied to make myself seem better. An excess of virtue strangles a book, and the writer becomes the villain. Books cannot come from righteousness. This is the persona battle that can take place in life, but not on the page: the only wisdom in books is the manifested struggle to understand, the deeply felt theories flung out in quavering courage only to be rescinded or corrected by the plot or a wiser or no-less-stupid character, a conscientious and intelligent fold of the author's brain unfurling to correct an assured overstep. When I used to read, really commit to it, I couldn't trust the character who seemed to be the smartest unless they said almost nothing at all.

Making a novel is teaching me something. We already know that the past stains everything, but I hadn't realized the extent to which the future grubs up the past. It's almost impossible not to lade a scene or a memory with grim foreknowledge. Penetrating, meant-to-be-shared retrospective insight leavened with the occasional wink at the pitiable callowness of the characters, trapped in linearity, doomed to the fate that their honest, fictionalizing author will be forced to inflict on his hapless avatar in the text. Restraining masochism and focusing revenge into a narrative instrument, not writing the equivalent of a running DVD commentary by a placid director recalling the misbehaviour of the stars crystallized in a series of false moments, requires me to remember that I'm creating an object, not pointing toward a past that extends into my known present. Thankfully, I'm unmoored from my right-now as well. It's easier to avoid foreshadowing when you are the bewildered victim of an accident that you haven't yet understood you caused.

I was proud of what I'd written, the first draft. Proud enough to speak it into my mother's voice mail at one AM PST, her phone ringing four times at four in her time zone before the rustling silence that began all of her outgoing messages since our first cassette-tape machine in 1989. *You've reached Sameen*, she then had the machine say for her, even though it was exactly what I had not done. The message sounded more like an admonishment, a calm reminder that I was attempting what I had promised not to attempt. I tried to find a photo of Sameen on my hard drive as I read, scrolling folders on an external monitor and reciting from my Word document until I was cut off, then calling back again and again, sometimes knowing I was only talking to the slim inert brick of my disconnected phone, sometimes not. Sameen honoured her promise by not calling me back.

Part Two

7

I chased the thrill of benevolence I gained from those messages with further late-night calls, voice mailing Mom pages and chapters of this. The entire first Part, redrafted and refined. The best I could do, slurred and spawled into the speakerphone. I didn't feel generous for what I was giving, but because I was letting Sameen take as much or as little as she wanted of me without having to tell me that she loved me afterwards.

To escape the sense that I was directly addressing Mom every time I thought or wrote anything down, I began escalating the frequency of my arguments with Dad to several times a day, muttering my half in bed, at urinals, while I walked to my car. I returned to my habit of screaming *fuck you* at my imaginary father when I took showers. My nudity, in the bright but ecologically conscious glow of LED bulbs that would last decades, reminded me of Ajit. And certainly not because my figure is an evocation of his. It's viewing the body I have and how it differs from the one I expected, especially if I catch a mirror when I'm drying myself and see, before a jiggling, vampiric recoil, the indenting slope of my strangely flat ass down to my thighs, the legs of a muddy sculpture that is unfortunately more prehistoric-fertility than Grecian. I had Dad's body for about two years of adulthood, but stretched and exceeded that form so completely that there is no visible genetic memory of it in my flesh. I don't think it's possible that I could lose enough weight to find Dad's tiny wrists, his consumptive Kafka chest, the full muscular bum built for the seated labour of writing and reading, projecting over his delicate, snappable legs. That form just isn't inside this body. I catalogued my vanished parts after a shower in my Seattle hotel in March. The bathroom had an incomplete modern glass-door shower that didn't slide, close, or function in any way.

Dislocation is a prime part of the AAP experience: having only 100 people qualified for our highest-end meetings with colleges and universities means we move, rove, that hotel points programs email us constantly and give us rooms with stoves and double balconies or sometimes overmodernized shitboxes that are more influenced by multiple viewings of *Blade Runner* than the shape and needs of the human body.

I didn't have a towel left for my in-betweens and crevices when I finished drying the floor, so the talcum powder I travel with was forced to do extra work in my folds. Five months had passed since the AAPC 2018, since Olivia Robinson's rise became inevitable. Under Olivia, there was a new internal plan to target university administrative roles for absorption, positions that we could assume as an institution-adjacent institution. It hadn't occurred to any prior president or board member that we could find a way to make eroding not just faculty, but admin, appealing to people with enough power to make the call. Olivia was driving everyone to pitch higher, to the sources of power and money, to the people who were sure that everyone beneath them could be replaced.

Under the distant commands of our new president, Nena and I were in Seattle to sell the newest AAP education product to Parnell, a small liberal arts college. It was Nena's creation, a limited-entry tenure-experience pack that offered a guarantee of seminar-sized classes, legacy professors, and a three-year Oxbridge arc (this last coinage my own). We had a parallel package including all of this with optional Arabic / Korean / Hindi / Mandarin Parallel Intensive Tutorials, the universal AAP code meaning degrees would be forthcoming no matter what level of English proficiency international students displayed in the classroom or on assignments. Our embrace of one of the company's founding tenets, *Language Is a Portal, Not a Barrier to Education*, had become a rib-liquefying bear hug that reshaped grading and evaluations in our institutions, then across the continent.

I counted down the appropriate number of minutes to wait after arriving at the hotel (I thought ninety-seven, about the runtime of a good action film, was perfect) before calling Nena. To pass this time I went for a walk and bought a sports beverage at a drugstore, where the clerk, an older woman with a soft Caribbean voice, looked at my forehead and hairline for a long time. She sleeved the drink in a bag of the waxy paper I would have expected to house a flat pint of whisky. My Gatorade Cool Blue wore the bag like a miniskirt, and I took it off when I walked by a trashcan.

I had stopped drinking the things I actually wanted to drink for two months because I wanted to remember everything, both what had happened up until then and everything that would come in the next several months, the time I'd allotted to the deposal or disposal of Olivia Robinson. I was worried that I wouldn't be able to call my mother and leave those successive messages while sober, but I could, and I did. (This sobriety, less substantial than a slip of tracing paper, ends soon, ensuring that spending time with me doesn't become too boring for either you or myself.)

I called in for a weekly update from Angela, mother's caregiver. Angela's outgoing message had pauses in it that humans don't usually make—*Please   leave a message*—but I theorized that this came from a career spent reading aloud to clients with slowing brains. Mom was insistent, that last day we spent together, that she didn't want a Filipino or Caribbean carer, which was embarrassing but not a symptom of dementia. She had been, along with my father, a genuine if selective racist her whole life, and was able to ornament this request with a desire to keep her mental faculties sharp by attracting a fellow reader and news-watcher, someone she could really talk to as the silt drifted down the walls of her neural pathways, before they began to collapse in earnest. I didn't leave a message, but Angela texted back an emoji and "All Clear" anyhow, her sign that she would call or not call sometime later, and that mother wasn't dead, declining, or improving.

At minute ninety-eight, I texted Nena. These were her last months at AAP, and this was possibly her last sales trip of note. Nena had an apartment in Seattle, one of the six she kept across the country. I was hoping she would ask me over. But instead she told me that she was near the hotel, and I felt that she had been waiting nearby precisely to avoid inviting me into a place that belonged to her, even if it was open to anyone who booked it online with sufficient notice and a deposit. Sex had concretized the distance between us, destroying the tension of possibility that had invigorated our friendship; we were now involved, together, but my inability to get through to her, to understand her, or to do anything close to fucking her properly was now confirmed, an immense clarifying relief for both of us, as brutally painful as it was for me. I had to think that Nena had known this, that sex with me would be a gravitational slingshot, pulling her into my furred, reeking sphere of self before bouncing her away.

I wasn't happy that she would be seeing me after a gap of months. I wish I had at least found a way to present her with photos every two or three weeks, so the change would feel less disastrous to me when I saw it in her eyes. But after the abortive video call, we spoke in text unless we were on a sales mission.

Nena would be confronted with the fullness of me, the growth and decay. I was larger almost everywhere, but briefly quitting alcohol had thinned me out in the face. It looked hollow and pulled, as though a coaxing hand was unmasking my skull. I put on jeans and a collared shirt, which I tried tucked, casually untucked, and roguishly untucked, cycling through the three options until it was so rumpled I was stuffing the tails into my pants to hide as much as possible when Nena knocked at the door.

"Change your shirt right away," she said. "I can't look at that. Please."

I straightened and sucked in to let her past me at the doorway. I slipped my shoes on when she was in, so I would at least look a bit taller.

At a dinner in January, just before an incredibly successful sales call in DC, Nena had been sure that Olivia was about to fire her. She'd survived by staying quiet about Brody's connection to Olivia, allowing Olivia to deploy that story when she wanted to, which turned out to be quite quickly. The Beagle Generation Knowing score had been notched as an Olivia Robinson triumph, with Nena credited for lending a vague connective assist, a deflecting tip that Olivia transformed into half a billion dollars.

"I just say those things because you seem to expect me to," Nena said.

"What?"

"Your shirt. It looks fine, and so do you." I nodded while she put her purse on the dresser and extracted ChapStick and a tissue to spit her gum into.

"What do I look like, besides fine?"

Nena seemed to genuinely contemplate this. Readjusting to conversation in reality was as difficult for her as it was for me; I think she spoke to fewer people than I did outside of work, because she never ate at restaurants alone.

"You look like a chocolate ice cream cone when it's started to go a bit melty."

"What's the cone part?"

"Your skinny calves and ankles, I don't know. Please don't ask me these things, it really makes it hard to come with you and I really like coming with you, okay?" she said. I pretended to be looking at the Keurig coffee maker. Nena put her arms partially around me and I hugged her back. Both of us shivered, at different times, for short moments that made it clearer how long we held on to each other.

"Have you talked to Beagle?" I asked, when she let me go and backed up to lean against the dresser. She scratched her back with her left thumb, at first over her clothes, then under.

"About what?"

"I don't know, something. Hanging on. Getting him to come into HQ or the Boston office. Not lying down for Olivia, finding a way out."

Nena stopped scratching and checked to see if I was serious, looking me in the face until I looked down at the floor.

"I don't want to stay, Osman. And I couldn't if I wanted to. There is no access to Beagle that Olivia won't cut off first. She's personally with him twice a week. They lunch. He buys out the Russian baths and they spend a Tuesday a month there. The board has approved any social time she spends with him as legitimate working hours that count toward vacation. She earned a bonus for going to Geneva with him and his college friends for a week in February. I can't win against that. I don't want to."

"Okay."

"I'm not enjoying how everybody's scared of us now, anyway," she said, when she was sitting on the bed. She'd peeled back the comforter and placed it on the floor without asking me first, and was lying on the bed in her skirt and blazer, with her green flats off. Her bare feet were clean, with prominent stony calluses just above each arch. She was getting smaller and leaner with age, but not shrinking: she looked gathered, concentrated, not withered. This degree of compression has more to do with astrophysics than Pilates. Looking at her, I decided to start drinking again, to replace sobriety with a new phase: eliminating every other sugar or carbohydrate.

"Scared of you and me?"

"No, idiot. AAP."

"They should be," I said. "No professor hired after this year, across the continent, will ever earn more in a year than a secretary in their department. And now we're coming for the secretaries. They can't handle that kind of efficiency. It is terrifying. It's something to be scared of." AAP had leaned into a zeitgeist that had the force of a turbine engine, and now that we no longer believed, just feared, Nena and I often had to talk about it to feel in any sort of control of ourselves or what the company was doing, to feel that we weren't simply being acted upon.

"Until Olivia we had the dumbest leadership of any 500 company right now and we were still murdering everyone." Nena sat up to pull off her skirt and then lay back. I didn't bother taking my pants off, because she didn't want that and neither did I, but I did brush my teeth quickly then came back to her. She flinched at the spearmint and water on my lips when I tried to kiss her, so

I gave up and spent a responsible ten minutes between her legs. I was rewarded with three moans and a clenched fist at my scalp that accelerated my balding by a couple of weeks.

Watching her coax Parnell into embracing our product would be thrilling. I'd seen her new approach in DC already. Resignation to the inevitable end of the job had invigorated Nena's sense of amusement in the work, had fused it to the professionalism and intensity that had fuelled her sales performance since her AAP beginnings. Now, she sold as an AAP satirist and apostle in one, a performance that animated her pitches with a trembling irreality. Awed buyers interpreted her simultaneous dual modes as the necessary dissonance that accompanied a paradigm shift. The laughter and self-referential winks alternated with Nena's fervid belief in the saleability of the product. Within the heat of the sale, she offered an upgrade of institutional educational methodology, a preview of the skepticism of cultural critics in liberal glossies and the NYRB, and a mordant acceptance and dismissal of the helpless emojis of forty thousand untenured, embittered unbelievers. And she constantly returned to the product and the buyer: its true audience, and the success of that product with that audience. Its success existed as soon as it was sold. That was the story. The notion of anything else mattering was laughable. So Nena laughed in these offices and conference rooms, and the college administrators laughed with her, and then they bought what she told them to buy. Witnessing her sell had become our closest collaboration.

"She moved AAPC to July. Do you know why? And how is Sameen?" Nena asked when I finished and fell back down onto the carpet, squirming back on my hands to lean against the closet. She didn't straighten her clothing out, and kept staring at the ceiling.

"Mom is still at home with her carer, and a nurse comes by once a month. It is very expensive." I hadn't mentioned that I no longer spoke to or saw my mother to Nena. I couldn't help but think that communicating Mother's fully lucid decision to tell me to fuck off would set a bad precedent for my relationships with women. But leaving this truth unknown to Nena also helped me maintain a crucial territory of fiction.

"At AAPC July, Olivia's announcing Vikram as VP of Development, but I don't think that's why she moved it up from October," I finished.

"I'm sorry."

"Maybe I'll have her gone by then. And I had no chance of being promoted against Chandra, anyway." Vikram Chandra was third-generation Californian and had broken his spine doing a skateboard trick over then under an Oakland BART train, but had allowed an undetailed childhood slum disease rumour to spread—polio or some other *City of Joy* stuff—that people were constantly asking me and the company's many other Indians about. I resented being asked and knew Vikram had started the story in the first place, whispering it to a small group from accounting, now all long fired, in a stuck elevator two Halloweens ago. But I couldn't betray him, especially now that he muttered a variant on the tale about contracting something-something during a summer trip his conservative Hindu grandparents had forced him to take and et cetera, et cetera. He was too stupid to do almost anything else but head a department at AAP, and God had taken his kickflips and ollies away. He could have this job. He could maybe even have Olivia Robinson's after I finished my campaign.

"Okay, Osman," Nena said. "And are you still having—"

I wormed up the dresser to stand at the foot of the bed, buttoning the top button of my shirt, and Nena made a general waving motion in the direction of my crotch. She would prefer to have asked directly, with compassion, but last time she'd done so I had cried and we were both very uncomfortable in a Oaxacan restaurant steps from my apartment where I can no longer eat.

"Yes. But it sometimes works when I'm alone, so I don't think I can count it as an official disability against Vikram's in an HR inquiry. I guess it is a form of partial paralysis, but it does move on occasion. Like a phantom limb, except it's still technically there."

"It's your health."

"I'll take care of it soon. I don't want to go to a doctor, not yet. I'm on a ten-year streak. And now I'm old enough to get the fingers, inside and out. I don't want that. And I don't want to see the numbers that describe what is happening with my body. I won't be able to forget them."

"I think you should be more serious about it but that's not my place."

"I do hope it's just cholesterol or rotten blood or a choked valve and not that I've transitioned to a zone of sexuality that my conscious mind isn't ready for. That I'll click on a video of a nest of spiders bursting open and suddenly find myself rock hard."

Nena took off the rest of her clothes and walked into the bathroom. She hated hotels, except for the opportunity to use unlimited towels that someone else would wash. She paused when she saw the terry cloth carnage on the soaked tile. I picked up the phone and called down for more towels, and Nena sat on the closed toilet as I waited for housekeeping near the door.

"Why did you ask about my mother? Who cares?" I was aware of a strong pull somewhere beneath my deep navel, a need for Nena to care, to care a lot more than I did.

"I asked about your mother because I didn't want to talk about your obsession with Brody Beagle. I ran out of other things to talk about and was afraid to start in on Olivia."

"Olivia's not a person I talk about too much. She's a force of evil."

"In a sense, yes. In another sense, she's a cancer survivor who has worked toward immense success."

"We have to make sure that it's the first reading that sticks when we finish up with all of this."

"Not 'we.' I asked about your mother because I know Olivia's all we're going to talk about while you're on this stupid mission," Nena said. This was two confessions of weakness at once—that she'd run out of ideas, and that she was afraid to talk about something. We both feared Olivia, but we hadn't ever dreaded talking about her, at least not in our chat window. Still, even though Nena had her hands in a praying posture and was nude on the toilet, she didn't look vulnerable. At most, she could be in an exoskeleton-shedding transitional phase. Not one in which she became delicate and open and the other things that she loathed, but a different kind of person than the one she had shaped herself into for AAP.

"I am changing the mission," I said.

"Lee Harvey Oswald tried to do that. The CIA wouldn't let him." Nena made many Kennedy jokes—her "second and most serious abortion" was a master's thesis on the overlapping conspiracy theories between the assassination, Iran–Contra, and 9/11. My politico-historical knowledge was so slight that I didn't want to get into a deep discussion with Nena by riffing back, so I always just laughed or gave a saluting head tilt. J.F.K. was, of course, killed by a Mafia / CIA / manipulated-Communist-rube trifecta, and I didn't want to lose myself in the weeds of Nena's superior knowledge of that, either.

"Olivia's parents live here," I said. "I found out. Redmond, about fifteen miles out of town. Oliver and Janelle Robinson."

The towels arrived and I extended an arm, holding a five-dollar bill that I had also made sure that Nena had seen, into the hallway, pulling it back in laden with two towels as thick as pillows. Nena started the shower and, before getting in, told me she knew.

"I know exactly where her parents are. I know about that woodland church they go to, even drove halfway there once. This was when I was still following up on her, before I decided to simply watch her become exactly what she is going to become, whatever you think you're going to do about it. I don't care what she does and I don't want to tamper with her past, Osman. It was weird enough I sent that crew to interview her aunt. Let her do what she wants, don't pretend you can do anything about it." Nena ran showers hot, not in a sexy film noir manner, but in a nerve-damaged way, like the Wild Boy of Aveyron scooping potatoes out of a pot of boiling water. She was vanishing into steam and I stepped back because I was starting to sweat, and once I start I can't stop.

"I want to go to the church," I said to Nena. "I have to close the door here, you're going to fog out the whole room."

Her hand emerged from the steaming bathroom, as smoothly as I had wanted my currency-clutching trotter to project into the hallway. Nena was actually able to do it, this light-umber limb emerging like a thin beam, the hand flat against the door, hot vapour becoming liquid again on the sparse stirred hairs below the moist bare saucer of flesh that had been beneath her watch.

"Come in here."

"The shower?"

"No. Just sit in here. On the toilet. Then close the door."

I took off the clothing I wasn't willing to lose to moisture and walked in, sitting in my boxers, which looked moth-ravaged at the crotch from repeated high-heat drying, and a greying white T-shirt I'd had since graduate school. Only the chrome of the shower door was really visible in the steam.

"Confess something to me," she said. "Something we haven't talked about in chat."

"No."

"Why 'no'?"

"I don't even know the kind of thing you mean. I need a category."

I heard lather being created in a hand and then nothing but the stream before Nena started talking. The air was almost half water. I took my T-shirt off, my rolls frowning over each other when I lowered my arms. Nena didn't give me a category, so I just talked.

"When my dad was still speaking to me, like three years before we stopped, when he'd come into the bookstore and front-face any novels he liked and complain about all the ones we didn't have, he would talk to me, too. For real. Conversations between men, between adults. This one day, he had on his casual-guy uniform, the Costco cargo shorts and a pink Brooks Brothers shirt with a candle singe near the cuff that he had to wear rolled up. He was ridiculous in it, but thought he was the everyman. He looked like a chain restaurant cocktail.

"He brought me a coffee and I followed him while he browsed. I had a rag with me, wiping shelves, but mostly chatting. It was a rare day when everyone inside was white. Something that just isn't going to happen in a room in Toronto or New York or Los Angeles, but it happened that day. Dad loved it, but he *especially* loved it when I had to go back behind the till to ring up an old man in a flat cap buying a Sunday *Times* that was making his wrist tremble. I could see Dad relaxing into the landscape." My upper lip was as moist as the inside of my mouth by now, but my throat felt dry. I took in breath, trying to coat my lungs with the room's amniotic vapour.

"I can't tell if you think that's a warm story or a trauma story," Nena said, her foot making a nautical squeak against the gelcoat as she turned her back or front to the stream. "It sounds true, but I don't know if you understand it. It's not a confession."

"It's a confession about the delights of knowing your place. Dad was pleased to be marring the unspoken white comfort of this classical liberal ideal, and me being beneath him, behind that register, perfected the image. It felt sweet and safe. It was so effective for him because I was doing a type of labour that was completely foreign to him, he who had never served anyone. He'd been below, but he hadn't served. And I wasn't done. A woman came through just before Dad left, Burberry overcoat and a blue claw chunked with rings, asking me to make a pile out of the books I'd just laid out on our Mystery: New Releases table so she could take a photo and Amazon them. He was delighted by that, so pleased at her gall. I actually made a pile for her instead of giving her the usual lite fuck-off line the store had us recite. I didn't want to let Ajit down. And I felt good doing it, not just because I was indulging him, but because I knew my place."

"I don't want to give you a category but I will give you an example. You're close but there's still too much story, too many characters, not enough of you," Nena said. "When I see the uneven oval of a crack by the seam in a cheap Easter rabbit or awards statuette, I think, *I could get in there*. It's not a penetration fantasy, it's one of occupation and concealment. If I'm inside that, they can't see me. Do you understand?"

"I don't know how to ask you about yourself. I really don't. I don't ever know what you want to know about me, and I constantly misstep, I bore you, so these conversations are hard."

"Say the same that I just did, but about you. Just reply in turn, Osman. That's a conversation. Don't push into another subject. Answer me." Her body had moved out of the stream of the shower. I could sense that she was against its back wall, looking in the direction of my voice through the analog cloud she had manufactured. The chrome had vanished. I couldn't see my hands or bare legs.

"My physical fantasies are aspirational, not sexual. Like what you said. But they don't deal with occupying objects, they're about becoming unmoored from my own dominating object, my reality. I think of, and this is often, almost every day, losing weight so fast that my skin becomes loose, comes away, is a separate, living organism I can collaborate with. At home I would run sterile fishhooks through it and attach miniature drones to float the skin upward, away from my bones and innards, the separation clean like peeling a properly adhered price off a book cover. I could rest in that safety of air between myself and my skin for hours."

"You're not big enough for that, Osman. You never have been. The walls of the outside of yourself are very close to you. You're wrong about how you look."

"You asked me to answer and I did it." I was soaked in what I thought was my own sweat, but it may have been the steam condensing onto me, trying to draw me into the cloud. There was no odour. I couldn't smell anything but the vague false almond of soap. No bodies. "It doesn't matter if I'm wrong about the outside, and you should understand that, with your thing about possessing statuettes. When you leak into one of these cracks, in that fantasy, do you get in there altogether, or is there part of you that's left out?"

"The leftover drifts off like exhaust. Dissipates. Every container I get into pares away the bits that won't fit inside, and I never have to regain them. That's why I've loved this current one for the years I've been at AAP, this tight, blazered one." Nena turned off the shower and I ran out of the bathroom, slipping on my T-shirt and smacking my nose on the slick door as I opened it. Not hard enough to bruise, but enough that I dragged my hand against it to check that it was water and not blood that had beaded onto the paint before I closed it.

I dried off with one of the sheets we'd done our near-fucking on, fucking that I consolingly told myself would have fully counted as fucking among many other alignments of gender identities and sexual orientations, and chose new clothes from my suitcase, ironing the part of the shirt that would be visible while it was already on my body. The fan and the blow-dryer in the bathroom provided the comfort of obliterating noise, like an amplified seashell.

"I know that was weird," Nena said, coming out with dry hair. "I just have a sense that we have to get into this shit right now or risk being mired in the stupid bantering mean way we cannot stop speaking to each other. Or totally spiralling apart and fracturing when we don't have Olivia Robinson as a focal point for our relationship. Okay? So it helps me to unvault this fucked-up shit especially when I know, and now I really know, that you can absolutely answer with something that is so reassuringly perverse I couldn't help pissing down my leg in relaxed celebration."

"I'm not like this with people. You know that. It's just you. It's because I love you." I had absolutely no expectation that Nena would, as she said when we were in the fog, "reply in turn," but I wanted points for being undeniably open. I don't know why I said she knew I didn't converse this way with anyone else. As far as she knew, and she would be correct, I didn't really talk to anyone else at all. I was counting on her to be kind, to indulge this extended illusion that we could draw closer despite the inevitable end to intimacy that started when we had sex.

"I know. I recognize that and I'm trying to—you will say this is therapy talk, sure, you'll think it but won't say it—I'm trying to honour that by helping you. But you should recognize that you don't know how to know me, and that you don't necessarily want to."

Nena saw me sniffling, saw the albumen tracers of sob snot starting to come and turned away from the bed before the yellow and green could emerge. I went to the bathroom as she started to dress, but left the door open, as she was still talking. In her usual voice, now.

"Parnell College is going to want us. The program. They're going to want to highlight the golden age of education while seeming innovative and keeping their campus as digital and minimal as possible in the next few months. A sessional—this didn't make the news, not yet. We're not going to use the name but it will be under each of my sentences. Edmund Bak. He was forty-two, Korean-American, and had been living out of two cars, parked side-by-side, in long-term parking. Had a deal with the attendants and security guys, they let him be. He brought them tacos twice a week out of gratitude, in addition to paying them. It was Taco Bell, which he also ate seven days a week, because price. So the attendants and guards called him 'Señor Gook' when he wasn't around, to cement over their genuine feelings of goodwill, liking, and pity. I found this in a Reddit post, researching for our meeting. One of the booth guys, fired now, he posts there regularly. I had one of our little basement ghouls chase down any data he could get on the handle to verify, and it is indeed a Parnell ex-employee, Dustin Carter. He's about thirty. Called that entry 'Señor Gook,' clearly took his time with it, probably better than most of what is coming out of Parnell's creative non-fiction classes. Fake introspection. There's real guilt, but you have to dig through the prose to find it. And he's obviously proud of the nickname and finds it hilarious, even if the title and every mention are cloaked in this false sense of shame and culpability that he continually upends by blaming Parnell and only Parnell. If you wrote like you talked for AAP, Osman, you'd write like this guy."

"Thank you." No more liquids were emerging from me, so I left the bathroom. I finished putting my clothes on, edging behind the large chair by the window to do the complicated bit with my socks, which involved a bend and suck and pull that had to be accomplished in one successful movement. Nena wasn't watching me. Just as I was my complete self within a doubt, she was especially herself in telling a story that was to be subsumed into a pitch.

"Please stop looking for the worst in everything I say, okay? If not for the sake of us, then for the pitch.

"Edmund Bak used outlets in the attendant booth to cook his occasional non–T Bell meals in an Instant Pot, and to charge his phone and laptop. He was an English lit prof, late modernist, and they had him teaching eleven essay composition classes a semester, to the business and engineering and tourism program students. He was sending half the money to his parents in San Francisco, where they lived above the convenience store they ran, dying from reduced footfall and property taxes, further fucked by a bad investment his dad had made in a company some home-country friend of theirs had founded, folded, then kept cashing investment cheques on for four years. A less ambitious Korean Madoff with a bit more shame, he flew to Busan and vanished when Edmund's dad and the two other people he'd been ripping off asked him for documentation.

"Edmund pretended to his parents, and to the off-campus friends that the cops were able to find, that he was tenured. Anytime he was invited to a department colleague's party, he'd make sure to have a picture taken of himself on a couch or in front of a bookshelf or at the kitchen table, using these images to lay out a hybrid luxury Seattle apartment with three bedrooms and a compass-spinning window in the living room that faced whatever direction the good light was coming from at a given point in the day. He had a specific album for it on his phone."

I got the socks on and returned to the bathroom to recover my breath and wash my viscous emotions down the drain, wiping off a straggling red-green dried one off the sink with two squares of toilet paper. Nena kept talking.

"School shootings. I understand them. I think that's the worst thing, don't you? Not that I'm going to bring that up in the pitch, but I think there is an instant understanding, if not empathy, from anyone who works with or around a campus. I understand, and you probably do as well? They say senseless, but I get why they happen. I've met these people. They have stared at my car and my body. I understand them on a deep personal level. When the shootings started to happen, really started to happen, I wondered why there wasn't one every week. Now I don't have to wonder because there always is one, another one, and it's something all of us in this business have to contend with.

"But I've always felt we were on the verge of a massacre from one of these Edmund Baks, these gossamer professors, some Ph.D.'d painful case who is absolutely aware of how terrible his life is, and can articulate it to himself and anyone who would want to listen, but can't do anything else worthwhile with his life. At least he doesn't think so. So he keeps drinking the way he did in graduate school, just with fewer people around, eventually saving money by staying out of bars, eventually saving more money by getting that discount vodka with the crest on it."

"Prince Igor."

"Try not to know things like that."

"We used it for watermelons in undergrad."

"Bak didn't keep a diary but he did start to babble for an uncomfortably long time to whichever attendant was working the final shift, before the parkade locked up at eleven. He started to give away books, to fish for interest in a given field, giving his personally annotated Routledge edition of *Frankenstein* to the attendant who said he liked *Child's Play*, giving *Mrs. Dalloway* to the one who Reddits now because he said he was buying flowers for his wife on the way home. Edmund implied he was going digital, that everything he needed from those books was in his head, which was balding at the back and had two eye-sized alopecia spots on the right temple."

"Is that from the parking attendant's post? It's not bad."

"Yeah. That's the thing—Dustin Carter insists he got a happy ending out of this, which I will skip to because the Bak part is inevitable, in that Dustin's boss fired him for his online criticism, but Parnell got scared and allowed him to enrol in the English department with comped tuition. Dustin's going to dedicate his life to telling stories of the hidden people, by which he means Bak but really himself. Like that's something Bak would have wanted, after killing himself with a length of hose over the exhaust and rigging a car bomb that truly proved he was an English major by falling off the undercarriage and rolling three feet before doing absolutely nothing when the paramedics opened up the Hyundai to pull Dr. Bak out. No explosion, just a dead, precariously employed professor, not a terrorist. But he did have a registered AR-15 in the trunk. No bullets, but still. He'd thought about it. He'd been thinking about it deeply enough to make the instrument real, to close his hands around it before he decided not to decide anything ever again."

Nena had dried and dressed quietly. She came into the bathroom and used a face cloth to wipe off the mirror. She started to do her makeup, extracting tubes and tubs from a small Japanese pencil case. I walked between her and the reflection.

"So," she said. "This is true of any college, but right now, it's provably and recently true of Parnell: this is a place where the teaching staff is at a point where they want to kill at *least* themselves, and probably everyone else in the world. That is a very strong bargaining position for us as we go in there and tell them that they can overhaul their image and how they work with one tiny and lucrative program."

8

I've figured out why I hate my body so much. I know you probably hate yours too, but as you've seen, it's more than that for me. I can't tell what any of this looks like anymore, or even quite how it feels around me. It's just tissue. I just know that this is where I'll be when they finally *get me*. I'm going to die in here. Whether I'm round with skin so stretched it bruises purple simply by coming in contact with existence, or whether my bulges flatten so quickly that I'm flat over my skeleton and my skin hangs off me like a folded collection of elephant ears underneath my sweaters, this is where I'll be when they come for me, this is where I'll be found.

It's tiresome to read about, to hear about. I agree. When I talk to myself out loud, or to Sameen's voice mail, or to my dad in the shower, it's to relieve the pressure of this one internal conversation. Emergency venting, that's what my schizo face-slapping babble is, my Bluetoothless arguments with the air. If I could get into anyone else's head, I would. I wouldn't choose this one for a second longer. As badly as you do, I want to switch into Nena's perspective at this point, to give her another, proper chapter where I'm finally able to expose every motivation and truth and intention. But I can't do that. The Beagle one was hard enough and I still think I stuck too much of my own horrible voice into her mouth and brain. My imagining of other people's conversations is bound to be unconvincing, because I can't properly imagine people enjoying speaking to each other, or learning something from their exchanges. So that's it. If I'm trapped in here, and I am, you should be too.

Nena looked at me hard after our intimate shower conversation and her sales pitch warm-up and rubbed a thumb over my cheek.

"I think that treatment finally cleaned your face. You've lost your favourite pimple, that one you've had since junior high. I'm so sorry."

We were able to go to the meeting after that. The ghost of Edmund Bak rode with us in Nena's rental car. We focused on the pitch ahead, on the exultance of the word and the threat of the unsaid, on the promises we could make, which was every promise we could think of.

9

Nena and I arrived at the campus of Parnell College and discovered that Olivia Robinson would be accompanying us to our meeting.

"And your incoming VP of Development—I'm sorry—"

The white secretary, a woman who appeared to be young but was actually just very fit and with unwrinkled skin that glowed a light chemical-seared red and had a Vaseline sheen, looked to me in imploring apology until I said, "Vikram, Vikram Chandra."

"Yes," she said, snapping her fingers with a dusty click that was quickly killed by the low-ceilinged acoustics of the provost's office. The reception room looked like it had been stone-by-stone rebuilt from some empire-raping Scottish industrialist's ascetic-aesthetic retirement humility chamber. It was hung with dim flags and covered with the kind of carpets that are better at hiding trap doors than lending beauty or warmth.

The secretary, Jeanie, who had told us she'd taken an M.A. and was only an abandoned dissertation ("Astrological London in Marlowe's Renaissance") away from a Ph.D., retreated to send in the officials and to get the laptop that would summon Vikram.

Jeanie left Nena and I facing the empty fireplace, which was devoid of ash or a grate, and smelled more like fresh pine trees than burnt wood. Nena was collecting herself, doing a reorient to take point position while assuming the correct degree of servility in the meeting, the silent demands of being a darkie working for Olivia Robinson. She wouldn't be able to push the product as she had in DC, with lambent humour overlaying the hard sell. I wouldn't get to see her do it again.

"Sometimes I think she hears every conversation we have," I said. "Every conversation I have, verbally or online, any time I mention her name."

"She's not magic. Don't start thinking she's magic," Nena whispered, then started mouthing something that looked like a list of numbers. Revenue projections, or privately gathered statistics about the college that the provost would be uncomfortable we had.

"We'll be fine," I said. "She didn't come here to embarrass us. She's here because she wants to be present for a success so she can take credit for it. She even gave Vikram his title early so Parnell could see how much she respects creatures like us. Her angle here is theft, not sabotage."

"You don't understand," Nena said. She smiled. "All that research and you don't understand a single thing. Our purpose here now is to fail. You and I, not AAP. Me, in particular. If she was going to work with us she wouldn't be beaming Vikram and his new title in. This is my execution. But let it happen. Don't resist. It won't 'deepen our bond,' I promise you."

Nena went back to muttering figures like a rosary. I gurgled stomach acid with my eyes shut.

Anthony Mockton came into the room, walking the strip of green carpet that ran from the door to just behind his desk. My gaze followed the carpet, which I hadn't noticed before: it encircled the room like a lawn path in an exhibition garden. When my father was at the university, there were fewer people like Mockton, and the administrators that did exist were mostly red and hearty, dressed in boring suits, and quietly worshipful of the professors, like my father, who were department stars. They'd subscribe to the TLS and humbly contribute to barroom conversations before paying too much of the tab and leaving early. Now they all looked like Mockton, had business degrees and new Ph.D.s in education administration disciplines that had been conjured into being by people with business degrees. Now they asked sessional professors to bring their own brooms and garbage bags to their shared offices, because the unionized janitorial staff was overtaxed.

Mockton paused behind his seat, pretended to remember he was being rude by touching his forehead and fluttering his right hand for a second, then did a friendly short jog on the circling carpet to greet us. We'd studied the college's financial records over the past ten years and determined that Mockton, while not in a role that gave him direct access to funds, was behind the majority of outside-service-provider investments. He was also the primary driver of the college's briefly protested decision to have the sessionals moved into one collective corral per department.

"Vastly looking forward. Had an amazing chat with Olivia— with your CEO last night and barely got my six hours, I was so inspired. Whatever comes of this meeting, I'm pretty sure I'm about to get schooled in office culture. Consider me tenderized for whatever you're bringing in."

Mockton had likely looked forty when he was twenty-eight and would continue looking forty until he was sixty-two. His tucked white shirt billowed nowhere and bulged only over his pecs. He shook both of our hands, inclining slightly forward when he had Nena's, which he held for an extra moment. To balance the contact time, he patted my shoulder before going to his chair. He didn't have a tie or jacket. None of the men do anymore, unless they're going to be photographed.

Olivia Robinson came in as we were watching Mockton sit, avoiding the green and setting her foot down, toe-heel, on the hardwood. He was only half out of his chair before she waved him down with a full-body move, as though she was playing a conclusive piano chord and curtseying at the same time.

"Don't even, Ant, don't you even. You guys are probably deep into Nena's amazing presentation. Her prep is second-to-none, I'm just in awe of people like her and my team is stacked with them—and I will not be interrupting. Just keep going." Olivia radiated pure attention at Mockton, a focus that made it seem impossible for her to look at us. She had perfect French nails, and a Batman Band-Aid at the base of her right thumb.

Vikram had appeared on the laptop screen at some point. I pointed to him. He waved, but no one noticed him, or me. Vikram was wearing a tie, a lavender one, with a blue blazer. His shoulders did that male squareness thing, and his long neck made me aware of how mine was only a frog-wattle ruff between my chin and chest. His skin was closer to Nena's shade. None of it seemed exactly fair, but I'm sure he had those thoughts too. Not about me, but you know.

We watched each other for a moment as Nena began speaking, starting with Aristotle before making the leap to Steve Jobs, who had to be mentioned at least once in these meetings if there was a man behind the desk. If it was a woman we went Oprah, Taylor Swift, or Sheryl Sandberg, depending on the administrator's age, outfit, and racial and class background.

Nena didn't joke. Nena didn't tremble, but she didn't unfurl, loosen into the sale. She simply delivered.

"The academy is still—and the student body that you're seeking, the elite, the ones who will define this institution's future—

they believe this with the utmost seriousness: it is still a temple. Just like those Grecian days, only now with new purpose and value in a shifting economy and world. And, of course, not so boringly Eurocentric. We have an entire world to embrace, and that's something that Brody Beagle, and his fund, are very interested in—his late wife, Gwen, was a passionate reader and advocate for the arts, and Brody says that she credited her education with helping her make actionable content, to create meaningful and sustaining connections with funders and clients—with humans. 'Humanities' means something, right? We've all been keeping a steady eye on declining enrolment in traditional faculties, your histories, your languages, your comp lits. We're impressed with the strong strides Parnell has been making toward creating programs that are active for today's market, hard job-skills-oriented degrees that still keep in touch with those wonderful disciplines of what Osman and I call 'the living past,'" Nena said, gaining on the conclusion now that she had landed all the numbers and couldn't make any jokes. There was a fatal politeness in Anthony Mockton's nods, one that I could sense Nena ignoring. He looked like he was rewatching a movie, waiting for a gag or action sequence that he vaguely remembered enjoying.

Olivia waited until Nena was about two sentences from finishing before getting up. Her eyes had been flitting in unquenchable curiosity over the plaques, paintings, mountings, and furniture before she visibly decided that she simply couldn't sit down anymore and was up and wandering. Nena surrendered the pitch. She shut up. She looked down.

"I'm sorry, Ant. I just had to get a closer look at this—is it a real—God, it is of course and rude of me to ask in any case! This is just one of those rooms that, that, and I imagine you must do this several times a day, that you look around and say—" Here Olivia came back to the desk, crossing the gap between her empty seat

and my full one, putting her hands on the glowing mahogany—
"'Hey, I deserve this.' You do that, don't you? I know I would."

Mockton nodded, smiled, a nod and smile he could explain
to himself as assent with Olivia, as appreciation for her pin-
wheeling, straight-shooting charm, and not acknowledgment
that she was right about his entitlement.

"And we must be about the same age, even if I do have this
embarrassing baby face."

Mockton was at least fifteen obvious, carefully managed
years older than Olivia. Olivia touched the dustless frame of a
photo with Mockton shaking hands with Obama on a low out-
door stage, both of them wearing similar navy-blue suits, a rev-
erent crowd of students in the background, their faces *ex post
facto* soft-focused into glowing beige orbs.

"Rooms like this, objects like this, interactions like this—we
grew up investing them with so much *meaning*. That 'Academy'
thing she was talking about just now. Nena and Osman get me,
they're old enough, too. Deserving a room like this means that
we respect the room, what it stands for, our fight to win all these
objects in it. I think in a strange way any room that we come to
occupy in our job, even any apartment or home that we buy—it
becomes a trophy room, a collection of trophy chambers. The
place itself as the trophy, you get me?

"Anyone born after, what, 2000? That's just not their world.
That's what AAP has been trying to understand in a meaningful
way, that in a very real sense we, the company, spend our lives in a
significantly different world from our ultimate consumers. You
know, we could have done this on Skype, but it wouldn't genuinely
have occurred to us. Other than having Vikram here, of course,
which is purely a practical technological solution to get one of our
most important thinkers into your office." None of us looked at
the laptop that Olivia waved the back of her hand at.

"But we know—you know and I know—that to take each other seriously, to know each other? We have to be in a room, facing each other, evaluating and knowing each other. The possibility that the kids out there walking your quad aren't actually missing out on face-to-face time with each other, but can actually form more profound relationships without ever occupying the same space—well, it's only natural that we'd be resistant to it. The tenure-experience, three-year-Oxbridge package that Nena and Osman were here to bring you today? You know it. You know it's good. We agreed on that last night."

Nena flexed her core next to me, rising an inch in her chair without moving any other part of her body. She stayed at her new height. Her lower left eyelid began to twitch upward, but she controlled it.

"You know it, you're the kind of guy who's already called other colleges that have implemented it. And you're going to buy it today, Anthony, because you already decided to. But do you know who you'll be selling this package to? Do you really know your buyer?"

Olivia waited for Mockton to shake his head, which he was reluctant to do. But he didn't want the story to stop.

"Parents. And I know there's potential here to say—*exactly*. That's who you are offering berths at Parnell to—that's exactly who you want to appeal to. They are, after all, making the financial decisions. But that leaves aside what I think is our most powerful recruitment force—and I don't think this is being abstract, if you'll stay with me. The students themselves. They're going to be here, they're the emotional drivers of every decision an invested parent is going to make. And only an invested parent, if I'm going to be unforgivably frank, will be able to afford Parnell.

"And those kids? They don't give one fuck about your office. They don't give one fuck about this campus. Students don't care about these walls. They don't give a single fuck about any classroom you have here." Olivia had turned around, risking a breakage in Mockton's attention, but he was totally arrested by her back and the finger she was jabbing through the window at the invisible students that she was sniping, plucking them into existence in the office, crowding Mockton with the paying bodies he risked losing, by the torrent of student loan dollars that Olivia hadn't needed to mention.

"But that doesn't mean they don't care about knowledge. Those Socratic values—that white outmoded Greek Western toga party that Nena was talking 'bout—there's even a purity left in that when all the layers are scrubbed clean. And that purity is the pursuit and exchange of knowledge. That's what people come to you for. But they want to get back to that purity, and for that, schools have to be able to abandon what people like you and me, Anthony, hold to be valuable and real. We have to let our idea of reality go and give our students the reality they spend the rest of their lives in." Olivia turned around; she wasn't crying, but she was misting up, the moisture more visible on her eyelashes than in her eyes. She clasped her hands in front of her, completing the shift from pitch to eulogy.

"The classroom is dead, Anthony. And that is a wonderful thing. This campus is a symbol. Your professors are symbols of the knowledge they impart. I haven't even been able to say this out loud in my own company's boardroom, let alone in any of the hundred campuses I've visited so far this year. Because you know what? As special as our talk last night was, I've been doing it every time I have a high-level team headed for a campus visit for the past three months. Because I've been waiting to find the person who would hear me. Who would understand that it's time for education to catch up to the digital real. Who would risk losing everything to be the first, the genuinely first, learning institution of the future."

Olivia sank into the chair she'd circled back to and spoke her last sentences to the floor in front of her as Mockton gazed at her extended, vulnerable neck. Vikram coughed and I could have leapt up to slam the laptop shut myself, but Olivia didn't react.

"I won't say this isn't compelling," Mockton said. He looked at the laptop in distaste, and Vikram's chair moved, as though he were dollying himself backwards. He didn't say anything, but I knew someone had to. Mockton was on the verge, had all the positive direction and reinforcement he needed, but he wasn't afraid yet. Afraid that if he didn't make this choice, everything would collapse.

"Edmund Bak," I said. It came out quickly, a nervous exhale taking shape as words, just as I'd intended. It required more muscular control than separating an urgent fart from a dangerous shit in public. "Edmund Bak, Anthony. Campus culture needs to shift, and you've just seen that demonstrated with alarming urgency. What Olivia is saying—and this is fresh to us, as well, I understand how unmooring it all is—what she's saying is this is an opportunity for Parnell to become a category definer instead of the case study it will inevitably become when the Edmund Bak story is more than just an internet whisper."

Olivia had watched Mockton instead of me, seen him tense and cover his mouth when I said Bak's name, his thumb rubbing his septum and even nervously slipping into his left nostril for a second. I was going to be promoted.

"This is the first Osman or Nena or Vikram are hearing about our new strategic direction. I wanted it to happen in this room because I need to be the one who loses something if we end up roasting our existing client base because of this. And that honestly is going to at least half-happen, Anthony. The last thing I want AAP to become under my direction is static, and it's going to happen if I don't extend what I believe in to the people we work for. That's you, Anthony. You, and the leaders under you, have the chance to start making the future real at Parnell."

We all watched Mockton pretend to think, as though he hadn't already decided. When I turned, just for a second, to Olivia, she was looking back at me. She mouthed a thank-you.

10

I drove with Nena for a speechless hour. I hadn't asked her if she was comfortable coming to the church with me, because it was clear she didn't want to say anything, let alone answer questions. It was a long silence through city traffic, and onto clearer stretches of highway. The trees and fog were familiar from family trips to Western Canada, but there was much more roadside garbage. The forest suggested itself more than it was visible in the fog. Even the initial strip of firs beyond the roadside ditch was more shadow than presence. I watched the ditch as well as the road, and had spotted four Charleston Chew wrappers and innumerable Snickers before Nena spoke.

"It'll be one semester of the campus totally shuttered, just to demonstrate seriousness, then a regular whatever e-learning supplement to real classes. Just fewer real classes. That is absolutely all. But that semester off."

"Will be huge news. A coup. Huge valuation bump for AAP."

"Olivia didn't do that expressly to humiliate me. Not expressly. It was about moving the AAP agenda," Nena continued, in the same tone, as though the subject had not changed at all. "But she did want me there, and you as well, for humiliation purposes. I used to love her. Actually love her," Nena said. I looked at her profile, that coin face. The business composure that she had kept in place throughout the meeting with Mockton was not quite broken, but fracturing like a cast that had been cracked against a pillar a few times. Movements of muscle under the eye and around the mouth formed and flattened like mobile vanishing wrinkles. She shifted the conversation.

"And that Chandra kid. He looks about twenty-four. I can't believe she gave him VP. Pushed in like a prop. Mockton couldn't close that laptop fast enough when he had us on our way out." Mockton was taking Olivia Robinson to an all-department admin meeting, her presence unannounced, but the meeting was a weekly one that she must have known about when she planned her invasion of Nena's pitch. Nena and I certainly had.

I was going to fumble near the gearshift to pull out my phone and show it to Nena, but understood it would be a bad idea. Vikram Chandra had texted me a few minutes after the meeting: *Need to talk to you bro*. I'd given him my number reluctantly after a lunch meeting in late 2017, when we'd been the first to approach the make-your-own-Korean-taco bar while the other two dozen people in the room dallied. Vikram hadn't taken a tortilla, only a small heap of barbacoa that he ate with a bamboo fork. He asked me something about Elon Musk that I couldn't answer honestly at work, then made a joke about desis in tech that made me wonder how many boats and planes over how many generations would have had to have gone down in order for this conversation never to have happened. I gave the number when he asked for it because it promised we could stop talking, and I needed to attend to my five tacos in privacy. When an office lunch involved hands and sauces, I ate it in the pristine disabled washroom.

But the text I'd received outside Mockton's office was the first he'd sent after the *hey* that allowed me to save his contact. The desperation of "Need to talk to you" would have been better mitigated by eliminating "Need," or at least the capitalized "n," than by adding "bro," but there was something frank and naked in the message that suggested an exciting possibility: Vikram wasn't purely under Olivia's influence. I'd save the news for after Nena's emergence from the chrysalis of hurt, analysis, and anger that currently enwrapped her.

"She sold Mockton the total obsolescence of his college as a goal to be purchased," Nena whispered. "Six campus shooters in a week couldn't shutter the place for a whole semester, for a year, forever. But Olivia's going to do it, and get two million from this idiot for the honour of having the status and function of his college evaporated."

"Two million?" I ran the numbers of our comparable AAP remote-campus packages to see where she'd arrived at this. "That's nothing."

"I mean that will be the board bonus Olivia Robinson takes home at the end of the year, after this deal. We can charge Parnell for this service, with the marketing rollout included—not just a sum. A chunk of their endowment. A lot. More than any one deal we've done before."

"A lot."

Hearing something as richly, as perfectly, as completely untrue as Olivia's pitch land with the absolute success that it had was—and this is what people who are unqualified to do my job would refuse to tell you—*thrilling*. Olivia had extended AAP's mission of fear. She was creating the same terror among administrators as they had created among professors—she had scared the absolute shit out of Anthony Mockton and offered him the opportunity to pretend he was inspired. When you hear a dystopian horror and the potential ruin of your job being described in positive, controllable terms, what you really want is to make an assertive move before being forced to think too much. And with AAP processes handling everything from onboarding to daily course administration and troubleshooting, we could offer infinite Mocktons at infinite schools the opportunity to survive and to pretend to lead without ever having to think. This barren campus plan was the logical endpoint. Olivia had offered him the chance to buy the illusory future relevance of the job he was already doing, in exchange for a huge amount of money and the complete elimination of his power and use value. To save his school from declining enrolment, to make himself an invaluable part of Olivia's digital education scrying that, if successfully implemented, would eventually mean the partial destruction of everything about his institution except the tuition rates.

So Nena and I were driving to a wooden barn in rural Washington to watch Olivia's parents throw snakes at each other and mutter in *Exorcist* gibberish to cheer ourselves up.

"Do you ever want to isolate?" I asked Nena. "Total isolation. Vanishing." The fog outside and within the car, the road invisible behind us, the eternal evergreens looming over this state road, made the idea of vanishing possible. Not simple retreat, but the oblivion of real vanishing, the kind I could most easily attain by pulling the steering wheel hard to the right. I stared at Nena's hand, at the tiny gnawing shadows of eczema between her knuckles. Beyond my window, between us and the invisible trees, one of those birdhouse structures full of donated books appeared and vanished before I could see if there were any Henry Green firsts or a mildewed copy of Poe's *Tamerlane* that had migrated from the attic of a hayseed. This road was smooth, new asphalt, with long driveways leading to hidden houses, and a hybrid SUV parked next to a delivery locker as we turned a corner onto a street potholed enough for it to feel like the car was being lazily chewed.

"I don't want to hear it. I don't want to discuss abstractions." Isolation wouldn't be an abstraction for long. It really was the word I used that day in the car, a few months before self-isolation became the greatest blessing in AAP company history and an international injunction, not a metaphysical option.

"I'm doing the same shit you were doing in the shower," I said.

"That was appropriate then. I was trying something with you, trying to approach you in a way you couldn't irony your way out of, that wouldn't completely freak you out, that was weird enough to have a chance at catching you in a moment of existence. The way for us to have drawn closer after that would have been some demonstration of support or loyalty when it mattered, Osman," Nena said. "You helped Olivia Robinson in there. You took the Bak thing and you helped the person you're supposedly bent on destroying. And she knew you would, that she could perfect what she was passively doing to me by having you in the room to pile on."

"You helped her by keeping quiet. And you fed me Edmund Bak before the meeting for a reason. Your instinct for the relevant. When you give me something I'm supposed to use it.

"I was fulfilling the basic obligations of my role by 'helping' her, Nena. To confirm the sale."

"You—and the parallel is so sickening here, you just seizing something I'd told you and using it for your own advantage—you didn't even try to marry her concept to mine. So yes, to answer your idiotic question, which by the way sounds more like something the dumbest person at a dinner party asks and has nothing to do with you knowing me or wanting to know more about me, really, I do kind of want to 'isolate' from you. But I'm tamping it down because you're determined to go on this stupid field trip. I know where you're taking me. I know."

"This stupid field trip is part of what I'm here to do. If I interrupted Olivia in that room, blustered all over what you know was a perfect pitch, we lose that contract. I was fulfilling the basic obligations of my profession as ethnic hype man with an academic pedigree and a memory for facts. You said you used to love this person. She just treated you like a wall sconce, did worse than taking your credit. You must, on some level, want to work toward her downfall with me. It's something we can do together, Nena."

"I'm not interested. I'll never be interested. It's what I had with Olivia that's interesting, not what she does now, and there is no point in my getting in her way. I want to get *away* from her," Nena said.

I didn't answer, because I am a poor driver and needed my attention on the vanishing road in front of me. I turned the high beams on, which only made the fog intensify and glow white around us, solidifying it. For the five seconds I had them on, all I could see more clearly were red reflectors on the mailboxes we passed. I tried to ignore the notion that this drive was a distraction quest, a way to avoid considering how badly we'd lost in the meeting, how far ahead of us Olivia would always be.

"You're right about one thing," Nena said. "There was no point in not helping her in the meeting. It changes nothing, really. And sure, let's quit any attempts to talk about anything else. It was my fault for trying to talk about matters that aren't explicitly Olivia. Let's honour her by shutting up about anything else. Your family, solitude, anything."

I wanted the fog to leak into the car, to obliterate the disappointed profile at the edge of my straining vision. I obeyed her and talked about Olivia.

"You have your apartments and your massive financial x in your accounts and investments, but you're still like a fifty-five-year-old cop getting drunk before his retirement dinner. You can't take it.

Olivia won't let you ignore the enforcement of your planned obsolescence. She's making you watch. Surprising you through Beagle,
this time turning us into her audience." The profile nodded, as
though Nena herself had been speaking, as though I were an
advanced autofill of thoughts she was too exhausted to voice.

"She didn't take my sale away, she made it negligible. She brutally assumed its existence as fact, she made it the semi-promising
soil for the real revolutionary product."

Olivia had demoted us into vapour. Mockton shook hands
with ghosts when we left his office, pulling his fingers away from
my lagoon-slick palm and trying to grip Nena's ectoplasm before
we drifted and melted out of the room.

"I want to keep going while I can, Nena. I can topple her. I
know I can. I'm trying to do something that is right in the larger
sense. Not just hurt someone for using me and humiliating you.
And even if I was just going for her because of what she did to us
in that office, I don't see the issue." Nena didn't bother answering, but my droning had relaxed her. She let her jaw hang open,
ending hours of clenched, silent tooth-grinding. When she
brought her lips together again her face had lengthened almost
imperceptibly, as unlined and peaceful as a death mask.

"Isn't this a strange time to be going to any church? It's not
going to be abandoned?" Nena asked.

"They do an evening service every night at seven. We'll make
some of it," I said.

"Seven's early."

"Evangelicals eat dinner at like four p.m. They're in bed
before nine."

The delicate turn of the conversation toward logistics allowed
me to ask Nena to help me with the directions. The GPS on her
phone told us to turn right in a mile, into what looked like a
logging trail with a steep incline but was revealed, after a bumpy

ascent of about twenty feet, to be a smooth, tended path. At either side was a colonnade of ancient evergreens, lonely and feet apart, sometimes with bald psoriatic birch trees between them, cannibalizing their own fallen leaves in their endless shaded winter beneath the giants. The landscape suggested private property and a congregation with an endless chore list.

Nena let our change in direction and surroundings function like an online pause, when she could pretend to have been called to a meeting if she wanted to stop speaking to me, and I could pretend to have a follow-up call if I needed time to come up with a witty response to her. We didn't speak for ten minutes.

"You're right," she said, when we finally came to what we had seen on the undetailed church website coming into view: a long strip of parked cars, from luxury off-roaders to defeated hatchbacks that would have to stay up here if the heavy rainfall that had just begun continued.

I braked. "Her parents have to be there," I said. "I know they will be."

Nena looked at me for a second before turning off the map on her phone, and I sensed she was wondering what my parents looked like, which one was the fat one, which one was the ugly one, which one was ultimately responsible, or if I had been an astonishing combination of recessive anti-jackpots. I parked next to a Range Rover.

The church was a long, flat building with frosted glass windows set too near the roof, windows that glowed yellow and let out piffles of screamed speech that couldn't escape the rest of the cement structure, with its high school red metal fire door entrance. I used the light from my phone to illuminate a path directly in front of us as we walked from the parking corral to the church, avoiding roots and slurping indentations in the mud made by heavy boots. Nena held my elbow in what I took as a reach for ballast, but she stopped and pointed to a clearing on our right, currently full of fog and white mushrooms. It was deeply trodden by swirling footprints orbiting a tall white tetherball post with nothing hanging from it except a sign reading, "The Gentlemen of the Pines."

"We should go back," Nena said, but she kept walking, staring at the sign as we passed it and continued up to the church. As though she were more perturbed by that slogan than by the place we were approaching.

"They're a legitimate organization. Pretty new, but legitimate. Tax exemptions. Food drives. I promise you I did the research." I had, but there had been nothing in the data on the Church of the Evergreen Advent, even from defectors who had set up their own rival churches, about "The Gentlemen of the Pines."

"What is it for, you think? The 'Pines' thing."

"It means that Olivia is involved in this place," Nena said.

"What? Why?"

I had seen Nena sell many times before, seen her subsume all of her personal beliefs, core, central truths, to a commitment to a product and an audience, but I had never seen her gather herself to lie like this. She was, once again, scared—as she had been in that Montreal bar when Olivia Robinson entered just as we stopped talking about her. I could feel the lie being born and could only hope that it was because she thought I wasn't ready for whatever truth she had, not that she didn't think I was worth sharing it with.

"Just sounds like her kind of thing, Osman. Part of her new patter, or some intermediate stage of development between when I knew her and President Olivia. It has a fake Robinson poetry to it that Brody Beagle would like. Maybe I'm remembering something from my interview with the aunt, I don't know."

"What do you think they do in their little faun grove?"

"They send the women home at some point after service to make dinner. Then they all take their shirts off and scream and run around this thing and pretend they don't ever masturbate. They hug and talk about the burden of fatherhood."

"I think it has something to do with the pole," I said. "They invest it with some meaning and then scream at it and circle it with crucifixes."

"Like you with Olivia," Nena said. She let go of my elbow.

"Don't metaphor me when we're trying to do something serious. If she is a symbol, to me or to anyone else, she's also a person. A terrible one. And her parents are right in there, so *shh*."

We entered the Church of the Evergreen Advent in the waning moments of the evening service, when the tongues were out. The back wall of the church was an enormous convex window that fishbowled out and magnified a mud pit: I had seen this on the one MPEG on the Evergreen Advent website. After Sunday service, it writhed with children and defanged snakes. But today only bluebottles and dragonflies swarmed the mud. The ululating was scattered and light, with pockets of intensity in the middle front pews, hands waving and babble emerging.

While a few faces turned, no one would speak to us, even if most of them seemed to be quietly tolerating the heavenly racket. The backs of branded T-shirts, blazers, cotton dresses and Carhartts faced us as Nena and I found a crucifixless patch of black wall and stood respectfully, hands clasped, focused on the man slumped over the pulpit, his bald spot pink and virgin white under the powerful beam of a central spotlight.

The elderly were confined to the perimeter of the pews. A type of aging white I had rarely seen in reality since those days and nights with Dad at the faculty club, where emeritus widowed pants-shitters expended part of their loneliness on the staff. I had since only seen people this old on social media: the grandparents who live too long, with their cobwebbed faces and dark trenches of mottled skin.

The bald spot vanished and was replaced by a hectic red face, bearded thickly at the chin and below, with wiry mismatched intermittent pubic thatches high on each cheek. He looked like a butcher or a bass player, and he stopped the pit moans with a conductor's sweep that ended in summoning hands held toward heaven. He lowered them and spoke as everyone sat. Nena slid down a couple of inches, but my knees couldn't take that tension.

"Jesus seemed a latecomer. Even a layabout. To the world around him. Perhaps to those who were close to him, but not so close as to be trusted, to be touched with the sure knowledge of his divinity. Jesus was never late. Jesus never *was*. Jesus always *is*. You cannot be late if you are eternal. Which is to say, hello, new friends. Do we have any congregants prepared to witness? Perhaps a freeform?" The pastor, or priest, or reverend, looked past the crowded front rows, came down from the pulpit after catching the rubber toe of one of his Hush Puppies on the stage lip for a suspenseful moment, cruised the side aisle and made Rasputin-penetrating eye contact with both Nena and me while trying on one of the wreathing smiles I've read about in Dickens. Little teeth surfaced in his beard like bits of barley from a recent bowl of soup.

I finally felt how afraid Nena was, beside me. Everyone here was white, a different kind of white from the day in that bookstore with my father, a less comfortable white. Our entrance had changed the room, introduced a volatility that made the backs seem to stare at us, every elbow cocked on the back of a pew tremble with magnetic attraction toward the centre of my face or Nena's. I squeezed her hand and she predicted my movement, starting for the door before I could touch her.

"Wait," said the pastor, when he saw us move. "Please. Please witness with us, friends. Please be part of the way in which we forgive each other before we ask the outside to forgive us." His face dropped, and elbows slid off pew backs, spines lost their tension as the gathering slumped into the humility of prayer. I took Nena's wrist and stopped her. She looked at me, without fear, but with a new certainty about me, about what I wanted and what she could expect from me. We rested against the back wall again.

The first witness was so ancient that her mutterings into the microphone from beneath the permed, crackling remnants of hair on her skull were amplified as breath and sigh, not words. Five minutes of this only intensified the reverence in the chamber.

The second witness was the youngest man in the room, a burly tattooed man with tunnel piercings, half of Henry Rollins's tattoos on his body and some uncertain prison work and black squares visible on the front of his neck.

He turned to me, to Nena, bowed and shut his eyes, then handed the microphone back to the roving pastor, who put a hand on his flannelled shoulder and said, "Thank you, Rick."

In the second row, a man stood. The Reverend Pastor felt it happen and turned, started a sigh that he cut off quickly, like yanking a just-boiling kettle off the stove. He handed the microphone over, then came to the back, standing against it a dozen feet away from Nena. His chest was still heaving from the effort of preaching, and I could feel his breathing through the wall when he leaned back.

The man with the microphone, who looked enough like Olivia that I didn't need the deeply painful rib prod from Nena, rotated in front of his pew, looked back over the audience, notably keeping his gaze at their eye level, ignoring us at the wall. He had a large purple skin tag on his lower right eyelid that I wanted to run over and tear off. The top of his head was so pointed that he must have been able to feel it when he had hair, must have dreaded his current baldness even more desperately than most men do. Otherwise he was quite handsome. Janelle, the wife, was a time-whittled strip, lightning-strike white and with two decades of silence between her slightly open lips.

"I wanted to, if you'll all bear with me, try a witnessing that I think is very in-the-moment. We don't have many new congregants, meaning we don't have any new accounts of journeys in the wilderness of our past sin. Unless y'all have been holding out on us." He laughed, but not to make it clear that everyone else should—this was an "I'll-laugh-so-you-don't-have-to" one. The congregation rustled, their synthetic rainproof clothing susurrating their discomfort and boredom.

"I want to discuss leadership, and how I've witnessed its degradation just over the course of my lifetime. I mean in the world, not in this house with you, my brothers, my sisters, and our dearest father, Pastor Greg.

"I want to talk about the cesspool we lock out of these doors when we immerse ourselves in the Lord for these hours, when we pretend that Pastor Greg's words are our world entire, when we feel His truth as part of ourselves in a way we cannot in the world. I want us to investigate what we discuss within these walls, if indeed our sins are sins, or if we truly need to reinvestigate what we mean by purity. I want to talk about the world we pretend to acknowledge, but that we willfully ignore, for fear that it will dampen our ecstasies of belief, for fear of the tremendous responsibility each of us bears. I want us to be honest so our hope can be honest."

He was containing his performance, orating in humble compaction, his arms now rigid at his side as his voice boomed out without cracking, climbing only in decibels, not register. But as his flat hands folded into loose half-fists, he did look a bit like he was going to explode.

"There's this phrase I've never looked up. I come from British roots, as many of you know. My family is long embedded in

America, my wife's as well, but culturally, I think it's safe to say that I grew up with a closer relationship to that once-great nation, that fallen empire, than many of you here in this room did. My father, in fact, left New York in 1940 to join up with the British Army. He was naive and just couldn't wait to get at what he called 'the Hun.' I wonder how he'd look at that war if he could see what has happened since, and where our nation is now.

"This phrase I've never looked up, it's something my father, who was not saved, used to say often, and often mockingly: 'Muscular Christianity.' If you know what it means, don't tell me. There's a truth in it that I've grown in my heart, in my soul, and I want to share it with you. It's what the words mean to me, and that's all the definition I need. What they mean is the loving, forceful leadership of the enlightened. That's what Muscular Christianity is, what it needs to be when we open those doors." He raised his arms to indicate the church entrance, but no one looked back. The congregants were closer to dread than fascination, but not me: I was studying the collection of speech acts that composed Mr. Robinson, the genetics in his talk.

"I watch the programs on Saturday morning, like so many of us here in this room do, hoping to find some sense of connection, of hope, in the greater evangelical community. I cannot but despair at the numbers. And the breakdown of those numbers. The muscle grows weaker, friends, in rooms that are not like this one. Leadership cannot be one man. It has to be—what leadership requires is supremacy, collective supremacy, if it is to lead to empire. That's what I've learned from my roots, from my Muscular Christianity.

"The ardent Christians the world over, the committed souls. When you look, when you don't rely on the numbers? When you actually look? They're blacks. They're blacks at best. And at least in blackness, there is purity. The others? The great mass of believers out there, when we open the doors of this, our church, our home? Mud Asians. A lumpen. And I know that we come to Pastor Greg to run from the conceptions that defined our past lives, the ignorance and violence of our thoughts, but what we cannot ever pretend to tolerate is the supremacy of that unguided mess of humans." I felt a pressure shift in the wall as the pastor left us. Olivia's father saw him coming and hurried to finish.

"America didn't need England. But that isn't a lesson of empire that we can expect to apply to these people. Our empire is the Word. I know you all believe that. These people—you watch them even as they take in the diluted Word from charlatans in suits—these mud folks need empire. They are so grateful to have it. We need to be strong. We need to bring them the Empire of the Word. We need to extricate the idea of hate from the complex work of supremacy.

"We must remember there is a humility in our strength, because it is also difficult, so difficult, to be strong. That is what has been lost in this modern morass, in the ingratitude of a world that pretends it could have formed itself without God's guidance and his hand pushing those of us who are equipped, who are laden with, the sense of responsibility, the intelligence, the compassionate sense of order needed to continue building His Kingdom on the sewage-sodden foundation of this earth."

The backs were staring at us again, some straight, some hunched, none bored. I had put my hand on Nena's back, my fingers grazing her belt, in preparation for a physically impossible scenario where I used it as a leather grip on her slight weight and slung her over my shoulder, charging the door with a pair of intact knees and pumping quadriceps that have never been part of my actual legs. Perhaps more frightening was that Nena accepted my hand: that she leaned back into it, for comfort, as we stared at the backs and waited for them to turn in response to the powerful summoning of Oliver Robinson's speech. I had felt the swelling duty in it, the authority of his gentle hatred. It marked me, as it must have marked these people, listening.

Pastor Greg took a short cataloguing look at Nena and me as he ascended the stage, perhaps sizing up how he could attack us if we turned out to be journalists.

"Our brother Oliver, as most of you know—please sit down, Oliver, please—is a veteran of many wars, within himself, with our Lord—and even a few pretty pent-up battles with me, right?" He unravelled a laugh that forgave, that begged indulgence, and Nena and I joined in as we made our way to the door, to the parking lot. The charge of agreement in the room that had followed Oliver Robinson's closing statement dissipated in the pastor's fogging words and laughter.

They let us leave. I took this as a form of generosity, not being murdered by hooded men wearing pine-tree air freshener garlands who would dissolve us and sprinkle our blood and bone meal over their vegetable gardens. I'd forgotten to feel something essential in there: the uncoiling certainty that I was capable of efficient, brutal violence in defence of Nena's bodily integrity and my life, if those benches full of the so recently benevolent turned and rose. I should have been envisioning scenarios beyond simple, impossible escape—*Get to that door and do not look back*—as my body became a fluid bulk of death-dealing movement. Nothing elegant, no wireless wuxia, just limb-rending violence. Reaching through pallid racist flesh to seize and crack the marrow from femurs.

"That was a mess," I said to Nena, when we were in the car and halfway down the forest path.

Nena was putting on lip balm and looking through her purse. I waited for her to put her seat belt on. She trembled, doing it, the same hand that had done her lips suddenly unstable.

Then she looked ahead and spoke, as I turned the car around, the trees and license plates circling us before I bolted directly away from the church.

"Can't call it that. It was not a mess," Nena said. "Oliver had a very cogent structure going. And Pastor Greg was pretty good at showrunning. Two natural pitchers."

The tremble was back, in Nena's voice now, urged out when she used proper names. We drove over the rock, the exterior shake stabilizing us both.

"I mean us going in there. Acting like we can walk into any room in America and be safe. The arrogance. I'm sorry I took us to a white power church."

"Anti–white power with some dissidents, I think," Nena whispered, before talking normally again. "You drove but I made the decision to go in. You know that. You know that you haven't decided a thing for me since I've known you, Osman."

I ignored the provocation, even though conflict would be a relief from fear, or from the unbreachable territory of the lie I'd seen Nena forming when we surveyed the ritual territory of "The Gentlemen of the Pines." We were still too close to that lie to speak of it, I sensed.

The car seemed to struggle even more with the slickness of the path when it was downhill, the weak engine and hesitant traction of the tires teasing the wheel out of my hands unless I gripped it and concentrated. Nena held nothing. Had she gripped my arm in the church, or outside of it? I couldn't remember, but I was sure that if she had, it was an instinctual accident that she regretted, like leaning back into my hand when I gripped her belt. She had let me take her to this church so I would again witness my own failure to do anything helpful, protective, or strong. It was another demonstration of our essential apartness in situations of intimacy.

"I was afraid," Nena said. "But not of those people. I know actual danger, and that wasn't it. Do you think Oliver Robinson makes that speech every service? That was for *us*. He wanted us to feel bad. And that's where a person like him stops, passively uttered threats that he can say were general statements. Olivia is far beyond that little man."

Nena tugged at her seat belt strap, made zydeco sounds against it with her thumbnail, graduated from shivers to a restlessness that seemed more me than her.

"A church full of sweating racists is scary because of Olivia, who isn't even there?"

"The scary thing about that church isn't what it has to do with Olivia's past, it's that it has to do with her present."

"Okay," I said, wary of the question I was being invited to ask.

"I was remembering and feeling something up there about my past relationship with Olivia, Osman. Something actual that isn't a fact or article of evidence."

We were back on the highway now, the humming asphalt scoring a silence that I knew was sulky and below me, but that I could do nothing to correct.

"If you don't understand by now why I want no part of your Olivia-destruction plan, I won't be able to explain it," Nena said. "She's scary, yes. She's unstoppable, of course. And we have a real past, Osman, an inviolable one that I already violated, a misstep that she's been punishing me for ever since. If I'm going to have any sort of win, any refuge, it's going to be *having nothing to do with her*."

"Continuing to blame yourself at all for what this psycho has been doing is frankly creepy."

"That pastor in there, Osman? It was Ogilvie. Pastor Greg is Ogilvie, Olivia's pet preacher. Her aunt showed me pictures of him in Oregon. You think he just ended up here coincidentally? This is a church of Olivia Robinson. She reclaimed that man from his Alberta hideaway, set him up here and installed her parents, gave him some sort of purpose that she's in utter control of. Are you scared of that?" We reached the highway, and I merged into traffic with aggression and acuity, concealing our car between two eighteen-wheelers. I wanted to drive well and hide at the same time.

I was scared, but also exhilarated. This was more than we could have hoped to glean from this field trip, this distraction. And the image of Olivia, grown and powerful, at some moment before AAP and her cancer, redeeming this broken loser from his Podunk congregation in order to set up a personal church playhouse for her pitiful and hated and erratic parents, her silent faith in her ability and in Ogilvie's channelling of it to develop an entire set of followers in the Pacific Northwest woods, the hidden, miniature success of this gambit, was an essential element of completion, a picture of her assuming control of her past by isolating all of the crucial players within a space she controlled and owned in the present.

"That's amazing, Nena. Can't you see that? How fucked up is that, she's literally a Christian splinter group founder? This is potent stuff. And look, Vikram Chandra texted me just after we left Mockton's office. Said he needed to talk to us. That has to mean something—he's never reached out before. I know it's about Olivia. This is absolutely moving in the right direction. God, I have audio of her dad making a fucking Klan speech in a church she founded," I said, waving my phone.

"You can keep talking, but I'm tired, Osman. Too tired to open this door and roll under the tires."

I did keep talking, about other things. My mother, my father. Trying to avoid all the questions that talking about my family made me want to ask about Nena's, all the conclusions I wanted to reach about Olivia's. Nena and I could speak at dinner. I could finish convincing her that I was capable of speaking of other things, that Olivia content didn't dominate my entire mind, but that it made sense to discuss the most interesting content first.

I thought in content now, retroactively if not in the present. I generated it and thought about its generation, I catalogued and edited time and reality as content. Today's content, bridging the archipelago of Edmund Bak's carbon monoxide-clouded car, my steam-choked hotel bathroom, Anthony Mockton's office, and the Church of the Evergreen Advent, had all manifested from the internet. People still think that virtual space emerges from real space, but it's no longer true. That part of Olivia's pitch was true. Even in the deep woods, in that sap-stinking barn of a church, the algorithm dominated: those pews were filled by a consensus created by content, by words and video pieces generated by slim whites in T-shirts and assembled on a framework generated by my slender brown cousins, wearing musty seventies deadstock shirts and moustaches of the same vintage, either ironically in Silicon Valley or haplessly in Bangalore, coding and connecting Mr. Oliver Robinson's discontent with a vocabulary and falsely world-encompassing vision of a fallen Europe and an elegant ivory sword and a past where children ran unmolested and never abandoned their families because nothing awful was ever visited upon them from the hordes.

Nena spoke as I stopped at the hotel, preparing to go into the underground parking, weaving between cabs and Ubers.

"Don't go down. I'm going home," she said.

"Dinner, though. I'm only here for another—"

"No."

I pulled up in front of a doorman who let his phone drop to his side as he straightened. Basketball highlights played soundlessly on the screen. The doorman stretched below his overcoat, his back arching, his calves rising and feet arching.

"We really loved each other," Nena said.

"What?"

"Olivia and me. That church is proof of it, and I don't think I'll ever make you understand how."

"You think because she invited her molesto-pastor back into her life that she's, what, testing you, Nena? You're doing exile desert-time while she treats you like shit before ushering you back into her heart and tells you all about her dead tumours and how hard it was to be strong and alone and—"

"Shut up." This was the first time Nena ever spoke to me the way I had longed for, with truth, with utter disgust, with her eyes full of me and her mouth spitting out the sight. A tremor started below my right knee. If I were standing I would have knelt.

"If you understand that you love her for whatever reason, then that's another way it was a worthwhile trip, Nena. It worked out perfectly. We both know more now."

"Can I leave now? Can you get out of this car and let me drive it to my apartment and go to fucking sleep, Osman?"

The doorman was watching us talk. I got out and she did too, walking behind the car as I circled the front. She got in, adjusting the rear-view for height. I bent toward the open passenger door, craning like a neckless dinosaur, clogging her sight with my torso, forcing her to talk to me.

"I'll talk to you tomorrow, Osman. Or text tonight."

"We know more, and that has to be useful. The fact that we know this much about her has to make her uncomfortable, Nena. We're getting somewhere."

Nena reached for the door, but I backed away and shut it myself, being careful not to catch her hand. I was so relieved to have finally lost her that my torso felt light for a moment, and a channel of hot sweat from my waistline descended into my boxers, embracing my chilly penis in wet fabric. I walked to the elevator.

11

I reveal nothing by telling you that Nena didn't discuss "The Gentlemen of the Pines" again until the summer of 2020, when we were living in extended and strict isolation in a compound of Muskoka cottages Nena bought with the sale of her city properties weeks before the worst of the economic shockwaves from the spreading virus. Nena had been tipped off by someone who would later be fired due to extremely fair but not-quite-substantiated rumours of insider trading. We were in an isolated lakeside Ontario community which suggested 1980s family films rather than wilderness with Nena's new German shepherd puppy, Horace, who lunged around the main residence on the huge adult paws that blossomed from his slim legs, stumbling from the bulk of those downy leather-soled clubs. I pretended to be comfortable with him, remembering that I had lied to Nena about having had a dog—a Labrador, I think—when I was a child.

Nena and I had spent the day taking the hard-wired surveillance and IoT hardware out of the wall with butter knives and screwdrivers. Stabbing drywall, cutting wires, grinding lenses into dust in the enormous basin sink in the kitchen. After we'd washed the glass and plastic down the drain, I put a vacuum-sealed Mennonite-raised chicken under the running tap to defrost. We cut the plastic off one of the sectional couches that had been delivered but not installed by masked workers who left before we could tip them, and I knelt in front of one of my boxes of books. I wasn't unpacking, just checking on them. I'd asked if I could have my collection delivered here after I sold all my apartments, and Nena had agreed. It was our first solid conversation, in a chat box or real life, since the end of the Olivia business. It had led to us being here, in this enormous, luxurious parody of a cabin, together for an indeterminate time.

"I was more fucked up that day in the woods than I let you know."

"You did kind of let me know, with the hostility."

"Sorry."

"Deserved it. I deserved all of it. It was stupid for us to stay out there once we saw what was happening," I said, as though I could entertain an idea of the past or myself where I left the Evergreen Advent before or during Oliver Robinson's speech. The idea of surrendering the memory of the experience for any danger we had imagined was especially unthinkable now that we didn't have anything to do. We did no work. Elsewhere, a hum of reports and press releases emerged from homebound employees who worked two hours a day and swiftly masturbated while their husbands or wives showered. My combat with Olivia remained incredibly significant to me, even as AAP evolved past it in a way I couldn't have foreseen.

"Not in the church. In the woods," Nena said. She had a rare pimple under her right cheekbone, and had stopped doing whatever she used to do to her eyelashes. She was eating a cup of ice chips.

"I wanted to ask about that a few times. I knew that if you were being shy about it, it was for a reason."

"I wasn't shy then or now. I was deliberately withholding information. It wasn't just the pastor I recognized." She threw an ice chip at the back of my head, and I hugged the Arkham House *Dark Carnival* in my hands to my chest as though it were an exploding grenade and I was sacrificing myself to its impact. She laughed and I rubbed smudges off the Brodart with the leg of my jeans.

"You just wouldn't ask me up there, talk me through what I'd seen and what it had to do with Olivia. I knew that it wasn't our pattern anymore, it was shared pathology. This veneration for me that your unasked questions carried in their unaskedness, as though you had every right to know and would probably figure out the answers yourself soon, but were graciously allowing me my privacy. You were attuned to me, I knew that and still know that, but you were so proud of sensing anything about me that the connection broke when you spluttered it out or said you already knew with that gross cow-eyed gentleness and hand stroke you do, every single time."

"Jesus Christ."

"Calm down. I've thought this through a lot, condensed it, even taken out some hurtful parts about sex. I'm talking about the past, the recent past but still the past, a set of circumstances and behaviours that doesn't exist anymore or else we wouldn't be in a room together in isolation. Don't be a baby."

I set the Bradbury book down on the snap-laminate that Nena would replace with hardwood when she could get people in. I didn't cry much anymore, out of exhaustion, partially, but also out of confusion at what my emotions meant, a recognition of the potential falseness of every reaction in the weeks since Olivia.

"I know you're thinking about Olivia Robinson right now. And you will anytime anyone reminds you of this past year. That was part of the rot between us: you only thought of me against her, or opposite her, and believed that making that clear would somehow draw you and me together. It didn't. And that was because you didn't understand what I had tried to let you know, even if I didn't exactly tell you.

"The Church of the Evergreen Advent was my creation. The substance of it, and 'The Gentlemen of the Pines' thing, even if Evergreen Advent was hers. The gospel-pagan-frontier thing. That was me. Evangelism against white supremacy. I made it up in a joke."

"She took the joke," I said. "Olivia. She has no use for jokes but she can apply their logic to ideas that would be—"

"Absolutely crazy to anyone who wasn't her, until they are real." We were speaking over each other as we used to type over each other, in the sodality of our new pod, the home that had been made for us by disease and Olivia Robinson.

Nena lingered in my pause and kept the silence long enough to make it clear that she was going to speak again and didn't want collaboration.

"Before any of my research, before I visited Olivia's aunt for that video interview, before I made a crying phone call to her that I'll never tell you about, that she treasured in a part of her so deep and real that she gave up any opportunity to leverage it, I came to know that Olivia was lying by lying to her myself; by watching ourselves believe ourselves as we built these edifices of unchallengeable bullshit, as we tested new stories every other week or day, as we hard-formed the right ways to deceive everyone else and eventually, hopefully, ourselves.

"This is why people confess, Osman. Most people. You spill for reassurance, not communication. But the substance of the act is different for people like me." In that moment I understood that Nena's strict delineation of our types was an assurance that we would never, ever have any form of sex again, even if she had invited me to a cabin at the seeming end of our economic universe. I tried to register this as a fact of little significance in the new growth of our relationship, but a cavity just underneath my bottom right rib announced itself with an altitude-drop rearrangement of organs around this new hollow, from a body truly exhausted with how reliably I spoiled everything.

"The attractive part of confession is the reality you're building with the person who's invited you to say that what you will announce is true. You reward the attention they're bestowing on you, the focus on yourself and your interior and your motivations that you haven't felt anywhere outside of that particular interrogation, with a confession. And with Olivia, she pays you back in kind. Paid me back in kind. I told her a portion of family truth, she gave me everything about the evangelical game show circuit, only subbing a parallel version of my dad as hers. My dad, Osman, who you'll never hear about again, buried his brain in pamphlet then WhatsApp fantasies of terrorism and the Deep State, tried six separate times to be the target of an FBI sting, lost food vendor licenses in two states, was in the newspaper for stalking the family of a Christian stand-up comedian who lived on the hill overlooking our duplex. I send him a thousand dollars a month. Olivia and I talked extremism. She talked her dad. I invented a church, and she built it in the Washington woods."

"Is that for real?" I asked. Perhaps hearing how shitty my attempt at a playful uplilt was, Horace came over to assist me. I held one of his limp ears, crinkling the young cartilage. The structure of my nose was one of the few parts of myself that I could still contemplate in the mirror or by touch and know that it was real, because I've never much minded it. I twitched a nostril, feeling my soft tissues pass over my septum, feeling Horace's ear, envisioning it all as the rubbery translucent material in a commercially deep-fried chicken thigh, chewable but not edible. I still thought in food, often, even if my body had shrunk within my clothes, the fat that I did have and the fat I thought I had both vanishing into this lack of presence below my brain, this flesh that I'd stopped thinking about as though by hypnotic trick after Olivia and I finished with each other.

"I have no reason to lie to you, Osman. No motivation, I mean. There'd be no purpose to it. My love for Olivia made for a private and true relationship built of mutual advantage and the narrow opening of intimacy that happens when two people need to use each other for a limited amount of time. You're not equipped to understand something like that. You would see it as exploitation coming from one direction, not as mutual exploration. You don't understand or respect me enough to see that I fed off what I took from Olivia. That her lies to me when she invented a father for herself, built out of pieces of mine, dressed in evangelical huckster suits and the comprehensible American earnestness of an apocalypse-embracing dance dad, was something that she was doing for us, to bring us closer together, to invite me to dwell in a bonded fiction with her for as long as I could resist seeing what she was doing at the company and finding out who she really was for myself. I lost something when I decided to start looking at Olivia Robinson's life as entirely separate from mine."

Horace whined and I realized that I was still holding his ear. I let go and he immediately nipped my hand, which I pulled back hard enough to slap myself in the face. The sound echoed down from the high ceiling, and I looked into Nena's expectation, her demand that I say something that would reflect understanding, but not a level of understanding she didn't feel I was entitled to—something that let her know that I knew I understood nothing, but wanted to, someday. That I had at least absorbed what she said. I turned away from her and stared at the hand that had slapped me. I remembered to close my mouth.

"Anyway," Nena said. "'The Gentlemen of the Pines' was a mangled translation from Farsi. It was *my* father's thing, the name for his little edu-anarcho-terrorist-junior group which consisted of him and a friend who owned a dried fruit and nuts store. They drank arak and vodka and talked about how various presidents deserved to die. That was it. I told Olivia about it, and the next time I saw that order of words anywhere was that sign in the woods. 'The Gentlemen of the Pines.' I just thought you might want to know that, because if you really think about it, it makes sense of what happened to Olivia and you."

I thought about it. It did make sense. Horace walked toward one of my piles of books and licked the spine of a Robert Aickman first, *Sub Rosa*. I screamed. Nena walked over and picked him up with one hand, clasping him against her chest, her hair hanging over Horace's face for him to lick instead. Nena let him, perhaps so she wouldn't have to look at me.

"I watched you take in what I said. I really did," she said. "I can see the sentences hit and sort of percolate in, most of them. But it's not what I actually said that registers. When you record what you believe I've said to you, it's absolutely you talking, not me. I've read the pages you have so far. I can't believe you've inflicted them on your mom, voice mail or not.

"It's so rare to recognize myself between your quotation marks that when I do the words leap, they become uncanny—it's as striking as seeing someone who looks just like me as a background actor on TV. It's really only that part you wrote with your father, that recitation of his—that, finally, isn't you. Must have something to do with you hearing it from him first then seeing it written down. Otherwise—" Here she set Horace down, and he chose to splay out his front paws in front of him and his back ones behind, flattening his whole body to the cool plastinated particleboard and falling into an immediate sleep.

"Otherwise I see and hear you the whole time. And it's agony, you know? Hearing all voices as the same voice must be what is happening in your skull all day long. At least Olivia is looking for an angle. Finding something to exploit means doing some preliminary exploration. But with you—I brought you up here for these weeks or months or whatever it turns out to be because you're as close as I can come to talking to myself while still having a body around, someone that will give me a reason to continue to interrogate what is happening with me and why. I need to be away from screens but you're as good as one. You take input. You hear me. You do nothing without explicit commands on how to react. Now that you can't frustrate me, no one makes me calmer."

Nena went to the bathroom after that, picking up one of my books to accompany her. I trusted her with them, even in close proximity to water, and it made me happy that she wanted to read them. I didn't want the kind of collection that only existed to be protected from the sun. I wanted it to be of use, and I could no longer use books in the conventional sense.

I ate a bag of beef jerky in front of Horace and decided Nena was wrong about me.

12

After Nena left the hotel that night in Seattle, I wouldn't consider "The Gentlemen of the Pines" again until everything was over. Which is fine, because there is no fucking way I would have guessed the truth about it, and I lost the chance to ask Nena when she drove away. The Church of the Evergreen Advent was the evening's essential content, aside from Nena's exhaustion with me, which had been such an inevitability I could embrace its arrival with relief.

To calm myself, I called Sameen's voice mail, even though it was barely nine, long before my usual time. I read her a thousand words or so, correcting and editing as I went along—a passage about Nena that hasn't survived into this draft, because I couldn't find a place for its sincerity. Sameen kept her part of our unspoken pact by not picking up as I left message after message. I drank water from a toothglass and rinsed with Scope in the mouldering wetness of the bathroom as the drywall sweated out the remnants of Nena's shower.

I couldn't grasp how to draw the relationship between the current Olivia and that church. It ran parallel to Olivia. It produced preachers like her. The pastor, once her pretend leader and now her pet, enthralled believers as Olivia had at AAPC and in Anthony Mockton's office. It wasn't a breeding ground for Olivia's thought, it was not a propagation chamber for her values, or more specifically her only value: the promotion and worship of the self. Olivia Robinson was an entire, specific form of church, and the Evergreen Advent was a reflected test case that I could use if I could only become a much more intelligent person capable of making the connective leaps that had been beyond me as a scholar and a writer for my entire life.

For dinner, I went to an oyster-and-steakhouse that Nena would very much have enjoyed and sat alone in our reserved booth, facing my heaped coat. Before setting it down, I had pulled a small notebook from a Canadian marijuana start-up from its pocket. I gently tore off the prismatic foil cover. I had a stack of these in my carry-on, from when they were thrust on me by a clipboard and branded-hoodie college kid at the Toronto airport after my final visit to Sameen. This one would be used to record my notes on Oliver Robinson's speech.

With Nena absent, I ate in my old style, with utter focus on the glistening rush of buttered salt on blood and bread, all taken in quickly enough to compromise my ability to breathe. This enhanced the high, if not the taste. As I ate alone, I felt reassured, confirmed that Nena's relationship with me had been a secret evidence-gathering mission to prove that a relationship with me was a terrible idea. Perhaps I could win Nena to the battle against Olivia for the first time, now that we both acknowledged that I was not someone she could ever fuck or live with. And surely I could love Nena properly, as I did before, with no threat of having to perform with her or exist in proximity to her.

On the walk back to the hotel, I called Sameen's carer again. She picked up.

"She's really sharp, Osman, at least until about seven PM," Angela said. I sat at the hotel bar. There was a basketball game on television. I pointed to a Pilsner tap and laid my wallet on the bar after shifting my ass high enough to extract it, creating a dull pain in my hip and a brief, bright, enlivening agony in the pinched roll beneath my rib cage. My right side glowed as Angela spoke. I wondered if the doorman from outside would come in after his shift to catch the last quarter. I wondered if he'd think I was gay if I told him I'd noticed him watching highlights on his phone when he let me in that afternoon. Probably not. No one wanted to picture me as homosexual or heterosexual, sexual at all. The doorman and any other man—Anthony Mockton, Brody Beagle, anyone who could properly fuck and be fucked and be fantasized about, or at least endured—saw men like me as ambulatory innards, as an exposed nervous system obscenely alive but with no place in this environment. We were meant to quiver and lurch toward an early, merciful death, dust entering our wet folds and lidless eyes until we were encrusted and invisible. The doorman wouldn't think I wanted his body, because he couldn't imagine my body as an object or source of desire. He'd think I was threatening to rat him out to his employer for fucking with his phone on the job.

Angela kept talking as I stared into the lobby. She lifted her voice in the middle of sentences instead of at the end, giving every statement a soothing, rolling-hills rhythm with a constant questioning note. Instead of listening in detail—Angela sent an email update every week, anyhow—I imagined Sameen being soothed by this tone, discussing television shows and novels with Angela, perhaps seeing her as an amalgam of past classmates and her few secret friends as the delineations of present reality and everything before and beyond it stippled and gapped with darkness.

"We're actually doing this thing now where we read a book in a public place, together, talking after every few pages—right now it's a Lawrence Durrell, she's in a big revisiting mode that I'm trying to encourage—just talking over what happened on the page and what happened around us in the Starbucks when we look up. It really helps, cognitively."

"That's amazing. Does she mention anything about my messages, ever?" I said. Angela, whose last name I could only remember when I was looking at it in my inbox, wasn't only hired for being white. She had an English degree on her CV just below her nursing degree. It was from a particularly undistinguished Canadian university, a dressed-up community college, but it had gotten her the job.

"What messages?"

"I've been leaving her some of my writing in voice mails," I said, into a silence that sounded annoyed, and eventually became quite long. I understood, for the first time, that Angela made these calls with Sameen in the room: that this quiet was Angela talking to my mother after brushing the phone onto mute, or simply staring at Sameen to elicit some truth.

"You're a writer? I thought you were in tech."

"I am. Education, tech. I meant that she and I used to talk about writing, that it could come up when you two talk books. Never mind. I just miss her a bit, that's all."

"That's sweet and I'll tell her. I promise you she's very comfortable. And we're thinking of a short trip, either a day on Toronto Island and possibly an overnight out there, or a cottage for the weekend. I'll let you know beforehand what the plans are, Osman. Okay?"

"Okay. Just let her know that we talked and that I love her." Sameen, Ajit, and I used to spend some time at the marina on that small island, on the deck of an enormous houseboat owned by Dr. Millie Archibald, one of the committed alcoholics in Dad's department, beloved by students and with zero publications after she secured tenure at age thirty-four. She had a cupboard full of

Christmas panettone that she fed to the ducks that clustered around the bow of the ship.

"Osman," Angela said, quieter but not quieter, stage-whispering a new seriousness into the conversation. She breathed into the receiver for two seconds, indicating a swift move to another room. "I have to tell you that these accounts I give you of Sameen's—I have to use the word, decline—are glossed. Just a bit. I'm always being honest with you, but I do skim some of the gaps and confusions your mother has been facing or manifesting. She really is fading. Slowly and not in agony or humiliation, but it's true. Your mother asked me to do this, to keep our conversations focused on the good. She doesn't want anything I say to bring you to a place where you feel obligated to violate her wishes."

"I won't ever do that. And I appreciate the honesty, but I have to admit, I admire your ability to abide by my mother's wishes even more. That's really meaningful to me. Don't take that as scolding, I'm grateful for you letting me in like this. But if she wants the curtain drawn, we'll leave it that way."

"She hasn't told me about any messages you've been leaving, but they may be a poor idea. In terms of upsetting her, that is. And her wishes. I'm going to leave that up to you, okay?"

Once, when everyone on Dr. Archibald's bobbing cabin cruiser was passed out, with fumes of Tiger beer and the gentle miasma of middle-aged hot dog sweat permeating the cabin, I tore off strips of the soft sweet bread and threw them to the ducks, urinating gently near their heads and bills as they swam close. I talked to them after I peed. Apologized, told them about my parents, whispered promises of what I would and would not do if they swam back. They left and I jumped down into the hidden world of the filthy water, with its motor oil and carp and my piss and the cummy fondle of lake weeds. I swam away from the boats and into the cold openness of the lake after a few dozen feet, floating and coming back after an hour in which I hadn't been missed. I can remember this, remember floating on my back when I was tired of movement, grasping hollow flutes of drift-wood and pushing them under me, letting them poke into my back as they surfaced. But I can't believe I was ever equal to an hour of activity. When I returned, pulling myself up the steel ladder to drip dry, Sameen had moved from below deck. But only to sleep, not search. She was on a deck chair, wrapped in Dr. Archibald's blankets and everyone's jackets, her small skull on a pillow, her body a heap of borrowed fabric.

I was so used to missing my mother, to looking and thinking right past her for decades, that I couldn't tell if I missed her more now.

The heat of my head left my phone as condensed as my glass of beer when I laid it on the bar. Vikram Chandra's unanswered text lay within. He hadn't followed up, which made me think he was a different, less desperate kind of person than I'd imagined him to be, or that his phone had died. I felt the urge to speak to him, to test him out with a submerging plunge into the develop-ing plot and theory of Olivia Robinson, a test of his alliances and of whether he was either stupid enough or secretly intelligent enough to be an asset. I was getting closer to the meaning of the church as I drank, but the alcohol and lack of an interlocutor didn't allow me to think properly, didn't allow my conclusions to arrive as they usually did, from someone else suggesting them to me or me lying and joking my way into their truth.

Much of fiction is asking ourselves what happened in the woods. When we were children, or when we vanished, or when the people we cared about most left our lives only to haunt, to be remembered, to return as altered beings who have grown beyond the control we have over them. Things had happened to us among The Gentlemen Of the Pines. Our presence had manifested a speech by Mr. Robinson. Nena had called her patience with me into question, perhaps terminally. And we had passed into Olivia Robinson's life in a deeper way than I would have thought possible, accessing the photo-negative of her politics, the authentic, pure racism that illuminated her progressiveness, the philosophy she hadn't rejected so much as reshaped. Oliver Robinson's rejigged white imperialism, his gentle missionary quest to shut us all up and help us all out.

Olivia appeared over my left shoulder, holding a square-cut glass with a heavy base. I saw her without turning, in the slanted mirror that encircled the bar. She was wearing a vintage suit, pinstriped and belted, more formal than what she'd worn in Anthony Mockton's office. Her eyes, the gentle blue of a screen saver sky, communicated no information, contained nothing but my reflected fear when they met mine in the mirror.

I once licked a broken nine-volt battery when I was a child, drinking the shock as I stared unfocused at the spume of crusted acid leaking from the shell. My pores were producing this same sensation and substance now, adrenalized sweat pushing through a melting aluminum barrier of antiperspirant. I moved on my stool, my clothes crackling like foil, my elbow twitching like a malleted knee when Olivia touched it.

"I was so hoping to catch both of you guys, but I guess Nena's being her usual responsible super-efficient self and sleeping or something totally dull like that, right? Sorry to just jack-in-the-box here but your company phone's off and I thought it would be less invasive to ask Amy where you'd booked in than to peel your private cell off your personnel file.

"You should really just use your business as your personal. It's very early-aughts not to, Osman. Not an order but I think it's a good idea, personally. And I hope you don't feel, like, intruded on." Olivia sat next to me, and we both looked up at the mirror for a moment, as though checking to see there was no one behind us, that the rest of the room had indeed vanished.

"Nena has a place in town," I said. Or really, found myself saying, as they do in books, when the words precede thought, when the interrogator's needle quill through the tear duct has prodded just the right area of brain to elicit confession. "A couple. So no hotel for her."

"We used to talk investments when we were at HQ together," Olivia said. The liquid in her glass didn't bubble, or act with any of the viscous cling of booze. It was water playing liquor. "I always admired that, how she could focus on all these projects she had going while still conscientiously doing her job. Which she does, obviously. I mean, how about that shit today? We have Parnell locked. It's over. Mockton and I had cocktails after that marathon admin meeting—God, I promise to forever forbid AAP from getting that bloated—and I really put a pin in the Beagle interest, showed him a couple of texts with Brody and maybe if I'm being honest accidentally scrolled past a couple of photos of Brody and me in Mexico City and he was so sold he sent six key emails from the fucking table."

I smiled. I felt beer calories settle into my tits. Sweat formed and simmered in the crease just below them.

Olivia tried to swirl her ice cubes, but there wasn't enough water left in the glass. She shook her head and laughed, at herself, toward me.

"I always forget who I'm talking to. After a day of hustles like this. I forget what company I'm in, that I can drop the sales talk and boardroom bro terms and just really be. Talk, really talk. Yeah?"

"Yeah."

"So forget all that. Let's leave it behind at Parnell. Let's just speak. I want you to know, Osman, that I trust you. I don't think Nena quite gets me, and that's cool. She was a total terminator in the right role, and the company is well aware of that. But she has defences in her that I just cannot ever see her letting go, and for a woman in business those defences are dead necessary but at a certain point all that steel turns you into your own anchor, you know?" Olivia paused, either because this was a line she had perfected earlier and wanted to make sure it stuck, or because it was a spontaneous one good enough that she was banking it to use again. She continued.

"Nena doesn't trust, and as a result, she'll never believe that she is truly trusted, that the faith we all have in her is unshakeable. You're not like that, Osman. You have softness in you. Nena's guard makes her more vulnerable than she could ever believe. I sense that, and I take on the pain of it myself. I know how humiliating it is to be looked at as less-than, as other, as foreign and despicable. What I didn't learn from being a woman, I learned from being sick. From what my illness triggered in others, I mean: I could accept pity, I could understand that.

"But so many people looked at me with fear, Osman. Not of what I could do, but what I represented." I recognized the evolution of her conference speech, how she had now integrated the genuine reaction she'd had to my joke—that fear created power. Olivia had found a way to acknowledge that this was still true, but when you are feared because of a tumour instead of a possible concealed AR-15 or dynamite vest, the tumour gets the credit and the fear-power. She watched me think, and pivoted.

"That's part of being an empath, accessing all this pain that others are going through, and feeling it nest into you, without totally overtaking your ability to function. You're not quite an empath, Osman. I would know. We recognize it in others. But what you are is vulnerable, exposed. And I want you to know, please don't let that go. It's specifically that quality that means there's a place for you in AAP leadership. I really do see a rising future for you. Getting this face time is half the reason I came up here. I knew that Nena could totally close Mockton on her own. Sold him that brilliant little package that she came up with. But I wanted to see you. I was afraid that when I promoted Vikram Chandra, I gave you the wrong idea of how much you're valued. You've seen Vikram. You know him. He glows, Osman, even from a screen, and we can't let that quality go. His value to us is unique. Have you ever talked to him?"

"No. A bit."

"He's not a linear thinker. I don't know if he's a lateral thinker, we haven't figured that out, but he's just entirely himself. You know? Like, he doesn't need to shift modes. He's just there, present, Vikram. And that's what I wanted to talk to you about." I couldn't tell if she was redefining the stupidity I'd always seen in Vikram as invaluable omnidirectional thinking, or letting me know that she thought he was stupid, too.

"I think Vikram was a perfect choice, Olivia."

"I want it out of the way that he wasn't promoted in your place. That title, that role, it's for Vikram. He'll fit with the team around him. But we haven't created a place for you at the top that can truly channel what makes you great, Osman. We need to create that position for you."

"That's kind."

"That's kind means 'that's bullshit,' right?" Olivia laughed, this one almost as much for her as for me, clutching the rail under the bar and tipping back slightly on her stool, barking and hiccupping.

"That's totally a part of why we need you, Osman. Someone who isn't afraid to bring up an almost-school-shooting to tie up a sales pitch. That's some of what makes you great. But we need the rest. We can't create a leadership role for you at AAP because you're not letting us know who you really are. Osman."

"You're saying my name a lot," I said. For a moment, annoyance overwhelmed fear just enough to make me forget who I was talking to.

"It's a clue."

"What?"

"Osman, are you Muslim? That question isn't for answering—I would never make a demand like that—but it's just one that I want you to know is being asked in some very important rooms. Ever since the last AAPC, where I accidentally ushered in your coming-out moment, which I still sometimes doubt I had any right to do." My right nostril was as dry as a callus, and my thumbnail would be just long enough to give it a deep, satisfying scratch. I tried not to twitch like a rabbit.

"You have to understand I did that for a reason, Osman. Channelling what you said to me. It's why we give each other facts, stories, emotions—we need other people to show ourselves to ourselves. And you did that for me. You fucking locked into place everything I was thinking about when I was sick, when I was in this half-world that no one who hasn't done chemo drugs or been dead half the day and incredibly, painfully alive all night could understand. The only way to see another person is to see yourself. And the only way you can see yourself is to force people to be uncomfortable, to beam an image of yourself back to you. You create this image, this burdened good-humoured brown barely-man being downtrodden by authority, by circumstance, by his body, by his mind, by his inability to exceed what is being forced onto him. You present it to anyone listening, and you wait for them to define you aside from that, against that, to make you more than your joke. I don't joke about serious things, so I never unlocked the exact way it's done until I watched you trying to impress all of us at the conference. Trying to borrow a moment for yourself that everyone would remember. It was beautiful.

"That's what you lit up in me with your little joke, Osman. I understood that everything in our HR docs was something that should be in AAP's vending approach. And the way you did it, just getting completely ethnic with those uncomfortable white people while inviting them in for a laugh—that is pressure. That is sales. You showed me something that day, Osman. But you didn't show me yourself. Getting up there on that stage and calling out to you—I was trying to show you yourself, but yes, I admit it, sweetheart, I was calling you out too." She couldn't decide if she wanted to give this last a Bogart dip or a John Wayne twang, so she did both and looked like the frenulum beneath her lower lip had been cut out.

"Just for optional fun, can you answer my question, Osman? Are you Muslim? I ask because of your name, sure, and because people have been wondering about you, about our company culture, about what we've done to invisibly force assimilation on people and what we can do to reverse that process. I've been trying to work up the courage to talk to you about this directly, but I knew it had to be offsite. This can't be a formal conversation."

"I've never practised anything. My parents wouldn't have let me if I wanted to."

"That." Olivia pointed at me, her fingernail close enough to brush a pill on my woollen blazer sleeve. My shirt was too wet to take the jacket off now, and I was too hot to live with the jacket on for more than a few more minutes. "You can use exactly that, what you just said, because it's the truth. We need more of you at AAP, Osman. That's all we're asking for—to get all of you, not just the parts you think are presentable. We need you to be real so we can be real with you, understand?"

The simple answer hunted me, tried to arrest my thoughts, stop them, prevent any complexity from being possible: that what Olivia was saying wasn't a reversal but an extension of the white supremacy she had absorbed in earliest childhood, at the feet of her unhinged father. But this wasn't the case. I'd seen Mr. Robinson's varietal of racism that evening, and it felt personal, his own, something precious to him and deeply religious, something he'd made as the rest of his life disappointed him, beginning with the flight of his daughter, or perhaps before, with his wife, who even now I can only remember as a slender grey animated wax dripping next to him on the curved modern wooden pew, listening with equal attentiveness to the pastor's hedgings and her husband's ravings, not humbled but hollowed, edged out of her own mind and body by years of failed combat with the people around her. Mom did not look much like Olivia. And Olivia didn't sound like her father any more than I sounded like mine.

"I am explicitly giving you all the grace and permission you refuse to give yourself: you can stop assimilating," Olivia said.

"I haven't."

Olivia stared at me, summoning sympathy which emerged as a head tilt and a minor tremble in the lower eyelids.

"It's something we don't even know we're doing, Osman. Believe me. Ask yourself again. Not for me, but for yourself. Please. Can't you feel it when people have been talking about you, maybe in a way that could threaten your future, behind your back? I really can. I developed a sense for it while I was raised in the church. Everyone with their eyes on you. I came to find it soothing when I just assumed I was being monitored, though. That's what I think one of the main appeals of God is, this sense that someone is watching in helpful judgment, allowing you to be better at being you, at finding yourself in the world. People just talk so fucking much, Osman. They research, they talk, they invent things, they talk, they do everything they can but ask you a direct question, which is why I'm speaking to you tonight. I just want to be direct. I want to keep you among us, and I want to know what that takes. What I can offer to retain your value at AAP. I need you to feel needed."

"I have to go to the bathroom."

In the stall I took off my blazer, my soaked shirt. I hung the jacket from the hook and laid the shirt on the toilet tank. I wiped myself down with toilet paper, rolled threads of it coming off in my chest and arm hair as I rubbed too hard and fast, until I was as dry and pilled as my hanging jacket.

My shirt was dirtier than the toilet it was resting on. This was a hobo situation with a third-world twist, exactly the life people would judge someone who looks like me to live. Dad didn't feel guilt when he made judgments. "Judgment is the essence of any decision," he would say. My father's increasing inability to tolerate me came from the purity and completeness of his success, from my resemblance to his nightmare self. In that unlived existence Ajit inhabited a subcontinental English crammer where he was Mr. Professor Sir. Trapped eternally with his original surname, smelling of the spices he later banned from making contact with hot oil in his home. I made the idea of Dad's own avoided failure real again, through the force of his shame.

Oliver Robinson was, according to the reality that Nena had managed to reconstruct in her documentary research, an addict married to an addict who lost his child to a wealthy sister, then cleaned up and reconstructed himself in the American religious rehab model, eschewing substances for a gospel modified by an intensified apocalyptic vision and his personal recommitment to white purity and power. But the Oliver I'd seen in that church possessed elements of the father in the story that Olivia had told Nena during her job interview, of the ambitious dad who wanted to take his scripture-memorizing daughter on the national circuit as a celeb-in-training before meeting resistance from his insistent wife, who was a clear fiction compared to the half-straightened paper clip with hair we had seen at the Evergreen Advent. Oliver had been changed by his daughter's story, by what he must have heard of it, by what he could have absorbed from it to rebuild himself as a man worthy of his daughter's outright rejection, even as he continued to worship at the pulpit of the pastor she'd replaced her father with as a teenager. The racism hadn't been passed on to Olivia, it had been constructed in opposition to the woman he imagined his daughter to be. Oliver Robinson was trying to stick as closely as he could to Olivia's story of what kind of man he had been by building that character into a future he now inhabited, absorbing traits and opinions and deep-seated beliefs that resonated entirely with the invented Dad that Olivia had cleaved out of her life. She had gotten to her father in a way that I had never reached mine.

I picked up the shirt and knew I wouldn't be dry if I put it on again. It looked and smelled as though it had been my only garment on a week-long jungle hike. Ringed with sweat craters that reached the bottom of my rib cage, wafting my odours and those of the animals I'd ingested before the beer.

But I did put it back on, along with the jacket, and headed to the elevator bank instead of the bar. Nena's roped towels still snaked across the bathroom floor in my hotel room, minimal amounts of her sweat and come still in the rumpled sheets of the bed. When Olivia was finished with me, I could contemplate screaming at housekeeping on the phone and reject the idea after a brief, perfectly worded fantasy of control.

I came back to the bar in a shirt that was almost the same blue as my discarded one, without a jacket. Olivia had a real drink in front of her this time, something dark and iced in a collins glass. She was talking to herself without moving her mouth, just tilting her hands slightly, raising her thumbs as she did in her video presentations.

"I scared you off," she said. "I'm sorry."

"No. It's important. I want you to go on."

"That is so good to hear, because—you know, it's a lot. I actively think about you, Osman. With Vikram, I don't. He's great, and he does everything right, but you're the kind of AAP pillar who could expand our definition of what 'everything' is. And that involves building on—you know, what we were talking about before. Come on. Pakistan. What a fascinating place of— and I acknowledge I know nothing—of extremes. Enlightenment and corruption sharing space in the same nation-state like that. There must be so much you could let out, Osman."

"I really don't know much more than you do. I'm not ahistorical but I've—it's more of an England and Europe and America thing for me. My family lived in Canada and came from India, not Pakistan, but I know almost nothing about it."

"You're the second generation of melting-potters in your family." Olivia said. "I've read about your father. I've even read your father, all eighty pages of one of his books that I found on Google. It was Wordsworth and countryside and wars that had nothing to do with his history. Sidebar, you've been on my mind that much, you've even got me reading way-above-my-head academic stuff on flights. And I guess I should have understood that the man who wrote that book was a man who wouldn't let his son access his own real past.

"I'm going to overstep again, Osman. I think Nena is critical to this phase in your progress. Both in a great way and in the slightest negative way. You sought her out—and I'm not making any assumptions about what is between you, other than that you're clearly close—when in the past I think you would have pursued someone who maybe looked and sounded less like her, and maybe looked and sounded more non-threatening."

"Nena isn't threatening," I said, and wondered if there was anyone in the world who had met her and could say and believe this. Anyone she wasn't selling to.

"Let's just say that's my mistaken assumption, then. But I will tell you that I've seen your interests fade away, just from looking at your socials. You haven't posted one of those old book covers in months, and I bet you're not even quite aware that you've dropped the hobby. You're not even drinking at interesting places, Osman. I find you in the hotel bar? Look at this carpet. Look how bright it is in here. You don't care about things anymore. You're moulting. You're becoming. It's beautiful and it's painful. I think you're currently seeking out permission to step out of the identity your parents designed for you by reaching out to some-one of a similar-different background, but you picked someone who is so entirely whited-out herself that you're only compound-ing your own shame. But I think drawing closer to her speaks to an instinct that you have to go back, to access the real stuff, the person you were never allowed to be. And that's a wonderful thing. A perfect thing."

I believed her. I believed those things about myself for a few moments. Olivia hadn't come close to being right but she had pointed out the truest inheritance I had from my father, whose genes had nothing to do with the shape of my face or body, but were embedded in my disguises. Ajit was from India, but he fre-quently pretended to be from Pakistan, floating across the Line of Control of the border in campus conversations eight thousand miles from his discarded home, advocating for whichever cause he felt would benefit him most with his interlocutor, whether it was a donor, a student, a student's father, or a woman he was whispering to in the living room while his son and Sameen slept upstairs. Father was the family's first man from no-place, and it suited him exactly, as it suits me.

"I screamed at my dad about this," I said to Olivia, who closed her eyes in a moment of pure ecstasy, like an actress in a commercial for European chocolates. It was triumph that she was trying to convert into sympathy. She looked down and put a hand on my shoulder, which had cooled slightly when I lied about Nena, and was getting even closer to the temperature of a correct body as I continued to lie.

"We were fighting about my work for AAP. Dad and me. It was our last fight, and I didn't know how to make it penetrate that the world changing meant my aims, my loves, were changing, and that was a good thing. He wanted me to be him. Wool-jacketed, tenured, in a teaching and research position for decades. But I wanted to do what we do at AAP, and he just couldn't believe I was being sincere. If it was just the money, he could have accepted it. But he couldn't accept that I was interested in the work, and that's when it got personal. I told him that I was tired of him lying about himself. I don't want to go into detail—I don't quite feel—"

"Of course. As much or as little as you want to."

"But I told him that he hadn't allowed me to have a foundation, so it was only natural that I wouldn't become what he thought I should. That it was his inability to be himself that had made our distance.

"We never spoke again. No one's ever come close to guessing this until you."

I was careful with every sentence. I was aware that to reveal any actual truth about myself to Olivia Robinson before I had a chance to tell Nena, or really any human, would be an unfixable error, a fracture in my ability to relate to myself or any other person for the rest of my life.

"I'm ready to become myself, and I want you and AAP to be part of that process." I looked thoughtfully at the warm pint of beer that I had just picked up, and put it down again. Realizing this was a bit much, I immediately ordered a cold one and started on that.

"I'm so grateful to you, Osman. For what you've just said, for today, for everything. I can't wait to get right back into this when we hit L.A. soil."

Then she did something—nothing sinister or vampiric, not a lizard flash of monstrous eyes, not a coquettish film noir flourish, none of that shit. Olivia relaxed, just as Nena had in the car when my dullness finally penetrated her. Her jaw jutted, the underbite lengthening her face, while two small lines appeared in her forehead as she focused on a sip of her drink and on what she was going to say to me in her true voice, which was both higher-pitched and more conventionally adult.

"I know what you've been trying to do to me up until now, Osman. It's more important that I know why you felt you had to investigate me, make your little attempt. I get it. I just want to make it clear that I admire you, and I know where you've been coming from. It's not my place to say I understand what it is to be you. But I do understand what being someone like you around someone like me would do to a person, Osman. I've watched it happen so many times. I watched you understanding what I was doing in Mockton's office, and how you couldn't help giving me that perfect assist even while you thought I wasn't exactly the kind of person you wanted to be onside with. And I respect that. Know that. I respect you. Oh—Brody!"

Olivia swivelled her stool and boosted herself off with the heel of her right hand, as though she were dismounting a novelty horse. The movement was for the benefit of Brody Beagle, who I'd been avoiding pictures of after Nena's meeting and the obsessive thoughts I'd been having since. He looked as I remembered him from the candid snaps of his vacation with Gwen Geffen in Calabria: a muscular Nordic Zuckerberg with a dick the size of Facebook, which was currently outlined against the inner right thigh of a pair of striding slim-cut slate-coloured chinos. I left my cool brimming glass behind and walked to the elevator.

13

I accepted the obscene surcharges of the minibar in my room and thought of what I could offer Olivia in lieu of a false Muslim personal history if she continued to press me. I decided that if she grilled me again, I would extend a tortured salaam alaikum and tell her to not to let the others know until I was ready.

I know what's demanded of me at this point. Not just by Olivia Robinson, or by you, but by the dictates of the very thing I've written. We are all getting frustrated by what seems to be my mania for avoidance. I have illustrated my disconnectedness from everyone except Nena and possibly Olivia, I have been honest about the fission of my family and the calm that it brought, but you would never believe me. From the way I've built this story, the Osman of the page appears to be the frozen surrounds of a cube broken out of the tray too early. But the unformed liquid at the core, the sloshing trapped stuff of life: you think I'm withholding it. We're all convinced that I'm hiding something, and that something is in the past.

An episode of warmth and truth in the home, and of course in the past: something that will satisfy in the way that my interlude

with Sameen in Toronto did not. The small brown father in wool
pants and an autumn sweater, the son described in traces and sig-
nifiers, a slender outline in a T-shirt and significant sneakers that
tread toward Blackness and whiteness at once. That scene, an
offering that hints at pain and loss so deep and inaccessible, that
confirms my life has been one of constant migration from a primal
loss of love and place, would push aside any doubts you have
about how truthful I'm being about who I am.

The pain here is that I do have a story that fits. It's one of
avoidance and pain and flight, even if it is more Ajit Shah's than
mine. His invented past, the flux between India and Pakistan in
his origins that eventually became a place of his own invention
that he could reach back to for convenient anecdotal arguments,
is as far as I ever got when discussing Dad here. By the time Ajit
and I had our ultimate fight, after that Sunday roast and before
the indigestion that would have me sweating gristle in my bathroom for hours, the job at AAP was only the surface of our arena
of combat. But not in the sense that I have told you. Dad was
disappointed that I was turning away from the academy so thoroughly that I was levelling a Gatling gun at its faculties and funding through my new job, yes. But he was also angry that I was
abandoning our shared project, the one I had taken the AAP job
specifically to avoid.

"I want you to quit the bookstore," Dad told me, in the basement den that housed his study and the chair he used for drinking and watching cricket on an enormous television hooked into
an illegal black box. He was wearing a home sweater with the
elbows blown out, a blue plaid sleeve visible through each hole.
There were worn patches on the arms of his chair that corre-
sponded with his reading position. His elbows were sharper than
standard. The skin that covered them seemed to be thicker and
more hide-like than the rest of his flesh. I was kneeling in front

of the television, trying to hook the house's legal cable unit into it without disabling the black box, which had been purchased along with a lifelong subscription to the sports channels subcontinentals favoured and hated paying for at a table in the back of a Queen West grocery store.

In trying to recover these moments, I can't think of Ajit without an image of Olivia Robinson imposing itself beneath the facial features, a distorting pixelated backdrop that appears in lags when I'm trying to remember what he said next. Their features aren't totally dissimilar: it's part of the Aryan mess, that confusion of free movement and imperialism and colonialism and invasion and rape that can make a Robinson and a Shah look a bit like each other around the nose and eyes and forehead two thousand years on. My recall is swiftest if I replace the head emerging from the blue and red collar with a rounded umber flame, a wickless heat with a moving centre gap for speech.

"Why? You need more home repairs? Is it your printer again?"

"You couldn't fit under the desk to fix it, Osman. No. I have something for us to do. Something I need you for. You have a style I can't affect. An unlettered, casual style. I've seen it in your emails, those ones you sent when you were in London last summer."

"I sent those to Mom," I said. There may have been a pout in my voice but it was probably a pant. My knees were beaming agony into my thighs, and my calves were so numb they may have been cushions of industrial pork that I was resting my ass on.

"She was impressed by them and shared them with me. The attempt at travelogue. Your little disquisition on the tourist-pastoral from Kew Gardens mutilates the young Coleridge and skims straight over Walter Pater, but it's genuinely readable for a popular audience. You have that, and I don't. I'm humble enough to recognize it, and I should hope you're humble enough to take it as a compliment."

I rocked back, which I knew was a terrible risk, but ended up sitting as I wanted to, butt on ground and back against the entertainment centre, a brutal piece of oak that three of Dad's graduate students had manoeuvred down here. I pulled my legs in, giving up on crossing them when my left knee made a sound like a can of Coke being run over by a bus.

"Okay. Thank you. What do you want?"

Dad flicked his right canine with his index fingernail. "I want a set of false memoirs as convincing as these." He'd had his whole set ripped out and replaced with implants in the early 2000s, at an incredible expense.

"False memoirs," I said. Ajit didn't need much back from his interlocutors in conversation, a personality feature that had intensified when his active teaching career ended. Part of the reason Sameen spent so much time in other rooms was her husband's building inability to shut up, a problem faced by the spouses of retired faculty for centuries, curable exclusively by death. That afternoon, Mom was at the movies, supposedly. I think she spent many of those days alone in hotel rooms, napping or watching television. I think this because I looked at her credit card statements, just once, after Ajit was dead and I had an excuse to creep through their shared financial paperwork, contained in a stuffed deep drawer in the central study that the family lawyer eventually pulled out and transported to his own office. Dad never looked at anything but his chequing account balance.

"Deliberately false, yes, Osman. I want to give a public who doesn't know me a story that they'll like to hear, one that will provoke interest in my deeper works. I can't be disingenuous on the page, but it comes naturally to you. That story you had published in your friend's magazine, with the old cinema burning down or whatever, the terrorists in the sand—"

"Dad, it was *not* at all about fire or terrorists. You're mashing together a couple of Rushdie books with my completely tame—"

"Yes, yes, but that's perhaps exactly what needs to be happening in your work and also in mine. If you're going to make progress, why not make your crutches part of your active process, why not make that falsity you can't shake the engine of a piece of fictive non-fiction? Why not write the story of Ajit Shah, a cross-border scholar who hid his atheist leanings from his parents and whose lack of dogmatic beliefs created a sense of fierce justice that drove him from both countries he tried to call home—"

"You only lived in one of them."

"Ask my dean where I lived. Ask the Danielsens next time they're over for dinner. I've told a dozen different stories of where I'm from, from the Caribbean to Joburg to the Seychelles to a village near a Himalayan peak that housed the last active Kashmir sapphire mine. The whites never follow up, I avoid the tiresome company of my generation's émigrés, and your generation just beams empathy at me even if they think I'm lying. They don't dare interrogate me. None of them."

Our dynamic had long been a franker, crueller version of the teacher–student relationship. These personalized lectures were an accepted form of bonding. I listened, because I had nothing to say. I could push in with a joke and turn a disquisition back into a conversation, but it would be disappointing to him and would bring a halt to any deeper exchange. When we ate together or watched a game I could understand, meaning anything that wasn't cricket, we spoke as men who were distantly fond of each other. But when Ajit leaned forward, the collection of small bones that were his chest clustering together until his torso seemed to vanish and he was all extended face and hands, pink and yellow palms and old sockets of skin that darkened in gradients until they reached inexplicably pure and clear eyes, he was my father, speaking to me because only I could understand him.

"I want you to join with me in thinking of this false autobiography not as an irresponsible act, a lie, but an act negating the idea of responsibility: to the self, to the race, to the culture, to every race. There is no responsibility. No personal responsibility. History is essential. Literature, yes, in some forms. The past does inform us, it doesn't reject us, it's there for us. But the idea of a personal past, of a knowable set of influences and events meshing over the early years to shape and dictate a future? That's an invention of the past two centuries, further distorted by the trauma obsession of the twenty-first. Now, this is what I have so far."

He leaned back and crossed his legs, his oration pose, perfected in his final professorial decade, when a wireless microphone allowed him to recline in a desk chair instead of clinging to a podium in the lecture hall. His dangling right foot bounced every paragraph or so. He sometimes made a twisting motion with his index finger, as though he were winding tape back into a cassette. He didn't look at me once. He spoke to me as I would later speak to his wife's silent voice mail.

My sister died like Isadora Duncan, but without the scarf. Vina was a dancer too, in the classical Kathak style at my mother's compulsion, and of the three a.m. go-go variety in the microwave heat of a roadside club built of discarded tin from an abandoned biscuit factory. I used to take her to the club. I was an escort with a paring knife tied to my thigh, sitting on a fruit carton behind the man with the black resin discs that conjured sound and movement. I don't understand music, cannot carry a melody or be carried by one, but I am stilled, arrested, paralyzed by a love for the impulsions of a dancer whose mind has vanished into her body. Vina danced that way.

Our overnight trips were disguised as labour, and we returned from them with a tiny bindle of rupees for my mother, who flipped two coins onto my sleeping father for the arrack he would need when he woke up and kept the rest. She needed the money, and therefore needed to believe our lie, which was that we were working for my friend Sanu's family, harvesting rotating crops of millet, mung beans, and potatoes from the vast unserfed tract of farmland and orchard on their estate. We needed to do this work before the sun came up, we told our mother, our feet and calves wrapped in snake-deterring burlap, filling pails with fruit and grain before the sunrise belched overwhelming sudden light over the flatness of our village and a heat that withered thought and muscle arrived. Only those who were born to it could stand to work during the days. Our mother had never farmed; she fled north from the servant's quarters of a great house, and began learning about the greater world too late to avoid marrying my father.

Sanu loved Vina. I loved Sanu and Vina. My mother was abashed by his family's wealth, more so when she couldn't refuse the money our offered labour brought in from their coffers. Really Sanu pulled our wages from his own monthly allowance, which was stored in a bronze box guarded by its embossed image of Hanuman. I was thin but Sanu was as slender as a betel leaf: his was a prisoner's body, engaged in the same rebellion against his father's wealth as his mind was. Sanu spent his father's money on us and on Soviet-printed biographies of his communist deities.

My mother finally met Sanu's father on the day that Vina died. Father was drunk at the arrack hut, and I was in the passenger seat as Sanu started up the road toward our unnamed tin palace of dance. Vina's long braid, the dark rope that was a measure of every year she'd spent alive, was drawn out of the open window. Then the rest of her was drawn out of the car, and then the life was drawn out of her body, as that braid wrapped all the way around the right rear tire axle of Sanu's family Jaguar.

When we recall the stories they told, dead fathers glimmer and crane forward out of oblivion to inspire us, no matter how small they may have been, how much we hate them, how wrong and neglectful they were, how absent we were from their living thoughts. Besides the obvious parallels between Ajit's racial politics and my own, which can only seem more inherited than clear-sighted and roguishly progressive to you now, this is why I've avoided much mention of Dad. He had a tremendously informative impact on me, beyond the obvious bits related to how constantly I let him down, but I don't want you to get the wrong idea of what a disappointment we were to each other.

"Isn't that great?" Ajit asked. "'Sanu's Family Jaguar' is our Chapter One heading."

I pretended to consider, moving over to the smallest of the basement bookshelves, where Dad had copies of both of V.S. Pritchett's memoirs. *A Cab at the Door* was a first, signed to a dead Toronto television host that Ajit used to drink with. When he went to sleep that night, I came down to the basement again to steal this book, the first serious piece of my collection.

"It is great, Dad." His recited speech was better than my prose—it was also moving, direct, palatable, *meant*. He didn't need me. He'd told me how much he needed me to emphasize how little he actually needed me, with this recitation of an ideal chapter. Ajit leaned back into his chair and waited for me to feel the hurt he'd intended. The expectant angle of his lowered, smiling face, the same look as when he announced our vacation to Tahiti when I was eleven, or when he invited us to Ottawa to watch him get a Governor General's medal, showed me he was waiting for something else: deserved praise. Love. All I could do for myself in that moment was give him neither.

I found 45,560 words of the book in his laptop after he died, the last of which had been written the morning he was taken to the hospital. I deleted the book in a slow-then-fast whirring backwards hum of the cursor, saving a lessened version of the document every few seconds, watching a new digital memory of blankness eat Ajit Shah's false memoir right up until that first page of "Sanu's Family Jaguar," which I left complete in an undeleted file that no one since me has opened.

I haven't put this digression here simply to satisfy you; it genuinely came to me that night in the hotel, with Olivia and Brody in the bar a few storeys below me, as I tried to reconstruct myself. I extracted a useful point from Ajit's false memoir. Lying. Everyone's lies. I thrust my thumb into the ungiving green call sphere on Nena's contact, knowing she'd ignore any chat or text nudge tonight. She picked up but kept the line silent.

"Olivia was never sick. She was lying about her cancer," I said.

I could hear Nena's effort at silence. I could hear her surrender it, and the last allotment of love she had for me, before she spoke.

"Of course she was lying," she said. "Of course."

14

We do need a last digression, a brief one, to explain my several asides on book collecting. While all these moments of collector's discovery, shopping, and theft did occur in the times and places I have described, there's a reason why they are accumulating in this text like so many dustless, Brodarted volumes of passé mid-century white British writers on a shelf. My limitations prevent me from quite synthesizing this reason through a direct telling of the story, so I'll explain. I do realize that a proper writer should be able to accomplish this type of communication smoothly, but as this section is about an admission of faults, and I am still quite shaken by the painful recollection of my father's prose, I beg for your indulgence.

Collecting coincided with my decision to stop reading. Reading is all that my inclinations and education equipped me to do, and even then, not quite at a professional level. I was a surface critic, an explainer, a thumbtack-and-yarn bulletin board boy, connecting elements of famous works with elements of less famous works and items in history that I figured were forgotten until I submitted my thesis and discovered the source I should have looked at first had made my points for me already. I can read, but not properly.

This is why I can't write with the invisible subtlety I long to achieve, creating a compressed jewel dusted with coal, a text so brilliant that the Olivias and Nenas and even Osmans glister and rotate under examination, become greater than the people I am describing, become the ideas that I feel they incarnate even when I can't quite define those ideas. I would be torturing you and myself if I tried to write that way, just as I tortured myself when I tried to read that way. So I write as I joke, with the determined process of a poorly domesticated chimpanzee rebelling against the placatory red wine and Xanax his owner has given him to suppress his post-pubescent yearnings for sex, freedom, his own kind. I find my subject and bite deeply into its face, deeply enough that my own rotting canines break off before I achieve my goal, realizing a depiction so real that my teeth meet in the middle of it. Then I call my mom and read it to her answering machine.

What was left when I finished reading a book, when I used to do that? The object, only. The item. I used to think that I absorbed the contents—not in full, but in large part. But I don't. I destroy books. My brain annihilates the contents of any text longer than a sentence. I've buried every one of the beautiful books I own inside my skull. The human mind is a grave for ideas. Mine is, and I imagine yours is too, but you're afraid to encounter the full truth of that—that when a concept hits you, unless it can be immediately repurposed for your own benefit, it crawls under the meninges to wither on the surface of your brain, sinking into the grey meat like housefly piss.

This particular book will absolutely not outlast me. Novels are born, especially now, to be lost in an endless churn of text, of forgetting, of new novelty. But it may outthink me. It will meet the eyes of someone who isn't like me, who can see the smallness of a man who can only attack, insult himself accurately, and fling hopes and false images at a bored Iranian-American woman.

You can take the book from me, like Olivia took my joke at the beginning, like I consumed my father's faked-up life story. I would welcome the theft, because I don't know what to do next. I did all I could with my abilities. I'm no better at absorbing people than books, but I am an excellent collector.

15

I vomited the morning of the operation that Vikram Chandra and I were running at the L.A. office, with reluctant online support from Nena. It was July 2019. AAPC was a week away. I had lost time waiting for Olivia to make contact again, and used it to plan, to pull all the digital paper on the Church of the Evergreen Advent that I could, and to make sure that Vikram was absolutely trustworthy. He was. We now spent part of every day together, online and even in public.

Recommitting to my drinking had been a good decision, especially when it came to bonding with Vik. He only ate proteins, avocados, and leafy greens in controlled portions, but drank straight, expensive vodka with abandon. We drank before our great operation, he wisely, I mixing cocktails with beer, Oreos, and post-midnight chicken karahi. I took a second shower in case there were stray vomit flakes in my chest hair, and because I had to be honest about the amount of effluvia that was still within me and emerging from my skin. I tried to boil it out with the hottest, highest-pressure stream possible, a brutal thumb of focused water pressing my pulsing brown pimple of a body.

Vikram Chandra was waiting in the parking lot, his van in its enviable space. The three disabled spaces next to his were empty, as they always were. Olivia had designated them in expectation of a focused hiring endeavour that was supposed to take place after AAPC. Vik nodded as I waved and walked past. The idea was that I should enter first, that the scenario should be in full play by the time the HR administrative assistant called me in. Vikram and I had looked at a scheduling spreadsheet we couldn't officially access to ensure that the admin assistant that day would be Tim Thériault, a Parisian language teacher who'd scored a mid-level position because he once taught the children of two AAP junior VPs before their family summer tour of Provence's organic farms. They needed their children to be capable of taking orders from the nanny. Tim had confessed that he hated his benefactors because they eventually replaced his tutoring role with an iPad that he stood next to in order to answer any questions that the children may have as they went through the lesson, and to make sure that they stayed focused on the correct screen. The VPs and their children left for France, promising Tim that lessons would resume on their return, but he told them that would be stealing their money, that the app had clearly surpassed what he could do for the kids. An AAP HR gig was Tim's reward for pretending to accept his uselessness. We knew all of this because Tim had dated Vikram for a couple months. It had gone nowhere when they admitted that their bond was solely based in sex and disdain for their workplace. Vikram laughed after telling me this so I did too, but I wondered how that couldn't be enough to sustain at least a couple of years together. Tim was an asset to us, but we had to keep him ignorant, for his sake and that of the operation.

"Does AAP know you're gay?" I asked during our first meeting, which had taken place in his parked van behind the Hollywood In-N-Out. Vikram had eschewed buns for two patties wrapped in double layers of lettuce. I breathed in odours from my empty fry bag as he started on his second burger.

"No. I kept it secret that I'm gay and I kept it secret that I'm not stupid as shit." I wanted to supply an equal confidence by telling Vikram what I'd held back, but the list was too long and non-specific, and not as goal-oriented as Vikram's. He was saving his gayness for his third act coup, a reveal that would aid him in securing the presidency if simply being nearby while Olivia was toppled and the company was shamed wasn't enough.

I walked by HR on my way to my desk, which was really a portion of one of six long desks in the room. Short walls of frosted plexiglass kept two thirds of our laptop screens private, usually forcing me to arrange my bag and perhaps coat to ensure that I could chat to Nena and read antiquarian catalogues without being observed. But it was Saturday, when the invisible company injunction to be visible and performing didn't really begin until 11. I sat down in an empty room at 9:20 and waited for Vikram.

Tim hadn't been at the front desk at HR, but perhaps he was in the back, scrolling Reddit or a dating app. Vikram's wheelchair was noiseless, but I still listened for it whenever the elevator door opened. Each time I heard footsteps instead, until the time I didn't. Ten minutes after that, Tim was in my office doorway, slim enough for the high-waisted pants he wore with a tieless white dress shirt and a creamy blazer with the buttons on the left side. He'd kept too much of the grad student about him to truly fit the office—he had actual style, like Nena, but didn't understand how to conceal it.

"I've got Vikram Chandra in my office with a request that's complex for me, Osman. I was going to move it upstairs but no one senior comes into HR on the weekend. He suggested that you could maybe, I don't know, double stamp, notarize—"

"Okay things? Yep. Sure."

I rose, bringing no odours with me, no cumin or gin or dried vomit. I was proud of this, of the soap I'd used to clog my pores, of the antiperspirant I'd rolled on like I was painting a swollen, flood-damaged wall, of the breath strips I'd melted in my mouth in three batches of two. I followed Tim, who walked in a peculiar leaned-back manner, like an elegant man in a *Punch* cartoon, reclining throughout each step but somehow advancing. He had what looked like a rubber thimble on his right index finger.

I saw the back of Vikram's chair and his significant shoulders above it. He was wearing a Smiths T-shirt, and both of his elbows were so ashy they seemed to have been dipped in talcum. When I got closer I realized it was powder, as there was some running up his right forearm as well. I poked a questioning finger at the trail as I sat next to him and Tim rounded the desk. HR got their own, real desks, with drawers and everything. There were eight of them. They all faced away from each other, and they each got a day a week to use the glass-walled central office in the middle of the room for calls, meetings, and even, with the blinds down, privacy.

"I was climbing," Vikram said. "Got a wall in my place. Slither all over it like a lizard, it's great. Custom build."

I had never heard Vikram speak like this in AAP, like himself. I'd been shocked to discover the person he was in our first con-spiring phone call, made from the hotel room as Olivia and Brody loured in the bar below me before undoubtedly scurrying to a much more expensive and fitting place. Hearing him talk as his actual self in the office felt like a loss of cover, a misstep, until I reminded myself that he was addressing someone he was plan-ning a secret coup with in front of someone he had fucked for several weeks.

"Stop shaming us for being not-athletic," said Tim, smiling at Vikram before realizing how fat I was and making a shocked, backpedalling expression that struck me as French in how it was regretful without being apologetic. Europeans excel at a colonial shrugging sorry-I-guess which feels laden with more historic truth than any land acknowledgment, imperial divestment ceremony, or molestation mea culpa. He looked at me then, bit his upper lip, and pulled a rightward rictus with his lower lip that he hoped I'd let him make into a smile. If not, no matter.

"I used to climb all the time but it was too hard on my manicurist," I said. The three of us shared a workplace titter before I added, "And I have the muscle mass of a can of oysters," which got a genuine laugh from Tim, along with a slight allowance of truth into his gaze, likely recalling the dead-eyed stare he gave the wall during his French lessons, that he gave the wall over the top of whatever he read when he reached home after a day in this silicon and glass destroyer of the profession he had signed up for. He would help us.

"I've started to discuss with Tim what you and I had floated to us by the board," said Vikram. He started massaging his right shoulder, pushing a thumb into the juicy cluster of tendons and muscles at the rotator cuff that was one of the only flat parts on my own body. "This will go a lot easier with Osman and I both here as verbal confirmation, because part of the point of this measure, at this stage, is that it's unofficial, secret. Not CIA secret, just gradual reveal secret, okay, Tim?"

"It's okay to say, yes, but I still don't know what you're talking about."

"This is about pressuring the government, state and federal, to start really looking into healthcare options that will benefit workers in the edutech sphere. We want to tabulate to the cent the exact AAP costs for every employee, in terms of treatment, lost labour, everything, of our frankly amazing health plan. We want those numbers to reflect a recorded truth in order to be able to apply real collective pressure to make some changes at the state and federal levels. Okay? The problem being, if we announce this company-wide, panic time."

"Everyone will think their health plan is being taken away," I offered. It was unnecessary and interrupted Vikram's flow.

"That's what you're doing, no?" said Tim.

"No. No." Vikram poked his tongue hard into the centre of his cheek, for a second in which the flesh bulged like a finger he wanted to plunge into my eye for breaking his roll. "We are totally not doing that—we'll never allow any employee to have less coverage than they do today, we just want to illustrate to the state that they need to start doing their part, or risk losing AAP to our satellite offices in Europe or the U.K., where we'll gladly reincorporate and rebuild, divesting whatever we need to down here. The board is bullish about this. They'll eat the cost of our further studies and a campaign. And Olivia Robinson is the woman who can make that case convincingly.

"And all this is why we need her files. Not just what you have digitally, but the hard copies that were printed out when O'Keefe was president and insisted. We want comparison consistency from our pre-blockchain record keeping period. And we want this to be done quietly, alerting no one, telling Ms. Robinson only when it comes time to present."

The three filing cabinets that Nena had told me about in the increasingly excited, pre-conscientious-rethink portion of our conversation about Olivia's potentially fake cancer had been shipped here to L.A. along with other moribund contents of the New York office when they switched to a 50 per cent remote work staff. O'Keefe was in the waning days of his power then, and had insisted that they keep the files, not shred them. By the time they reached this coast and were entombed in the basement storage of our building, it occurred to no one that they were worth either keeping or destroying.

"If we start with the president's files, do full disclosure within the company of those financials and details—getting Olivia's okay on that first, of course—none of the other employees will feel threatened. You get us?" I figured if I came in more confidently this time, Vik would forget my gaffe. I liked him, and admired the strength of his forearms and resolve in retaining his mask of total idiocy and inconsistent lies in the workplace. I felt bad about all of my previous inward and outward jokes about him. It's because I hate skateboarders, not the disabled, I wanted to tell him. But to do that I would have had to let him know about the insults in the first place.

"So the possibility is we throw it all away in America, start maybe offices everywhere else. In Paris, right?" Tim smiled and I knew that no matter what, he would be quitting and moving back home within a few months. He didn't even need to tell us he was about to get the files. He pushed that rubber thimble deeper onto an index fingertip and walked past us, telling us he would need to go downstairs. He noticed me staring at his hand.

"For sorting, grabbing paper. Dead technology," Tim said. "I like its feel. This will be the first time I've flipped through papers since maybe November."

He left. Vikram and I did a strange sideways fist-contact handshake. I made a note to joke to Vik, when we were closer friends, about the sexual applications of Tim's rubber thimble, and was warmed by the vision of a future where I was still in contact with him, where my first real Indian friend emerged from this odd battle that had been forced upon us, or that we had created, depending on whether you asked Nena or the two of us. Nena had given extended notice to AAP in late June, and was tying up her final sales and killing projects she didn't want anyone else to touch when she was gone, or she wouldn't have agreed to help us at all.

I texted Nena that everything was fine, we didn't need an assist. If Tim hadn't been there, or if he had been resistant, Nena had agreed to call in with an official authorization that would pair with Vik's new status to be unshakeable, and to add a threatening insinuation that Vikram wasn't being taken seriously for exactly-what-reasons-she-didn't-want-to-say because it was simply too vile, no? Nena didn't answer my text, having been somewhat against stealing Olivia's insurance and medical records in the first place. But only somewhat, or she would have told us to stop, and I at least would have listened, I'm sure.

16

The night before AAPC 2019, I wanted to pick Nena up from LAX. She said that her ground transport decisions for the past few years had amounted to an ethnic betrayal of Iranian cab drivers, and she wanted to start atoning for that.

This was the lengthiest "no" of our relationship, of our friendship, and I wondered if she wanted me to start in on an argument about whether the total erasure of her origin culture from her food, manner, and conversation was just a foible or also a determined betrayal, like using Lyft. Unfair and inaccurate, yes—Nena had been eating that rice stuff with the burned potatoes on the bottom when I called to confirm that she would be meeting Vikram and I to finalize our plans in the lead-up to AAPC Los Angeles—but some of our best conversations had come from baseless accusations. Maybe she wanted to fight again so she could remember why she liked me. Maybe she just wanted to take a cab and not listen to any of my shit until she had to. I never found out, because my question sounded like a rip-off of one of Olivia's anyhow.

We met at a Starbucks near Vikram's and I gave her the water and the green juice she usually ordered when she was forced into meeting at Starbucks. She poured half the juice into an empty coffee cup on a just-vacated table, and diluted the rest of the bottle with water. It was as mysterious to me as most healthy or supposedly healthy foods and supplements. I watched Nena's neck move as she attended to the drink. Murky spirulina and kiwi fruit, the crushed testicles and ovaries of dynamic but sustainable jungle plants, apple cider vinegar. She pulled it all down in eight vivifying gulps while I opened with some conversation about Vikram and Tim, a speculation on how they fucked, perhaps with slings or just Vikram's upper body strength and cleverly placed handholds or pillows. Vik was never without someone, but never attached. I was hoping Nena would tell me the exact shape of her moving on from me, the number of men, their races, but no. I left spaces to be filled by interruption, insult, questions. The gaps stayed there, neither of us attending to them. I wanted to order a venti medium roast and pour the whole thing into my unbuttoned pants with a manful Sydney Carton expression on my face. I wanted her to crush my larynx in her best shoes to make the pauses last forever. I wanted to be close to her.

"Throat's dry from the plane. Skin, too," Nena said when the drink was over.

"Dustin Carter."

"What?"

"That security guard you told me about. The one who wrote the Reddit post about the dead shooter manqué, Edmund Bak. Nena, he's going to be at AAPC. He's going to be part of the goddamn press release and the keynote presentation. It's supposed to be a surprise, but Vik has gotten intelligence on everything, people just trust him. As stupid as I thought he was before, apply that same intensity to how smart I know he is now. He could be running this. Even has Olivia's presentation title, because she asked him to contribute a disability vector. *Anxiety, Trauma, Violence, Learning: Is Distance Our Cure?*

Nena pinched the skin on the back of her hands, seeing if it stayed pursed.

"Are you still calling your mom?" she asked.

"No," I said. It was true. I'd stopped leaving her the messages, thinking of Ajit's laptop in its basement tomb, of the book I'd tricked his computer into eating. I was afraid that Sameen would connect what I was doing for myself to what I had done to him, that she would go looking for my crimes against him, especially if I confessed them into her mailbox.

"No, I stopped because I got bored," I said. "Are you?"

"What?"

"Bored."

"I'm not bored around you. I'm close to peaceful and I'm extremely resigned. Maybe that's what you're seeing."

"I thought you'd want to at least see this if you didn't want to participate."

"I'm coming along to see if I can protect you from whatever you're inviting onto yourself. And for the same reason that I'm going to AAPC even though I'm through with this fucking company: I have to see the end of things myself, or else they never end."

Vikram Chandra lowered himself from the chin-up bar when Nena and I entered his floor of the Santa Barbara house he shared with his mother and sister. The room didn't smell of sweat, but of lemons and cinnamon. I checked for a vaporizer or incense and saw neither. Vik was one of those mystical browns who sweated the nicer spices. Nena and I sat down on the couch in front of an immense video game set-up I would have mocked in anyone else's house, while Vikram towelled off and wheeled over to us in a compact chair of minimalist black metal and brass spokes, a tasteful

Scandinavian-looking mechanism that I'd never seen him use in the office. There were no books, the only print material a wall of framed *Thrasher* magazines.

"Oz, you told her about the files," he said. "The results."

"I did." I'd done so over the phone in my thirty-five-minute overture to Nena, who was packing up her Greenpoint rental in advance of her departure from AAP and the city. She would have been fired just after AAPC, in that week when the company would evacuate its depleted corpuscles and hire the sub-Olivias and next Vikrams and never-me's who were going to take the reins in the fully digital campus phase. I could hear a suitcase zip, and something in Nena's apartment fall over. Then a man's voice, perhaps a mover. Then her again. Mockton and Olivia were cutting the ribbon on this new movement, aided by an extremely expensive video presentation currently being assembled in our offices and paid for by Parnell College money.

I told Nena it was true, but instead of her at the other end of the line, surrounded by boxes and other men, I could only envision Olivia at her bar stool in that Seattle hotel, swivelling and praising my little attempt at investigating her.

"Olivia is definitely tumour-free, had always been tumour-free. She never had cancer."

"It still could have been any number of other extremely serious things she didn't want to announce. Or something undiagnosed."

"Don't walk *back* on this, Nena, come on. We knew it was true, you knew it was, and now we have papers. You know that's not how she works. You know. She was on the cancer ward with Gwen Geffen and Brody Beagle. She infiltrated it to make the connection, knowing Gwen's chances with that stage of that cancer when she posted that chemo drip and red lipstick Insta. Knowing Gwen's education ideas. Olivia predicted the fund before it existed, before you ever heard of it. The insurance material Vikram and I found, it covers the negative tests, then that's it. Optional unpaid leave after that, reasons undisclosed. No one checked up on her because she didn't gas the insurers for money. Someone on the AAP board might have, must have known what she was doing."

Nena didn't have any more arguments for me on the phone as the movers worked, but she had some for Vik just now. He had unsheathed an oat milk and protein concoction in a cardboard cylinder from a pouch slung crossways over the back of his wheelchair. His lunch. I suspected he preferred pissing to shitting, but again, it was an area of detail that I couldn't venture into yet. Our relationship had reached a stage where I would speculate about him, but not turn those speculations into ugly, dehumanizing jokes that would either wipe the thought process away or deepen it. Soon we'd be able to talk with complete honesty, and I looked forward to it.

"I saw Olivia, Vikram. She was sick. Chemo-sick. I've seen it before in my family, as I'm sure almost everyone has," Nena said.

"I was around Olivia back then too. New York was where I interned. Different floor from you, Nena, but I guess my Clark Kent thing worked better than I thought. I wanted to be invisible for the first few months, just efficient, a bit tragic if that was going to help me. You and I have met thirty, forty times. Not just at big meetings, either."

"We have a large churn of interns," Nena said. "I'm not very sorry. But sorry."

"She was on chemo. The home edition," I said. Vikram had promised I could have this part. "The doctor who booked her tests, the only things insurance paid for—he also did her prescriptions, and she paid for those herself. They're not in her AAP record, but his files are part of a court case."

"So how did you get those, then?" Nena asked.

"Vikram did," I said. Vikram sucked liquid oats and smiled.

"Once you have a doctor's name," he said, "And once you know that doctor has been in trouble, and might still be in trouble, it's not so hard to get him to have a frank conversation. I know this kind, anyway, from when I ran a painkiller side business just after my accident. Olivia's guy was Dr. Julius Lyall, has been on the edge of dis—what's the medical for disbarred?"

"Revoked. License revoked," Nena said, closing her hand around the air for a second as she hunted for the term, squeezing it into speech.

"Yeah, since halfway into the opioid crisis. He overprescribes. But no opioids for Olivia Robinson. She got the chemo cocktail. And the take-home drips. She went to the ward as a visitor, but not a patient. But she went a lot when Gwen and Brody were there. And she took the drugs: Cytoxan, Abraxane, Adriamycin, Ellence. Lyall confirmed it, but it's nowhere in her AAP file. And from the looks of her, she actually did take them. You saw her, Nena. She committed."

The list of drugs, like alien car models or a forgotten pantheon, flavoured our tongues with the chalk and copper of cures that burned holes in tissue, that ate muscle, that harrowed. This story felt much more Olivia than cancer did. I watched Nena sink back into the belief she'd reached when I first called her from Seattle.

"What do you want from this, Vikram?" asked Nena. "You're not out for justice like Osman pretends to be." I started to answer but she poked my arm and smiled, our first contact since Seattle, a fingernail through wet linen.

"The presidency," Vikram said. "Just for a year. Maybe two. I want her out and I want myself in."

"And you think degrading her publicly is—"

"It's a shortcut, and I don't think it's undeserved. And I do care about the justice element, actually." Vik looked at me, wondering whether he had made an enormous error in trusting my certainty that Nena was with us, and I willed him a request as best I could, quivering my lip in *Shining*-fashion without the little bead of psychic spittle, to explain to Nena, to talk instead of attack.

"I've been focused on Olivia Robinson because she's directly in my way, and for months she's been treating me like a fucking Segway that happens to talk occasionally. But I can definitely get self-critical. Or brown on brown violent. I would love to. I don't get much of a chance for frank conversation, any conversation. My pre-spinal friends are all dumb as fuck. And I play very nice with everyone I've met since, in order to get paid, even shutting up and putting up with the disgusted glances of people like you, Osman, who I always knew I'd get along with if you put even a second of thought into whether I was putting on an act."

"Thanks, man."

"Yeah, well, I ended up reaching out to you, but that's okay. And my act was nothing. The ones that can actually compete with the Olivias are the Nikki Haleys, the fake-drawl Bobby Jindals. And the ones that make fortunes minstrelling their mothers and fathers in sari-moustache cosplay on YouTube, worse-than-Apu imitations of their father who worked sixty-hour weeks then dropped dead to be memorialized as an accent in a Netflix special.

"I'm obsessed, man. Because I do it too, to function, make another me, but what *these* fuckers do, shit. There's no moral equivalency, but I keep seeing them all as the same person, the same combo of effects that works every time on every audience except the secret network who whispers at home and does nothing and I'm beginning to wonder if I can do this semi-whiteface-as-brownface thing without being entirely owned by someone as master-faker as Olivia. The only way out is to go all the way up," Vik said.

Nena stood and started to walk the room, making Vik rotate slightly to keep watching her, a movement he accomplished with a gentle ongoing suggestion of the wrist.

"And him," Vik said, pointing at me. His palms weren't rough from wheeling and climbing, but moist and muscular under the chalk, a rare-steak pink melting the white. The backs of his hands were dustless umber, with only tiny, dignified resin stains from the weed he smoked. "I'm sure Osman told you he thought I was faking. Faking, not lying. With that Calcutta thing he over-heard in the elevator, the mysterious disease shit, the *City of Joy* meets *Trading Places* combo Penelope from product fucking longed to hear from me, imagining my legs pulled behind while I slug-trailed forward with my forearms and fists wrapped in rags until a white couple swooped in to adopt me and discovered I was whatever fucking kind of genius AAP thought I was." Vik had started to talk to me, not Nena.

"It's the *blanks*, Osman, that's what you've never understood. You know that about him, Nena? His cluelessness about his own strengths? The blanks are what they want. All you give them is one fucking big blank that you feather with jokes and brush-offs that must disguise depth, that absolutely must mask pain and the real shit. Your whole routine is a dead zone and that's why it worked better than mine until Olivia arrived. Olivia hates blanks. She prefers the concrete of a lie that doesn't permit challenge, something she can help you shape, something that you can't go back on. I had one, so I got promoted above you."

"Okay, Vikram," Nena said. "I really enjoyed and absorbed what you had to say here, and it's absolutely confidential, and you can count on my silence and passive support. I believe parts of your little manifesto, because it's tied to an honest ambition. I get it. Just not the identity crisis dilemma stuff. You want the big chair and you will do what you need to in order to get it, and that's not always evil. It's not evil when you do it. Right?" Nena stood in front of the framed magazines, in the centre of the wall, herself framed by endless photos of wheeled planks and athletic white bodies shrouded in branded baggy clothing.

"Believing you even that much makes it clearer to me that I don't believe Osman. I never have. I'm not saying he's a traitor, I'm just saying he's a liar at the deepest level and we need that clear before we move on to any irrevocable decisions. You want power. Osman doesn't want anything he's told us."

Vik took his wrist off the wheel and looked at me. I wanted to share a meaningful shrug but I couldn't move.

"Take your shirt off," Nena said.

"What?"

She knew I had heard her. And I knew she hated repeating words that she knew had been heard. Nena was across the room in a second, both her hands on the panels of my shirt. She ripped it open Superman style, but with no logo or even an undershirt behind the void she'd created in the cotton, and the metal buttons of my quite nice if overlaundered rag & bone shirt pinging off Vikram's cement floor. It took her two thorough pulls to do it.

"Leave it, Osman. Leave it or I'm out of here, and we don't speak again for anything that isn't explicitly business-related." Nena was calm. Even her ponytail hadn't shifted from its position, lying on her right shoulder, the upcurling ends facing me like a tight nest of living wires. I dropped my hands and felt Vikram's eyes on my sweating ruin of a chest, on the moist, private dent below my breasts.

"Osman has to accept something," Nena told me. "That his fantasy of destruction is based completely in envy, not justice. You've been with Vikram three days and you want to be him. You're obsessed with Olivia's dimensions and her power. You don't want to be her, no, but—what do you see when you look at yourself? Not emotionally. I mean at yourself, in a mirror, the glass of a bus shelter, the mini-you in the lower right corner of your video calls?" The fingernail that had gently prodded my sleeved arm now poked, hard and constant, into my naked breastbone, as though she wanted to split me unevenly and get a wish.

"What?"

"I would ask you these things privately but there's no need. There's no sense that you even want intimacy and privacy with me again. You don't even notice that I have to talk to you like a fucking analyst or I'll lose it and tell you what I actually think."

"There is a reason you two would talk about this privately," said Vikram. "It's making me uncomfortable."

"I got him to take his shirt off so you can understand who you're allied with, Vikram. You're honest about wanting her job. Osman wants out of himself and into something else. Osman thinks he's three hundred and fifty pounds, covered in hair, sweating constantly, that he reeks of whatever food he most recently ate, melted together by alcohol on the inside and pulled down by gravity on the outside. That's your partner. I can tell you that he will be absolutely reliable and trustworthy on this Olivia thing, but not because he has any internal notion of justice or reality. This has everything to do with his self. There is no matchy-matchy between what he's looking at and what he sees and thinks. You're fucked, Osman. Please understand that I say that with love." Nena backed away and sat down again.

And then the palpitating grip of an idea at my root, the rope of gut between my prostate and aorta, overwhelmed what was being said. I was having what another Nena, the one who still enjoyed me, called one of *Osman's Realizations*, the kind I could make a book out of. The thrill of non-existence that had filled me as my father made up his life for my eventual transcription united with everything Nena had said, with everything we knew about what Olivia was and wasn't, and I knew there was nothing I loved better than being told who I am, because then I didn't have to think about it myself.

If I could remember this, if I could cling to this realization that was now a stone-tablet prescription for future peace, I would never have to think about myself again. I could just take it, take it from someone I loved and trusted.

"You're right," I said to Nena. I held the flaps of my ruined shirt over my flattish, smooth chest, noticing the button casualties ripped all the way down to my stomach, which was fuzzier but only bulging in a pre-adolescent pooch, which would vanish if I just moved up an inch in my jeans size.

"Can I borrow a shirt, Vikram? Not a Skull Skates or Vans one, please."

"Screw you," Vikram said, moving to the metal wardrobe that stood just outside his open bedroom door.

I walked to Nena's chair and let my shirt go, putting my two hands out to her.

"Thank you. Thank you so much, and I'm sorry. And I still have to follow through and do what we started planning, and what I planned, but at least I know why now, okay?"

I think it was that moment, the authenticity of that thank you, that made me the person that Nena thought of first when she needed an isolation companion at her cottage complex. But all she said just then was: "I'm disappointed in us, Osman."

Nena looked at her fingernails, seeing that her right index was broken off. I could feel the sharp fragment of cuticle grazing my body from the buttonhole where it had torn off. I would keep it forever. It's currently in an orb made of craft-store resin that I keep on my desk. Don't tell her.

"I looked deeper into the Church of the Evergreen Advent records," I said.

Vik had apparently taken the shirt request as I'd meant it, both seriously and as a request for him to exit stage left. He was in his bedroom, and had pulled the door shut with a double-thwack, simulating wheelchair awkwardness that he couldn't possibly have had, especially in his own place.

"Legally?"

"No. Olivia's their most consistent major donor. She keeps the lights on for them if they promise to keep their profile low. What she pays in takes care of the rent, some of their land, and gives her parents a place to go. It's a fantasy camp created specifically for them, she pays the pastor's salary, and the other followers were just gatherings from along the way."

"I would have guessed most of that, but how did you find out?"

"I found the last lawyer they fired and paid him for an unofficial conversation. I'm just telling you this, with Vikram out of the room, so you know that we're dealing with someone who isn't purely selfish, who does have a sense of misplaced responsibility to her past. Whatever it is she's doing up there, she's doing for her parents, and that pastor."

Nena kept staring at her broken fingernail, looking past it at the story she would tell me at her cottage when we were in lockdown. That the church was as much for her as it was for those others. That it was the edifice of a friendship that had perhaps not quite died, only transmuted.

"Okay, Osman. Okay."

17

The site of AAPC Los Angeles was a dead molasses millionaire's recreation of Fort Moore, a stone-built landmark from the Mexican–American War that had been demolished to make way for the Hollywood Freeway. Erasmus Daiches had used a third of his money to loosely adapt the plans of the fortress into a scaled-down version on the grounds of his Santa Monica estate, and would hold all of D&D Molasses Co.'s meetings there. He wasn't as devoted to military history as he was to the hatred of Mexicans, and the company's firm and unwritten hiring policies had played a much-written-about part in its downfall. Olivia Robinson had heard the story and liked it; she'd toured the site and liked it. AAPC 2019: RECLAMATION was booked, and the entire mansion rented and portioned out as lodging for our employees. This wasn't just a top-level conference for the core 100 of upper management. For the first time, the conference invitation had been extended to key personnel in development, HR, and marketing. Especially marketing, a division that Olivia had added thirty people to per month since she took over. Every one of them would hear what I had to say about Olivia.

One of the inaccuracies of the reconstruction was a large central hall, a room that could fit one thousand on the floor and more in the bleachers. We would look out at an exact thousand. The digital banner behind us, a loose riff on the Obama "Hope" poster with a multicultural Picasso'd monster-stitch face instead of the president's, read RECLA at the top and MATION at the bottom, something that must have been forced on the graphic designer.

The first time I saw Olivia after the hotel bar was on this stage, before the crowd came in through the two stone archways at either side of the room. I'd come in early with Vik, and she was next to enter, walking the centre aisle of the clear auditorium. She slipped off a loose black T-shirt with a slogan reading *Don't Just Disrupt, Detonate.* The hair and makeup people who would be attending to us swarmed her with a flat iron and lipstick. Under the T-shirt was a blue sheath dress with a turtleneck. Olivia faced me as she was being flat-ironed. Vik checked his phone and hummed Green Day.

"Osman. I hope I'm making a step or two toward a sorry-for-being-out-of-touch by making sure you're up here where you belong for the Parnell College frame around my keynote. Anthony's going to talk for quite a while, but I think Brody will balance that out by barely speaking. Should give you all the time you need."

"I'm looking forward to it." A muscle in my inner thigh started to twitch. Olivia looked at me with meaningful charity, her version of apology.

"I really did find our talk fascinating, Osman. It cemented for me that I wanted you up on this stage. Not anyone else. I really think you heard what I had to say." Olivia took out her phone and took the lip pencil away from a small Filipina makeup woman and pointed to Vik. She started to do her lips herself.

"I've been thinking about being more open. About the past, my family, all of it."

"All of it?" Olivia finished with the lip pencil and held it out for a few seconds. When the woman didn't notice, Olivia let it fall to the floor.

"I've been struggling with the religious aspect," I said.

"I've been through that myself," Olivia said. "Not with Islam, of course. But maybe you could make that struggle part of your openness? That wouldn't detract at all from what a crucial vector of *you* being Muslim is, and how clear it would be to anybody who has any doubts that you are an essential voice for the future of this company."

Before she could effect the first forced Islamic conversion by the secret owner of a backwoods Washington church, Brody Beagle and Anthony Mockton arrived and Olivia began discussing seating arrangements with them, wheeling Vik into place personally as she illustrated the layout she was going for. Vik played willing roller. Surrounding screens showed us how we all looked to the crowd. Having these monitors would help me immensely when it was time to speak. I couldn't quite occupy the form Nena had given me through her helpful humiliation, but I could do an effective voiceover for the figure I saw on those monitors, for the one that everyone apparently saw when they looked at me.

There were six of us on stage, each mic'd, even though Vik would not be speaking. Olivia had explained that there was a slight time crunch that had to do with the evening's Calvin Harris set: they needed every spare minute they could get to maximize the fun part. Vik cut her apologies off and told her he was relieved, that he was just looking forward to hearing what everyone else had to say, and that it was an honour to be on this stage as AAP crossed into the future.

"That's so good, Vik," Olivia said, stooping a half inch and smiling at him. "I am totally stealing that with your okay, okay?"

The hall filled. Olivia sat forward and centre, with Vikram and I slightly back from her on either side. She needed us there because it had worked out that everyone else onstage was white: the uneven triangle continued with Anthony Mockton behind me, Brody Beagle behind Vik, and a man in the uniform of a parking attendant behind Mockton. Dustin Carter.

When it began, Carter spoke before any of us, meandering to the front of the stage as though lost, causing a few nervous laughs. He was in his twenties, extremely short, just over five feet, perfectly built for his former work at one of Parnell College's parking garages. Slim with a fuzz of brown hair that would have to be shaved entirely quite soon if he wanted his career to advance.

"I'm a racist. That's why I'm here. Because I know it," he said, staring into the audience with the earnestness of a parenting YouTuber staring into their webcam.

"I would love to stand here before all of you and say that I *used* to be a racist. But that wouldn't be progress. The only progress, and this is something I've learned from the people I'm on this stage with, from Olivia Robinson and Anthony Mockton and Mr. Brody Beagle, who I can't believe would ever be willing to talk to someone like me. But he was.

"I just wish I could introduce you to my greatest teacher. The reason we're all here tonight, united. I wish you could have met Edmund Bak."

Bak's image appeared on the monitors around the room, a half-smiling headshot that would have looked infinitely sinister if he'd carried out the AR-15 plans he may or may not have had. Dustin Carter told the story as Nena had told it, more or less, alluding to but leaving out the nickname.

"He was an amazing professor. The faculty knew it, Mr. Mockton knew it, and Parnell was in the process of making more space for him. A process that you guys out there and Ms. Robinson—Olivia—up here have finished. The way Parnell is going to teach next semester would have given Edmund all the online courses he could have wanted, all the freedom and flexibility and fulfillment—I just know he would have flourished, you know? I know how much a life can change when you embrace education and change at the same time. I know because I changed.

"We had a disgusting thing we used to call him because of the fast food he ate."

Dustin stopped here, a hitch in his voice, a quick look away from the audience and at Olivia. Bak's image vanished from the monitors, replaced by Olivia's pale glow, by the shimmering crescents of liquid pooling in each eye. Dustin kept talking and I looked at Olivia, peripherally, wondering what would happen to the tears. I didn't see them vanish, exactly, but they gradually began to be gone—reabsorbed, evaporated, I don't know. I never will know, because I won't see or speak to her again.

The audience shuddered when Dustin said, "I'm not even supposed to tell you what we called him, because it was disgusting, but I just have to be honest about it. Fully honest."

Olivia had a fail-safe for all of the speeches, and she used it then. Not a hook or a trap door, but an apparent failure of technology that was in fact an efficiency; she thumbed a control, probably in her pocket, perhaps on her watch, and our wireless mics were all disabled. Dustin whispered "Señor" and not even the front row heard him. Olivia put a hand on his shoulder and ushered him offstage personally, smiling to the applause that she raised with a finger. Olivia stopped at a podium with a questing antenna of microphone at stage left, leaving Dustin to the escorting hands of two men I'd never seen at an AAP conference or anywhere else before, black turtlenecked scenery changers with massive deltoids and biceps.

Olivia ignored the order of things and craned the microphone toward herself.

"Tech company has technical difficulties. I always knew I'd go viral for the wrong reasons."

They laughed out there. I looked down at my hands, which were offering a no-contact clap. Olivia was silent, willing the room to change gears with her, to be serious with her.

"I wasn't supposed to follow Dustin, you know. And now I'm wondering why I chose to speak last, why I wanted to treat all of these amazing, diverse individuals here like my opening acts— well, I can tell you what my surface logic was. I'm the president. I have to go last. It's my place.

"But that's not it. I wanted space between what Dustin was talking about—that hatred, that hostility of a campus, the unthinking ways in which men like him reinforce the minimizing and violence that people like Osman and Vikram and me have to deal with—I wanted space between his truth and the exciting way forward that I wanted to talk about. What I want AAP to become this year, with our partnerships with our paradigm breakers: Parnell and the Beagle fund.

"But you know what? Responsibility is a punishment. Power is a punishment. It's important for people like Anthony, like Brody, and even me, to remember that. I had the power to speak last, to make all of these voices precede me, to headline—but it was irresponsible to want to do that. To flee from the racism and violence that Dustin Carter brought to life for you tonight."

Dustin Carter was still at the side of the stage, flanked by the attendants who would soon escort him to a black car. His mouth was slightly open, his finger scratching the surface of his wireless mic, hoping for static.

"Do you see this stage? Do you see the folks behind me, do you understand what we're looking at, what we're part of, through our AAP hiring strategies, through the programs we've so carefully constructed to give people of colour, the disabled, the gender spectrum, all of the richness of humanity the place they deserve? Do you understand the incredible responsibility reflected in my duty to channel these people and everyone like or unlike them, before we can appropriately uplift them, and hear those voices that have been so long suppressed?

"And do you know where these communities already speak, where they already have a voice? In the world, yes. In the classroom, even, yes. But not behind desks, not behind podiums. No. We haven't gotten there yet. In online space. The only real success of diversity in education is in the virtual space, in a world that is a more real reflection of the place we want AAP to architect."

The backdrop vanished, replaced by a digital shimmer of letters: *Presence*.

"That's why Anthony, myself, Brody, and I created *Presence*. I've been thinking about what it means to be in a place. What a place even is. I've been afraid to bring a discussion like this into the workplace, and it's only the courage of Brody and of his late wife Gwen that have made me understand that not discussing *Presence* at AAP would be the end of our business, and worse, the end of our purpose."

Brody, despite having had his speech cancelled by Olivia's summary decision, clasped his hands and beamed a namaste at her. He even peeled off his wire of microphone, let it drop to the floor.

Even to the end, I was scared. Scared that what Olivia said when she spoke would convince me to take back my campaign, to convert, to live resurrected and good and beloved and rich, the way she'd let me. She'd turned a parking attendant who tried to take ownership of a Korean-American near-stranger's suicide into a motivational speaker. She made me believe her for a moment, at that hotel bar. She gave me a second of serious thought about embracing Allah. She could do anything.

Vikram knew we had to stop her, right then. That's why he fell out of his chair. I didn't see it happen, but I knew he must have sold it with his athleticism, hiding the rocking tip he used to launch himself sideways. When I looked, he was truly sprawled out, the chair feet away and rolling. Beagle was immediately out of his chair and assisting. Olivia turned to follow the audience gasp, the exhale of a thousand AAPers watching her conference-screen rage for a moment so brief only the naked eye and the screen combined could really capture it in memory, and then made the only decision she could. She left the podium to run toward Vik, who had added some twitches to his flop.

I let Olivia pass me, took out my phone and pressed the slide-show control I'd worked out with AV for my presentation. I took a last look at *Presence* on the main monitor before it was replaced with highlighted scans of key passages from Olivia Robinson's medical files, which would soon cut to shots of the Church of the Evergreen Advent, and an old mugshot of her father that would spur a precisely-cut audio loop of his speech from that evening in the woods. I ran for the podium. I couldn't look at Olivia, and Nena's pending retirement had moved her from the second row to the back of the room, where I couldn't see her.

I can only remember what I said first, before the adrenaline flooded my system and the best parts of my brain stopped working properly.

"Olivia Robinson never had cancer, and she runs a white supremacist church in Washington State."

18

Vikram was still mic'd up. Olivia's deactivation of the system prevented any breaths or whispers from interfering with my brief speech, which Olivia had interrupted with her controls before abandoning Fort Moore. But Vik's voice came from above as I looked at his body below me, seated again in his chair, looking toward the audience and away from me. Mockton had upended my chair in running to catch Olivia as she ran offstage.

"Folks, please—we all have a lot to process, so let's just break things off for the evening and head to the club social, okay? I'm fine, by the way. Call your person, talk to your fellow AAPers, just don't feel anxious—we'll see each other again right here, first thing tomorrow. Right after I scream at the company who made this stupid chair, okay?"

Vik got his laugh. By the end of the conference, he'd get the unofficial offer of presidency. There was a need for a press release to combat the news, and that press release was President Vikram.

Brody Beagle was still on stage. Quite close to me, in fact. His palm landed on my shoulder, pushing down and gripping at the same time. He waited until my knees buckled slightly, then pulled me up to my normal height, holding me.

"We are going to speak."

On the upper floor, past the empty stadium seating, were a series of small stone rooms that usually held exhibits, displayed in glass cabinets, on the fort's history. AAP had paid to have them safely transported offsite: we meant to have seminars and exclusive breakout sessions with guests in them. The first door Brody pushed on—pushed me into, rather—was the smallest of the six rooms, which I'd toured earlier that day, like Oswald casing the book depository. It was the most dungeon-like, the smell of stone that was permanently damp under the surface trapped by the lack of a window—the other five rooms were ventilated, a concession to basic modern comfort. Brody let me go, and I realized he'd been holding me a half-inch above the floor as he guided me forward. I fell, briefly but painfully, onto my own feet.

"She was lying, Brody. I can't lie to you now and say otherwise," I said, deciding to get close to the opposite wall before turning around. Beagle filled the doorway, its height cut for a generation that ingested fewer hormones and less meat, then stepped forward and shut the door.

"I know everything about that. I knew early on. Pretty much day one of Gwen, Olivia, and I getting away from the hospital, holing up at the apartment."

Beagle's rage didn't come across in twitches, fervency, or heat, but as what someone like him would call centredness. It was a meditative intensity of cool hatred, impossible to place in his features or posture or voice. But I could feel it. He was someone who had created nothing, but had made his biceps and billions of dollars, and these had engendered a godlike confidence that I couldn't argue with, certainly not alone in that little cell. Beagle could choose who he regarded as properly human. He had afforded himself that right.

And we both knew he was talking to something less than himself in that stone room. Something that would crack for only a moment before bursting. I could only calm myself by thinking of how much he could potentially lose if he did something too terrible to me.

"How?" I asked.

"Olivia told me. There was no mistruth, after a very short time at the beginning. No hiding. The day after everything was set up, the equipment, the room for the aide, the doctor in the condo I bought next door to ours, Olivia and I were talking about spiritual honesty while Gwen slept. Gwen slept as much as she could in the last few weeks. And during one of those naps, Olivia told me about her journey. The journey she decided to take. The one my wife and I were lucky enough to witness and be a part of. That I'm still a part of.

"That's what you're not understanding. Olivia chose to take on pain and despair and punishment that you could never imagine. Whatever it is you were born with, whatever advantages or disadvantages that came from being you, you had no choice. Olivia did have a choice, and she chose to put herself on a path that united her, Gwen, and I forever." As Beagle drew closer, I saw that his shirt was made of a rippling athletic material that was painted obscenely over his hard chest and clung to the long flatness of his stomach as it narrowed toward his crotch. When he leaned toward me earnestly the fabric resumed the casual hang of a cotton T-shirt.

"She lied about having cancer."

"Not to me. Not to me. Never to me. She used her own money and time to explore what she needed to explore, and in the process endured pain, sickness, downright agony. She went through what Gwen went through. Almost everything, except the last step. Olivia taught me about humanity and strength. She taught me respect. And AAP got a lot out of me. They got their money back plus a half billion. And they will continue to extract value from our relationship, from my respect for Olivia's transformation of this company.

"You and people like you understand other people and charity from the outside. I'm sorry, but that's just true. And it's not just you, I just want it to be clear that I see through your pose because I have Indian and Chinese and even Black guys working for me who just take it for granted that I can't possibly have had it as bad as they do, even when their parents made six or sometimes seven figures and they went to private school and every fucking hacker day camp they wanted to and their dads sponsored the tech fairs that they won with kit builds stuffed with Korean chips that weren't even available on the American market. Then they look at me being the boss and just think oh, of course, I stumbled into it. Like you do. Because you don't understand people. You've never had to. You've never had to work for it. People like Olivia and me work for it, and people like you and your Nena friend coast and lie and accuse and collect glory and paycheques. Olivia knows all about Nena's Swiss hot chocolate skiing private school childhood. And she tells me some bullshit about a slum New Jersey apartment that I was stupid enough to swallow until Olivia told me the truth, the way she always does to anyone who is equipped to understand it. But I let it pass. Because compassion.

"You don't have compassion or courage. You think it's hereditary? It's not. You don't just get to be born kind and perceptive and brave because you're not white. Olivia loved Gwen more than she loves me, and she proved that over months of suffering that you tried to turn into a car bomb up there. But it is not going to work, Osman. People are good. People understand goodness. Olivia's making it through this."

I thought about Brody's dick resting in his jeans, smug and flaccid because it knew how hard it could get anytime it wanted to. I stared at it and realized that I could get angry at Brody without plotting or prevaricating, without imitating anyone but the self I had been several years ago.

"You haven't accomplished shit and your compassion is a pathetic third-act add-on to your success. Every single company you've made is a bullshit invention. Unpresentable inventors pay you to bloviate about nothing in funding meetings. To disinform. Your talent is making people want to believe that you can't possibly be as stupid as you seem. You and Olivia shared all that nothing while your wife died ignored in a bed behind you."

I was expecting Brody to hit me hard enough to change my outlook. A series of expert punches and soccer kicks that would give me cause to rethink my choices as my wired-shut jaw healed, as my eyes emerged from puffed slits with new clarity. Brody didn't hit me.

"You're trying to hurt my feelings." He leaned backwards and looked at the ceiling in abstract puzzlement, as though he were a scientist who had just realized he'd been lured onto a creationist's talk show. Brody smoothed the fabric over his thighs. The penis rolled like a sleeping cat. "You're not equipped to hurt my feelings, Osman. You're just not. I've been through so much that I get to decide what hurts me now. Didn't you take anything out of being around Olivia all these months, other than this stupid hating?

"You know Olivia worked every step of treatment with Gwen? Like she was getting sober. I watched that woman turn green for my wife. Lose weight so that clothes hung off her, so her bras became pointless."

"She was lampooning your wife's actual illness. You allowed her into your house to do that?"

"Lampooning?" I could see Brody, puzzled, picturing Chevy Chase on a roof, cream shooting out of John Belushi's mouth.

"Making fun of it. Mocking it."

Brody walked past me to the stone wall of our small room in the fortress, scratching at a copper-red runnel in the grey with his thumbnail.

"You don't understand. You can't possibly. Have you watched it eat a person? Not the disease, but the drugs. That's what Olivia Robinson had the courage to live, to do, in solidarity with my wife. In some ways, I'm almost as weak as you. I couldn't do it. Take those pills that changed the blood inside me, that made food impossible to look at. Olivia used to climb into bed next to Gwen. Take her shirt off so she could show Gwen that she was the same as her, that it wasn't weakness that was the killer, it wasn't disease, it was the inadequacy of the treatment. Olivia risked dying so my wife could die knowing that she was strong, that her body was strong, that it was the world that had failed her. That's not something I would have been able to do or pay for myself. Do you understand that? Or does it seem like a joke? A joke."

I thought about that, while Brody scratched at his stone, unable to look at me, because he had already implemented his one-time-use convert-rage-to-Zenlike-pity option. I thought about it and it did still seem like a joke: an obscene, long-form, committed prank. Brody was right that I wouldn't have the strength for it. I couldn't imagine anyone but Olivia committing to finding and taking those medications. Filling IV bags with poison and holding hands with a dying influencer. Applying lipstick and trading wigs, not allowing for even the suggestion that she had designs on the soon-to-be-widower across the room whose collective, spread-out capital a dozen recessions wouldn't be able to kill off. Olivia undercover as a patient, as a saint with beatific eyes glowing out of deepening sockets, as a machine of empathy that couldn't possibly hide ambition.

"Of course it's a joke. The only funny part is that you still believe it wasn't, Brody, you fucking idiot. I feel sorry for your wife."

I got my beating, but it was brief and did nothing for my personality or courage. Brody just punched me once, so hard and specifically that I felt I was being penetrated, that the knuckles of his index and middle finger had split the skin and his hand followed them into me. But when he walked out and I clutched my side, there was only pain, no wound. It was a punch in the kidneys, which I understood later when I saw my summery pink piss. I hummed and rocked and dreamed about suing him.

19

I stole one of Nena's cars to drive to my mother's house from the Muskoka cottages. It was almost a year after my last AAPC, two months into my isolation with Nena. May 2020. Nena, Vikram, and I didn't speak or chat or interact for months after the conference, at first by mutual accord, and then because neither of them wanted to speak to me. I sold my apartments, started the lawsuit, and moved money during those last months in Los Angeles. I became more comfortable doing nothing than I had been since I was a student. When Nena asked me to join her at the Canadian compound where she'd chosen to vanish, I hadn't spoken to anyone who wasn't serving me food or wrapping a thousand-dollar book for two seasons.

The car was a Prius we'd crammed with lean organic meats and Nena's business wardrobe for the ride up. She intended to separate it into donation and burning piles. The meat had long been packed in the fridge and freezers, and I left the bags of clothing by the woodpile on the front porch before dawn, before getting into the car and killing all the midges that had flown in the open door.

Vikram was someone I would always miss speaking to. Nena had given us a chance to finish with each other, but he never would. In the winter, I'd called his home after the tenth ignored text and the second call to his cell. There couldn't be a third because he blocked my number. AAP was deep into the implementation of *Presence*, but he was flailing in the press and in industry gossip, considered a failure, a credit-thieving substitute, despite or because of the growing momentum of the product. Vik's mother had a listed landline, and his sister picked up the phone, answering with a soft politeness that was ready to turn into a scream or hang up if I was a robocall. She handed me to her brother.

Vikram sighed first, long and rattling, close enough to the receiver for the air to pixelate.

"I didn't know you were the breathing tube kind," I said.

"What? No, fuck it. Don't explain."

"Then you explain. What do we do now? They're going to get her back, you know."

"We don't do anything. I might do something. But you and I are not alike. At all. When did you forget that?" Vikram hung up on me and was offered demotion or a layoff before Christmas. I don't know which he took.

There was a last midge in the Prius, and when it settled on my lower lip, I bit it to death. I was violating Nena's trust, government injunctions to limit travel, and my mother's express wish that I stay away from her. Angela, whose last name I had never written down and whose email address, debokovvalentina@ yahoo.com, only identified the sender as D.A., had stopped phoning me. It had taken me five weeks to notice, and four unanswered calls to decide on this course of action.

The Prius had been plugged into the outer socket that was just below the sliding glass door of Nena's room, which was open. She would have heard me leaving, and therefore had decided not to ask me what the fuck I was doing, either by yell or by text. Confinement had imbued us with an Edenic lassitude that I couldn't have imagined when we worked at AAP, a relaxation that was sometimes so overwhelming it was indiscernible from despair. Most days, I really enjoyed it, but this morning, I had not. I felt the new lightness of my body, its reality and averageness, the way it conformed to my skeleton in a way that made boring physiological sense. I would be an easy forensic reconstruction if I were fished, bleached and greenteethed, from the bottom of the lake.

After two hours of driving, I was in the alley that led into our driveway. A neighbourhood tabby, a cat I'd memorized from frequent petting during breakfast over a decade of visits, waited for me on the first sloped stair of the back patio, his collar green and gently fuzzing from wear at all of its edges. I petted him, thinking that these mackerel tabbies were somehow a species analogue to German shepherds like Horace, who had successfully whined at me for an early breakfast before I left the cottage. I only seemed to touch animals when I was in Canada. I envisioned a conversation where I pointed to this fact as the reason everything had gotten fucked up when I was down there, laughing over a pint with a figure who remained a void across the table from me at a bar that couldn't be open again for months.

It was May, but fat quick-melting flakes descended in the bright sunlight, a Northern Anthropocene sun shower. They soaked my face as I attempted to enter the house through the back, which involved pulling the sliding door gently twice to create a rocking motion in the dowel that prevented the door from opening beyond five inches, then three hard tugs to change that rocking into an unmooring. The tabby vanished. I heard the wood, a smooth piece of broom handle I'd held, moved, and even wielded as a play sword since I was eleven years old, splinter. I pulled the door open all the way and saw it cracked on the guest bedroom floor, the gentle Cape Cod grey fade of its outer form irrupted by the needling yellow shards that had always been clustered around its core. I finished breaking it and left it on the floor next to my shoes.

Pulling on a breathing mask and yellow rubber gloves to lessen the chances of killing Sameen, I walked into the hallway and toward the living room. There was, again, less of everything in the home: fewer pictures hanging, the shoe rack at the front door gone and replaced by a rubber mat, the wicker basket below the full-length mirror gone, the open coat closet half-cleared.

I sat on the last remaining couch and waited. When the keys entered the lock and the door swung open with the same sound it had for twenty years—a reluctant unsticking gasp from the poly-propylene seal, an initial hinge shriek and two smaller, disgruntled whines that Ajit had oiled away exactly twice in his lifetime, inci-dents separated by a decade—Angela came in. I immediately remembered the text of her last name on her CV, in Helvetica font: Aitken. She had three grocery bags in each hand and looked star-tled, but not scared to see me as she set them down. I pulled my mask up for a second, and held up a reassuring hand.

"Keep the mask on, Osman, please. Your mother's seventy-six and she's just finishing a phone call in the car."

"I'm sorry I took the space—"

"We park out front when we go on big shops. Kitchen's closer that way." Angela picked up three bags. "Since we're washing all of this anyway, you might as well help. But please, once you set these down on the counter, come back and wait on the couch, and touch as little as possible."

"I should be angry at you for not replying to any of my calls or texts," I said, carrying a net bag of oranges and what seemed like an infinite depth of frozen spinach and peas. Angela was taller than me, a good six-two, with black hair and grey eyes.

There had been a photograph clipped to her CV when Sameen and I had gone through the stack, but this face didn't return to me the way her last name had.

I hadn't seen a face other than Nena's this closely for three weeks, and I did stare, putting Angela's age at about ten years below what my mother had told me. She wasn't quite forty. My age, or a couple years younger.

"That is something you'll have to talk to your mother about, and let me tell you, this is a moment I expected. She was sure you wouldn't come here, absolutely sure, and I told her she was crazy. When you stopped leaving her the messages she was especially sure, but I knew it would just build up, that you'd have to come." Angela washed her hands under a steaming tap, leaving it on for me afterwards. I waved my gloves at her and she grimaced.

"You're not exactly supposed to be taking her orders, and why are you saying 'crazy' in an I guess lucid and casual manner when you're discussing your dealings with a dementia patient? And why the fuck is she in the car alone?" I started toward the front door and felt a wet hand on my shoulder before I hit the kitchen doorway.

The grey eyes had large black pupils. The look wasn't beady or void, but generous, suggesting a superior interpretation of the light bouncing off me and everything else it took in. The expression on her face, which tilted as the eyebrows lifted and the lips drew slightly in, was a familiar one that I had missed: pity. Angela, backing away from me to achieve the requisite gap to prevent the invisible transmission of a disease neither of us was likely to have, told me she was sorry.

"There is a lot you don't understand, and will feel deceived by, but trust me when I say your mother, your wonderful mother, is safe and she will stay that way for as long as I'm around at least."

"You're planning to leave?"

"No." The pity flinched a bit before my undoubtedly cunty tone, which made me feel a bit better. "Just know that I haven't chosen to deceive you, that Sameen is safe, and that you'll need to get everything you need from her, directly. I'm going to stay in here."

She dismissed me, from a room in the house that I couldn't stop thinking of my own. Mom was right when she said so during my last visit: it felt not only mine from the past, but mine in the future, the very near future. I missed the apartments I had given up in Los Angeles, both the one I lived in and the one I kept empty. My purchased space, my sections of air. But this was even more than that, brick and cement that extended into the earth and into my past and belonged to me through rules of blood, ovaries, semen, money, and time. It meant more than anything I could buy, which was why I'd broken in when I could have merely entered with my key. I sat on the couch and waited for Sameen, who was outside for at least ten more minutes, undoubtedly answering texts from Angela that warned her of what was waiting.

She watched me from the entry to the living room, watched me stare at my socks. I could bend at the waist easily now, with pants that fit and an understanding of the reality of my body that I'd developed through avoiding mirrors and other people. There was a tear at the large toe of my right sock, lanced by a long toenail that I would cut someday.

"Hi, sweetie," Sameen said from the doorway. Her voice didn't quiver with emotion, apology, with thwarted authority, with anything. The purple glasses looked less silly on her now. It wasn't that her hair or face had changed, but that I understood that she had picked them out with Angela, and hadn't been hustled into the purchase by a mall optical store worker.

"I broke the stick at the back door. The locking stick. I'm sorry."

"That's okay. You didn't want to get the doorknob germy?"

"Yeah. And stay there, please, Mom, I don't want you to—"

"I was going to stay. Wait." Sameen vanished for a moment, to the kitchen, for reassurance and the chair that she returned with, a wicker-backed one that I'd once poked fingers through, leaving gaps that I could still see, grins prodded in the weave that Sameen blocked when she sat. She had a small blue track suit on, loose and completely unlike her, an expensive but tasteless thing.

"I've been really worried, Mom. You must know that."

"You haven't been worried, Osman. I know you haven't, and don't think that I was testing you. I was letting you be, and it took a lot of persuading Angela to allow you that. To allow us that." Mom had a way of looking as exhausted at the beginning of an argument as she would at the end, as though her body could predict the ordeal it was about to go through and sent messages to her facial muscles that would perhaps ward off the worst of a counterattack. It made me feel a pang of the love that hadn't occurred to me from the beginning of my drive. It quickly faded into a soft inhaled-nosebleed sensation in my sinuses.

"I was giving you the space you asked for and trying not to be overly worried and choosy about it. But you're losing your fucking mind, Mom. Sameen. That's no small thing, and respecting your wishes doesn't mean that I don't need to be kept updated in strict detail, on an agreed-upon schedule, of exactly what is happening to you." I could sense both of the postures I was assuming, speaking these unnatural words—first pretending that I was a devoted son, who was then pretending to be masterful father. Sameen had tape-recorded me babbling to her for hours in this room when I was small, just before I started school, telling her about the toys I wanted her to buy me or that we could build together, commenting on her clothes, asking endless questions about butterflies and grass and contact lenses that she couldn't possibly know the answers to, with that relentless pushy insistence that little kids ask questions with, blending entitlement to an answer with absolute faith that the parent will have it. Sameen usually spoke quietly and further away from the tape recorder. She filed the Maxell 120s in a shoebox that would eventually be half-full before I discovered it and listened to what I could stomach, after digging a red cassette player out of the AV armoire downstairs. My needy, wheedling voice. Her love and indulgence, the way her accent sounded frequencies in words like "trunk" and "bat" that they didn't anymore, as her English flattened and whitened out in the house. What I heard most in her voice, though, was the effort. Not impatience, not strain, but effort, similar to the effort I was making now in being her son again. Perhaps a father or mother would be able to explain to me that what I was hearing was just the regular tone of parenting, but more likely they would tell me that I could never understand. But I do know what it sounds like when people don't want anything to do with me.

"Osman, you're not at work. Don't talk to me like I'm a secretary."

"I don't have work," I said. "Nena and I were both laid off, fired, from AAP."

"Oh!" Mom laughed and clapped her hands, as though she had finally gotten an answer that explained my presence. "But you're okay for money?"

"Yes. Forever. I hope you're not implying money is why I came here." Brody Beagle's personal corporation had sent me a statement to sign and a cheque for four million dollars after he'd punched me; I assumed every one of his lawyers advised him not to do this for fear of further litigation, while Olivia Robinson had supplied an amount she knew that someone like me would simply accept.

"No, you came here because you had nothing else to do. But I can tell you what you think you need to know. I am not losing my mind, not going crazy. That doctor you met at the diner. The African you spoke to. He was an actor. He was in some of your father's classes, actually, and I told him that we were doing a—Angela would remember the words we used—a sort of reality-like movie shoot with hidden cameras, mostly amateur actors, improvisation."

"There were cameras?"

"No." Sameen smiled again, and I saw the same pity that had been in Angela's eyes, the same reserved and not entirely generous pity, a pity that couldn't help blaming. "There were no cameras. I had the idea for this when your father was in hospital, told him in his last weeks that I wouldn't be long for the world after him, that I was fading already. It was the only thing I said that made him feel better at the end. He almost lit up, a yellow glow under his skin, knowing that there was so little left for me after him. And when I got out, talked to Angela about it all, started phoning you with the same stories I told Ajit, I realized that I could make you happy this way. And myself. Make myself happy." Sameen's accent, the Englished Frenchness of the way she said "happy," learned from the governess that she'd had on her grandfather's tea estate from ages five to seven, lanced me first with that same palpitation of copper-scented love, then surfaced in a restrained movement of my own tongue re-enacting a memory of saying the word in kindergarten and being mocked with the words "'appy meal" at every lunch hour for six months, the white and Indian and Tibetan kids uniting to spit a mangled Quebec French at me, all the more when I tried to explain exactly how they were wrong to be making fun of me in this precise way. Barry Lun had pissed in my orange juice at the end of it, turning his stream away just at the point when the colour was changing too much for the gambit to work. I only spat it out when I saw the stares, before the orgasmic laughter that I decided to join, putting a foundational crack in the campaign against me.

"But your stroke was real. Just not the Alzheimer's."

"The stroke was real. And I never said I had Alzheimer's, it was you who kept forgetting what I said. Dementia. And I will have it, soon enough. It's a genetic promise on my side of the family. Don't pretend that I did you some great injustice, Osman. You dealt with my two cancers perfectly well. I don't think you even remember much about them. You haven't asked about my fibromyalgia since you were in high school. I had a knee replacement the year before your father died and you never asked me about that once. So I had proof that I wasn't burdening you nearly as much as I was relieving you with this."

"Did you really visit that neurologist that Dad pissed off?"

"No." Sameen smiled, here; it had been an excellent, believable Dad tale, one I could see him telling himself to a colleague, or to a student who had announced his intentions of going to medical school after her English degree.

"Why didn't you just tell me you wanted to see less of me, let it trail off? You hired actors?"

"Just one actor. You never would have believed me, Osman. That I wanted to be done with it all. And I thought we deserved to have a story that would make us both feel best about staying apart. I wasn't lying. My mind isn't quite as it used to be, and that's a path I'm still on."

"You and Angela—"

"Don't say anything coarse. You wouldn't be able to stand the memory of it. Don't. Angela and I are blessed friends, companions, equals, nothing mother-daughter about it, and not lovers, nothing like that either. I wish I could imagine you understanding this. We met two years before your father died, and I didn't tell anyone about her, because Ajit would have tried to take her away from me."

"But I would never do that. I wouldn't even care enough to

do that, if you want to put it in a way that suits the rest of your vision of me."

"By the time I could tell you I realized I didn't want to. I let you play a part in the hiring of her. She's not a personal support worker, of course. She's a psychoanalyst, sometimes a landscape designer. I gave you and I both a good reason not to feel obligated to use our time on each other, Osman, and I let my future come to me. And it's been beautiful, even in this dead, quarantined time. The house is the only tie I have to those strange decades I had, and soon I can leave this, too. We're moving to a beautiful apartment Angela and I bought, to—"

Past the front garden, Ajit's wooden magazine racks were piled on top of the plastic city garbage cans, waiting for collection. I would take them myself when I was finished with Mom; they were still useful. My estrangement from Ajit had been the most passionate and enduring moment of our relationship since early childhood. My dad, who on those faculty club steps smelled more like old meat than old books, was not ordering me to see the world correctly, but entreating me to stop contributing to the destruction of the world he valued and to help him construct a new past. When it didn't take, he simply banished me from his presence, from his life, from his consciousness. This was the purest our relations had been since he'd dislocated my arm when I tried to run into traffic to retrieve a fallen Ninja Turtle. We fought about me and what I was, we allowed the heat of a fight to become personal, not a flirtation of issues, not a matter of criticism, but a rejection of the differing lies at the core of both of our beings.

"I could live with you being a pharmaceutical rep. A lobbyist. A gigolo. Any other kind of whore you can think of," Ajit said on the steps, while his professorial tic, the ongoing air handshake he would do to mark his syntax, closed into a fist and extended finger. Inside him the unknown tumours were swelling and milling.

This tiny old man, who dyed his eyebrows with a certain brand of grooming pen he could only get in a Gerrard Street Indian grocery, who never managed to excise all of the boar bristles that poked out of his nostrils, shook and almost slipped down the steps that were our fighting arena as the enormity of his disappointment alerted us both to the continued existence of his love, just as it was finally being extinguished. I grabbed Dad's arm, Ajit's arm, as he got his footing back, gripping the two bones above the elbow as I pulled him back to balance. Those bones were so close together now, any muscle that had ever been there wasted to nothingness, the whole arm something I could take out of his socket with a gentle tug, as though I were flushing a Victorian toilet. The quiet vacuum of our exhausted, now absent feelings engulfed us as I let him go, and I think if we had looked at each other then we would have smiled. So I left before the moment could be spoiled or altered.

And now this gentle, untethered feeling had returned. I would have been able to find counterarguments if I'd wanted to, and not only appeals to traditions that had little value for Sameen and me, but to love and connection. She still wanted people around, didn't long for isolation. There was a Sasquatch-tall white woman in the kitchen to prove this. But any argument I could think of was one that eliminated what she'd been too good and loving and kind to say: she didn't want to be with *me*, specifically.

"Mom, did Dad have a sister who died with her hair getting wrapped around a tire axle?"

"What?" Sameen looked at me the way she used to look at encyclopedia salesmen or Jehovah's Witnesses.

"He brought it up downstairs. I couldn't tell if he was joking."

"He never had any siblings. I had two sisters, one's married to a jeweller in Hyderabad, and one did die when we were kids, run over by a bus. Is that what he was talking about?"

"It may have been part of his source material."

"This goes a bit to show what I mean, Osman. You don't even want to talk about me or you and me at a juncture like this. And that is fine. But let's see the end as the end, okay?"

"You didn't listen to my messages," I said.

"I don't know if you could have listened to them either, Osman. There was so much slurring and breathing. You weren't making much sense and the sentences seemed very long. I'm sorry."

Sameen pushed her sleeve up to put a calming hand on a dry patch of skin above her wrist. She had excellent discipline about scratching. When I'd had bad skin, I had flaked all over the bedding and couches and my clothing, digging through epidermis and dermis until every one of my adolescent white tees bore inner streaks of blood that wouldn't wash out, only fade to light chocolate flickers. Sameen wasn't making a sociological case, she was doing the same thing that she and Ajit had done with their own families before: distancing, waiting it out, finally cutting any ties that death hadn't severed with an awkward or stern finality. Both Mom and Dad had sent final cheques home sometime in the late nineties, avoiding the intermittent WhatsApp group messages and video chat marathons that would have been their lot if every uncle and aunt hadn't got the message and condoling dollars.

This was the real end of our family, the end of the journey that I had thought had occurred on the staircase of the faculty club: we were each adrift individually, now, abandoning any idea of a future together, and only lightly nostalgic for the past we'd been forced, by genetics and social structures, to share.

"I love you, Mom."

"I love you too."

"How soon will you leave?"

"You want the house now? Right now?" Sameen smiled and we discussed moving in lockdown, what it might look like, while my mind crawled with the questions I should be asking, with the hatred I should be feeling, with a sense of rejection on the scale of myth that I expected to take root at any moment, but wouldn't ever. From my phone, I transferred ten thousand dollars to Angela. I was pleased to find that her last name had already vanished from my mind.

"What's this money for?" asked Angela, appearing from the kitchen with her hands and forearms coated in suds.

"Wait, Osman," Sameen said. "We'll move as soon as you want to take ownership. As soon as next week, if you want. But you should hear this. I did love being your ma, being with you and for you for so long. I just found out that it's possible for any relationship to end, even this one. I feel that deeply, sweetie. Don't you?"

As Sameen spoke, I checked to see whether the questions had stopped roiling within me, that the gaps left for emotions which hadn't arrived were silting full. I felt peace enter me, cool and smooth, like the chocolate mint I stole before Christmas dinner in 1998, the first in a tray of twenty that I would take and eat upstairs as my parents talked to a pair of visiting professors from Oxford who had been given my room.

"I do."

20

The core of my new happiness has been the removal of any expectations of myself. This sounds like received wisdom from the most vapid elements of the culture, the ones we've been making fun of together all this time, I know. I understand. But if you really commit to it, the way Olivia committed to her treatment, you understand that you're embracing an abyss so profound you can't believe that people have noticed that it's right there, behind words that are supposed to reassure you into a state of self-loving torpor.

Take away everything you expect of and for yourself and you have found the dark backing. There is a soft, deep felt behind the shards, I can promise you. I have removed hope, a horizon, a future, any idea of an existence different from what I have right now, any notion that I could change within that existence or learn to endure it differently. I am no longer an actor or a participant. Verbs happen outside of me. They are visited upon me when they occur. I expect nothing; that took immensely hard work. When I sit on the front steps of my home, looking at the gnarled tumble of green and brown that is my mother's abandoned garden, I don't fantasize about becoming a person who wants to garden. I fantasize about hiring a gardener, about having a bantering friendship with her, about ceding to four out of five of her ideas and gently pushing back on the last so I achieve some sense of ownership over what I have paid for. But these are all preparation for the fantasy that ends each rumination: the one about doing none of these things, simply thinking my way to the end of a story that never has to happen, ending it in an ether of vaporized images and time that I can inhale until I'm unconscious.

Months in, and the house is mine, my books installed. Nena asked to visit twice, but I knew that she was being polite, and I reciprocated her politeness by never contacting her again. Angela and Sameen are gone with the same finality, even deleted from my address books and contact lists. I roam the three bedrooms and four bathrooms, I work on dismantling my father's basement dwelling and transforming it into the office where I finish what you will read. If my body still tells truths about me, there is no one to see them, and I barely feel it around myself, except when I'm using the toilet. I felt that this body was where they would finally get me, where they would finally find me: now I'm certain no one will ever look.

I belong here, doing nothing, contributing to nothing, letting any identity I have possessed in public or private reality vanish. I am confident that I can achieve this if I spend enough time alone, if I get through this notion that anyone ever needs to hear from me by saying my last long piece, putting it before you, and disappearing behind it.

I chatted with Nena before telling her that I preferred some time alone, just before deleting the last of my social and email accounts. She'll stay at her cottage for as long as she can, training Horace to hunt wild turkeys with her, once she can find online tutorials that will allow her to feel confident with the crossbow we ordered from Taiwan during our last big drunk together.

We barely talked about Olivia Robinson, but we did, just a little bit. She is, irresistibly, back at AAP as president. Nena and I had been waiting for it from the moment the isolation curtain descended. It was a matter of how they would do it, whether they would fashion a redemption narrative, create a scandal around Vikram, or simply ignore everything she had done. I leaked my recording of Oliver Robinson's testimonial at the church, and it was embedded in the articles about Olivia for those two weeks of the cycle when it seemed she was utterly defeated. But that time ended. Brody would aid her return, that I knew, holding hands with the woman who ushered his wife into dignified obsolescence when the time came, who programmed him to mourn her in a directly productive, capital-building manner.

Nena found the answer in her feed, the evening before I left the cottage to drive to my house. A twelve-minute film by a director hired away from Vice, beginning with a shot of Olivia's ear, elfin and slightly fuzzed, zooming into a digital canal of veinous red, coasting along the whorls of a computer-generated cochlea, and dwelling in the inaccurate Bubblicious pink of her brain before the first words arced across the cabin's wireless speaker system: *I didn't predict anything. I just followed the knowledge all of us had to the solution all of us needed.*

Then Olivia's face, beamed from Nena's laptop onto the flat screen in front of us, with a new smile that no longer had to be humble or knowing or anything but itself. There may be a mention of conquered-struggles-with-mental-health four breakout press releases on, but Olivia was cleansed, irradiated by the pressurized torrent of money that was about to hit AAP.

The outbreak had revealed her as an edutech sibyl: a prognosticator of the ineluctable fate of the classroom, professors, and students for the coming decade, the century, forever. AAP's *Presence*, all the remote systems it encompassed, was more efficient and integrated than any existing system in the academic world. The bug shut down every campus in the world more effectively than any thousand sexless message board crusaders with assault rifles. Every professor, every adjunct who would never become what they were promised, installed an app, became the app, delivered product to the end-users through AAP facilitation. This was all shown in a tidy transitional cartoon.

The last four minutes of the video start with the same drive Nena and I took. When it started, Nena clenched my hand, the last time she would touch me. Olivia descends from a Range Rover, wearing a Barbour jacket and flannels over yoga pants. She passes "The Gentlemen of the Pines" sign without explanation, making a soundless gesture toward Brody Beagle, who is walking beside her as the handheld follows them.

And then Olivia hugs Oliver Robinson, presses her mother's two papery hands in hers, waves at Pastor Greg in the closing moments of his sermon, which appears to have been entirely about the Indigenous history of Washington state and the misguided evil of missionary work. Olivia whispers to the camera, speaks without turning, lets the lens find her lips.

"This is my church, like the rumours said. I pay for it, because in this country, evangelism can be an incredibly powerful tool against racism. Perhaps it has to start here. With our personal, white, shame." Olivia turns, smiling, a mist of tears shutting her tiny eyes for her, the crescents of liquid turning into perfect ovals.

At the close of the video, which Nena and I watched in silence, a silence that remained unbroken until I started to make dinner and talk about my missing mother, Olivia sits cross-legged behind her presidential desk, leaning against its leg, typing with an agile hand on a tablet, using all four fingers and the thumb of her right hand. She spots the camera she has been spotted by and smiles, swiping her screen to black, turning to look out the window. The film swipes black too, minimizes automatically, and vanishes in the scroll.

"She called yesterday," Nena said, her hand moving away from mine, vanishing under the grey fleece blanket over her legs.

"Olivia."

"She wants me to oversee the spread of the church. Its franchising, I guess. Work the sponsorship angles, get more than just tax exemptions from the government. I said, 'heartland missionary work,' and she laughed the real laugh, the one you never heard. I can do it remotely."

"You would even consider this? Nena. She stole this from you."

"She took a joke and made it into an idea and that idea is an actual building with people in it now. I didn't do that. Olivia did."

We talked more and drank more and I went to bed. Nena took the job at some point the next morning, while I was driving away from the cottage and toward my home.

AAP's *Presence* technology became the universal educational standard within a semester. AAP is everywhere now. They made it. Olivia made it.

And so did I. I'm alone, for as long as I can afford to be.

ACKNOWLEDGEMENTS

Rudrapriya Rathore, the Ruthnum family, the Rathore family.

Andrew F. Sullivan, Michael Lapointe, Sam Wiebe, Patrick Tarr, Amy Jones.

Sam Haywood and everyone at the Transatlantic Agency.

Haley Cullingham, Stephanie Sinclair, Laurie Grassi, David Bezmozgis, Andrew Steinmetz, andrea bennett, Trudy Fegan.

Jean Marc Ah-Sen, André Forget.

David Bertrand, Waubgeshig Rice.

The Ontario Arts Council, for a grant that aided in the completion of this novel.